THE JOSHUA FILES

Praise for *The Joshua Files*

"An exciting adventure and coming-of-age story with plot twists and cliff-hanger chapter endings that will keep you up all night to finish."
San Jose Mercury News

"It's the Mexican and Mayan flavorings that give Harris's adventure yarn that bit of extra bite as she weaves a satisfyingly twisty plot."
Financial Times

"Josh's race to decode clues, sort out the good guys from the bad and his feats of derring-do make for an absorbing read."
The Australian

"M.G. Harris proves she has a deft touch and a real skill for writing heart-stopping adventure in her code-cracking debut."
Glasgow Herald

Also by M. G. Harris

Invisible City

Ice Shock

Zero Moment

Dark Parallel

The Descendant

APOCALYPSE MOON

M.G. HARRIS

THE JOSHUA FILES

darkwater

First published in 2012 by Scholastic Children's Books, UK

This edition published in 2014 by Darkwater Books
An imprint of Harris Oxford Limited.
41 Cornmarket Street, Oxford, OX1 3HA

ISBN 978-1-909072-11-4

A CIP catalogue record for this book is available from the British
Library.

Cover design by Gareth Stranks

www.themgharris.com

For Reba Bandyopadhyay,
thanks for a treasured friendship, all your advice, ideas and
support, and the memory of The Aquitar Files.

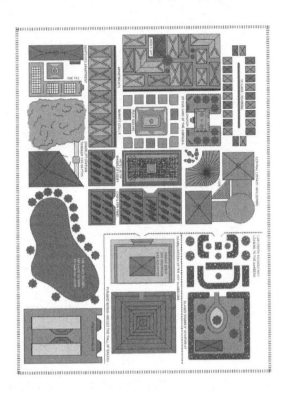

'Ek Naab' Map design by Megan Evans from Birmingham, winner of the *Joshua Files* "Design a Map" competition.

BLOG ENTRY: THE JOSHUA DOOMSDAY MANIFESTO OR HOW TO DEAL WITH THE POSSIBLE END OF THE WORLD

1.	Keep busy. Learn a skill or trade. Do your exams. Take me, for example: I'm learning to be a pilot. OK, I'll admit that I'm partly doing it to impress a girl, but also, it might come in handy, especially if the end of the world starts to look likely.

	Mainly, keep your mind off the possible impending doom. The trade/skill/exam thing is just a bonus.

2.	Stay in denial. The world is NOT going to end. Tell yourself this a few times a day. Thoughts of what might happen may spring up on you when you're least expecting it. In those moments, you'll need that denial to be rock solid.

3.	DO NOT look at videos on YouTube about the world ending. Most of them have got it badly wrong anyway. They talk about asteroids crashing into Earth or the Planet Nibiru or some other rubbish. You won't find much about a galactic superwave and a gigantic electromagnetic pulse wiping out all the computer technologies. That's so much less photogenic. Instead of massive fireballs, there will be a massive no-show. No TV, no interweb, no money going through the banking system and no twenty-pound notes in the ATMs. No food trucks going to the supermarkets, no power in the hospitals. The whole developed world relies on computer technology. Very definitely don't think about what would happen if there was suddenly a great big OUTAGE.

4.   Make a bucket list – a list of all the things you want to do before you "kick the bucket". Quietly. Show it to no one. This is just for you. You'll never have to use it, probably, because the world won't end. It's a just-in-case. Look at it for a long time and think about what really matters, what you really want to DO or BE. You might surprise yourself. I did.

5.   Stop reading this blog. How did you find it anyway? What makes you think I'm not making it all up?

6.   Trust the adults to sort everything out and save the world. Hey, they usually do, right?

7.   If you've tried all of the above and you still wake at three a.m. with a cold, vacant pit where your stomach should be, wondering if civilization is on the brink of destruction – then there's always this: GET INVOLVED.

Chapter 1

Lately, I've been having the feeling that people aren't being straight with me. Or some people in particular: my parents.

By "parents" I mean my mother (Eleanor) and her partner, Carlos Montoyo. If it weren't for the fact that my real father died pretty recently, Mum would probably already be married to Montoyo. They fell for each other after a few months. Now they're definitely a couple. But when you marry a widow, I think you're probably meant to leave a polite interval.

Montoyo is an interesting guy and I won't deny that I respect him. He's been on the ruling Executive of Ek Naab – a hidden "invisible city" – ever since the last proper Bakab Ix died: my grandfather. Now I'm the Bakab Ix; I'm next in line to succeed to the ruling Executive. When I turn sixteen.

That's if Montoyo will give up his place for me. If ever there was a wheeler-dealer, it's him. About nine months ago Montoyo played a sneaky trick on me. Since then things have gone downhill. Nine months ago, he tricked me into travelling in time in search of an ancient Mayan codex – the Ix Codex. Montoyo might say he had his reasons for tricking me, but it's not easy to get over being conned into risking your life. It's probably fair to say that if Montoyo could have managed the time travel bit, he'd have done the deed himself. If he could have touched the Ix Codex, that is. Like my dad used to say, If we had eggs, we could have ham and eggs, if we had ham.

Of all the people in Ek Naab, only I can use the time travel device, the Bracelet of Itzamna. Only I can touch the Ix Codex. It's not a magical power, it's a genetic ability: I was born with it.

Until nine months ago, Montoyo didn't think twice about risking me on a dangerous time-travel adventure. If the Ix Codex went missing, I was the guy for the job. It's what I was born for, after all. Prince William doesn't whine about being second in line to the British throne. And I try not to whine about being what I am, the Bakab Ix – genetically tweaked to be the protector of the Ix Codex.

There's an ancient legend that the world as we know it will end in December 2012. The bad news is that it's true. What is going to happen, has happened before. It will all happen again, too. The good news is that this time, we're meant to be prepared – thanks to the Ix Codex.

The instructions for how to save the world from the coming galactic superwave of 2012 are in the Ix Codex. But the cover of the Ix Codex is impregnated with a poisonous gas. Only a Bakab Ix can touch the book and survive.

2

There were times when it was very hard to carry all that responsibility. I didn't ask for the job; I was born into it. I wasn't always keen. But I did what was needed; I risked my life again and again. I've been shot in the leg, attacked with knives, experimented on, watched people I care about being hurt by my enemies, seen my father in prison, seen him plunge to his death saving my life.

All to try to protect the Ix Codex, to do my bit to save the world from the galactic superwave.

So when apparently I'm too young and too inexperienced to play a part in this incredible plan to save the world . . . when I'm completely sidelined and ordered to "Get on with your studies and leave everything to us" . . .

I get pretty annoyed. I get a bit suspicious too.

It has something to do with what happened nine months ago, when I time travelled. That's when everything changed. Before that, I felt like I was on the inside, allowed to know what was going on, how the 2012 plan was coming along.

Now – nothing. No part in it for me. I'm surplus to requirements.

On the upside: you can get a lot done in nine months, if you really focus. I had no idea. Nine months of intensive maths coaching and I've covered a decent chunk of the A-levels in maths, further maths, physics.

Not that I was a huge fan of maths before I came to live in the city, but for trainee pilots, maths is essential. My cousin Benicio passed his pilot exam when he was fifteen. I'm determined to at least equal that.

And there are only six weeks to go before I turn sixteen.

There's a knock at the door to the apartment I share with my mother. Right now I'm here alone – Mum is off with some new friends, teaching them Irish cookery: soda bread, Irish stew, things like that. She and I are the only foreigners, the most exotic people to have lived in Ek Naab for over a hundred years. After months of determined friendliness, my mum seems to have won over even some of the more xenophobic residents, who weren't too happy when we moved in. But after a while, her relationship with Montoyo made her quite popular. It seems people have been keeping their fingers crossed that he'd marry again – either that or leave town. Being alone didn't suit him; that's what I've heard.

I zip up my flight jacket, empty the pockets of lint and a half-eaten flapjack. Still only half-dressed for my flying lesson, I move out of my bedroom and into the living room, open the door. Standing outside is my girlfriend, Ixchel. She's smiling and carrying a basket of something wrapped in a white linen cloth. It smells delicious.

"Surprise!"

"Hey! What are you doing here? I'm supposed to be out. Already late for Benicio."

"You've got time to taste a cookie, though, yes? I just came from your mother's class."

I put my head on one side. "Aw, honey, you baked!"

She grins. "Try one." The grin vanishes for a second, to be replaced by a look of mock ferocity. At least I'm hoping she's joking. "You'd better be nice. It's the first time I've baked anything."

She opens the cloth and hands me a crisp, warm shortbread biscuit. I take a bite and the warm, buttery pastry crumbles in my mouth. I close my eyes and give a long sigh of appreciation. She watches with a hopeful expression. I'm silent, experiencing the delicious sensation of the freshly baked biscuit while I gaze at her shoulders and neck. They're tanned the colour of honey, a wonderful contrast to the strappy purple top she's wearing.

"Good?"

4

"Amazing. Marry me."

Ixchel is momentarily taken aback. So am I. The phrase just tripped off my tongue, a joke, yet not a joke, because for Ixchel and me, the whole subject is a bit tense.

After a second or two, she recovers her composure. "Josh Garcia, you don't get away with proposing as easy as that."

Thank goodness. We're back to joking about it. "Why not?" I mumble, mouth full of shortbread. "We're already engaged, after all. I'm the Bakab Ix and you're my betrothed. It's all been agreed."

"Engaged, betrothed. Do you even know the difference?"

"Give us a kiss, sweetness, and I'll tell you."

She plants a kiss on my cheek and grins as she pulls away. "Engaged is when you give me a ring and get down on one knee, and since you're only . . . what age are you again?" Silently, Ixchel pretends to compute my age in her head.

"I'm fifteen, almost sixteen," I growl. "And you're already sixteen, I know, I know."

"It's not that you're a few months younger. It's that we're both too young."

"Who says I even want to marry you, anyway? I'm just being accurate about our relationship."

"'Betrothed' is just something our parents decided on."

"What's going to swing it for you, my good looks or my charm? Or the massive political power I'm going to wield when I'm finally sixteen? They say it makes you irresistible, you know."

She gazes at me. "Josh. Be serious. We both know you don't care about power."

"But they could at least listen to me, right? I know the rules say that a Bakab can join the ruling Executive of Ek Naab when he's sixteen but. . ."

". . .that's never actually happened."

5

"Right. And can you see Carlos Montoyo letting it happen? He's doing everything he can to keep me out of the planning for 2012."

Ixchel shakes her head in sad agreement. "I know. I've heard that he's going to try to change the law. Make it so you have to be twenty-five. He's arguing that the ancient law exists because life expectancy used to be so short."

"Twenty-five will be about ten years too late. This 2012 stuff is going down in December! Now is when they should be asking for my help."

From behind us a voice calls out lazily, "Maybe they don't need you."

Ixchel and I turn swiftly to see my cousin Benicio standing at the door to my apartment. He gives us a sheepish grin and knocks twice on the door jamb.

"Whoops. Knock, knock."

Benicio is fully kitted in his flying gear: black trousers and a navy blue flight jacket that hangs open to reveal a clean white vest underneath. All ready for our lesson: me, Benicio and a Muwan Mark II, the nimble little "sparrow hawk'" aircraft based on the technology of the super-ancient, lost civilization the Erinsi, whose writings are inscribed in the Four Books of Itzamna, including the Ix Codex.

"I guess you forgot about the lesson," Benicio says with a nod at my shoeless feet.

"I'm nearly ready. And what do you mean, they don't need me?"

"I'm not denying you're handy when the Ix Codex is around," Benicio says lightly. He's teasing me, but there's just a bit too much truth to what he says. "But what we need now are grown-ups! Experienced soldiers in the battle to save the world from the galactic superwave!"

Ixchel says quietly, "Benicio, don't."

It's too late, I'm already getting annoyed. "People like you, you mean?"

"Hey, buddy, I've saved your life more than once."

6

"I know. I'm grateful. But you know what I'm talking about. You know I've been in dangerous situations, right? You know I can handle myself, yeah? And Ixchel is, like, this total genius with ancient languages. We should be on the team to decipher all those ancient instructions. We should be helping with the 2012 plan."

Benicio's easy grin falls away, replaced with an expression of caution. "Yeah. Maybe. I couldn't really say." And I know Benicio well enough to recognize this behaviour – hesitant, as though he's afraid to say any more on the subject. This is how he acts when he's been ordered to keep information from me.

"OK, Josh, but right now, let's focus on turning you into a pilot. Today, I'm teaching you a flight manoeuvre that's sure to make you vomit." He snatches a second piece of shortbread out of my fingers before I can put it to my mouth. "So, no more cookies for you."

Chapter 2

We all leave together. Ixchel goes to the gym, and Benicio and I head for the aircraft hangar. It's still very bright, even in the underground part of the city, which streams with sunlight filtered through the wire mesh of the artificial ceiling. In the recesses, though, beyond the reach of the wire mesh, the solid rock overhead hems in the light. In such corners of the hidden city, electric lights are already in operation, powered by the city's own generator several kilometres away, on the surface.

Anyone who looked at Ek Naab from the sky would see nothing but a huge plantation of bananas, coffee and vanilla, and the eco-resort section of the city with its cabanas, thatched-roof restaurants and swimming pools.

Just another private estate belonging to another Mexican billionaire; that's what most of the outside world thinks this is. Most of the world has no idea that underneath is a vast complex of caverns and tunnels, and a hidden city of futuristic technology that would make generals in the Pentagon drool.

Only the enemies of Ek Naab have any idea we're here. And even they don't know exactly where.

Some people in Ek Naab want Montoyo to stop keeping Ek Naab's mission top secret. Tell the world, they say. It's too much responsibility for us.

But Montoyo has lived in the outside world. He knows how things operate. He knows that there are people who'll kill us all to get their hands on the advanced technology in this city.

Well, I'm with Montoyo there. My father was captured by the National Reconnaissance Office, a US government organization. They wanted to know the secrets of Ek Naab, too. They faked my dad's death and imprisoned him in Area 51. What happened to my dad is a direct result of the greed for the secrets hidden away in Ek Naab.

Benicio gets on with telling me about the new manoeuvre that he's programmed into the Muwans. But it must be obvious that my mind is half elsewhere.

"Did you hear me, Josh?"

I turn to him, more than a bit embarrassed. "You've programmed a new thing. Yeah, sounds good."

"Listen properly, OK? You need to be focused to fly one of these machines."

"I'm focused."

"No, I don't think so. Something's on your mind."

"Nope."

"What's up, Josh? Still worrying about conspiracy theories? Maybe you think we have spies in Ek Naab?"

"Conspiracy theories. . .?"

"Your blog – The Joshua Files. I saw you updated it. A Doomsday Manifesto. . .?"

"Well, you know what, turns out there was a conspiracy. . ."

Benicio laughs. "Just because you're paranoid. . ."

". . .doesn't mean they aren't after you. Yeah, I know."

We walk in silence until we get to the entrance of the hangar. The smell of hot grease and sparking metal fills the air. It's intoxicating, a total rush. That's even before I've got into the craft.

"I think you're gonna enjoy this, cousin."

The Muwan Mark II we're taking out is being given a final once-over by a technician named Rafa. He's about thirty-five years old and worked on the design and build of the Mark II. There are rivets on each machine that Rafa put in with his own hands. It's a decent-sized craft, a four-seater in brushed, matt titanium, not as handsome as the Mark I Muwan but smoother, sleek and cunning like a snake's head. We watch Rafa walk around the craft, tapping information into a hand-held computer. I notice that for the first time in any of my lessons, the craft is fully equipped today, including the motorbike that's stowed in the belly of the craft. An innovation of Benicio – who has the most field experience with flying in the outside world.

"The Muwan is fully weighted today," Rafa says. "Full survival kit and bike."

"We need to see you handle yourself with a heavy load," Benicio says.

"But there are only two passengers," I point out. "The maximum load is four."

"Passengers don't change the balance as much as having a Harley in your lower regions," Benicio remarks. "Carrying a motorbike, that calls for a slightly different technique."

He and Rafa exchange a few quiet words about the Muwan. I'd love a cool job like Rafa's. In the outside world, I don't think it would ever have occurred to me to go into engineering. I wasn't good enough at maths. But after a year of living in Ek Naab, with intense study, it turns out I'm actually not so bad. And there are other good things about moving to this city.

When I first moved to Ek Naab I hated it. I missed Oxford, missed normal life. Getting Ixchel to be my girlfriend made all the difference. Before that, she'd been dating Benicio. Now that I'm with Ixchel, I don't much care where I live, so long as she's with me.

Benicio hands me the remote control for the Muwan. I open the cockpit and hit the button. A metal arm pops out and drops an extending steel ladder made of light tubes of metal connected with woven metallic fibres. I climb in first, slide into the pilot seat. Benicio follows me into the co-pilot seat. He takes off his jacket and tosses it into the rear passenger seat.

"You're supposed to keep your jacket on," I remind him. The flight jackets are equipped with essential survival gadgets in case you're forced to eject. Removing them is totally against the rules.

"Ha ha, I know. However, on this occasion, I'm officially allowing you to relax this rule. Go on, take your jacket off. I'm pretty sure you'll hurl. I'd prefer not to worry about a dry-cleaning job."

With some reluctance, I do as he asks and throw my jacket on top of his. If he's trying to psych me out, I realize, it's kind of working. . .

I decide to force myself to ignore Benicio's obvious relishing of the oncoming challenge. Instead I concentrate on going through the start-up protocol. Until a week ago I still had to use a checklist, but now I've managed to memorize it. It's a whole bunch of systems checks that have already been done by Rafa but need a final double-check. As I work through the checks, I'm conscious of Benicio's eyes on me, smirking, judging.

"Something wrong?"

He keeps on smiling. "No, no. Keep going. You're doing great."

Finally I put on my headset, lower the eyepiece and run through the final checks. Benicio lowers his own eyepiece; a yellow light fires up, casts a glow over his cheekbones. Engine is good to go; all routine manoeuvres are up to date in the list of autopilot programmes.

"OK," Benicio announces. "So you see how to bring up a list? Hit this button here. Or start typing and it will find one of the system programmes. Some basic flight programmes are included in the system. These are all the hard-coded systems, stuff that's taken straight from the pages of the Kan Codex."

For a second I can hardly believe what he's doing, going through basics again as though I were some total newbie. "Yeah, Benicio . . . I know all that. Are you going to show me something new or what?"

Benicio pretends to be hurt. "Oh, smart fly-boy too clever for teacher? I'm just making sure you remember your way around the hard-coded systems, and fast. It's been a few weeks since we used one."

"So no more lessons on manoeuvrability?"

"No. You're not bad at that now. But when we ran preprogrammed missions, you were still pretty green."

"Then why go back to the basic preprogrammed stuff?"

He grins, widely and with a glint in his eye. "Who said anything about 'basic'? Today we're gonna start with a personal favourite." In the empty air Benicio appears to press a button. In the display I see that he's typed a C. A list appears, with one title highlighted in neon blue.

CRAZY BENICIO

"Crazy Benicio. Your personal favourite. . .?"

There's a grin in his voice. "Like you cannot believe. . ."

Amazingly, Benicio and I still get on OK. Some guys would be mad if you nicked their girlfriend. But he took it relatively well. "I guess technically she was always yours," he once told me. "Seeing that you two were supposed to be betrothed."

Very philosophical.

Benicio takes out a hand-held computer and starts clicking with a stylus. "OK, all your systems checks are good. Start the engine and select a programme."

12

I follow his instructions and scroll through some options. Underneath our seats I sense the vibrations of the anti-gravity engine as it gradually warms up.

"Becan 6?" I suggest. It's a launch programme that takes the Muwan out of the hangar through a vent which opens in the ceiling, and into a course that flies just six kilometres east of the Mayan ruins of Becan and continues for a hundred kilometres without flying over any populated centre.

"That's fine," Benicio agrees. His voice has finally become serious, businesslike. He loves to joke around, but underneath the playful exterior, I've come to realize, he's actually a very intense guy. Half the time, I have no idea what he's thinking. I think he likes it that way.

BLOG ENTRY: CRAZY BENICIO

My cousin Benicio pulled a gun on me. A real one. And he screamed like a psycho.

I was flying a Muwan Mark II. They're amazing aircraft – they practically fly themselves. The main reason for the many lessons I've had is in case there's ever any into trouble with the National Reconnaissance Office, flying aircraft whose technology they stole from Ek Naab.

I'd just turned off the autopilot, about a hundred klicks out of Becan. I'd taken the controls, popped a holographic projection of a satellite map in front of my eyes, and started to fly to the contours of a mountain ridge about a hundred metres below.

Then I heard Benicio say, very coldly, "Land. Now. Quick."

"What. . .?"

He snapped in fury, "Land! Are you deaf? Land, now, or I'll blow a hole through your neck!"

I was so startled that I could only laugh. But words stubbornly refused to follow.

"Land this craft or I'll KILL YOU!" he screamed.

At that point I turned to see that Benicio was pointing a gun at me. He eyes were round, wide and livid. "Land this goddamn plane, you lousy *pinche gringo*, or God help me I'll. . ."

"OK, OK, OK!"

I began to lower the craft.

"Faster, *cabron*, like you mean it!"

My heart was thudding. So I did what he asked. And said, just to relieve the tension, "Jeez LOUISE, what is your problem? Put the bloody gun away!"

Benicio leaned back, visibly shaking. "*Hijo de. . .*"

"Watch your mouth," I warned. "Say what you like about me, but don't diss my mum."

The craft bounced to a standstill a couple of metres above the ground. I popped out the undercarriage and felt it thud to the stony ground beneath. I lifted my visor to find Benicio had once again raised the gun.

"What's going on?"

"Spies in Ek Naab?" He smiled nastily. "About time you found out."

My mouth dropped open. "What. . .?"

Benicio nodded. He leaned forward and hit the control panel, opening the cockpit. He stood up, towering over me, then leaned back, making space for me to pass.

"Get out."

"After you. . ."

He screamed again. "Get out! Caray, Josh, don't you know when you're in trouble?"

I held up both hands and stumbled past him on the way out of the craft. "All right, all right, don't have a cow."

He had to be joking, surely? Why was he going on about spies in Ek Naab? There had been constant rumours and fears that our enemies might infiltrate Ek Naab, but as far as I knew nothing had ever been proven. It was such a strange thing to joke about. Was he telling me that he knew about spies, or maybe that he was one himself? Or that he suspected that I might be a spy?! My mind raced, trying to make sense of what he was saying.

15

Before I knew what was happening I was on the ground, with Benicio following me. I glanced over my shoulder to see that he still had the gun aimed straight at my chest. It was beyond surreal. I couldn't even feel fear; disorientation obliterated everything else.

"OK, Benicio," I began. I felt a firm yank at my waist. In the next second I was pulled off my feet, dangling. A surge of panic hit me; I twisted around in the air to see the Muwan rising slowly off the ground. It took me another second to realize that I was connected to the open cockpit by an almost invisible thread, a thin cord that had somehow been attached to my belt. I swivelled back to look at Benicio, grinning and waving at me from the ground. I spotted the Muwan's remote control in his right hand.

"Ha ha, Josh. How do you like Crazy Benicio so far?"

Chapter 3

I open my mouth to reply but the air rushes out of my body. An unseen force flings me against the side of the Muwan. There's barely time to protect my face before I slam against it.

Benicio calls out, "Hold on tight."

Then the aircraft takes off. It hurtles along, fifteen metres off the ground, for about twenty seconds. It comes to a juddering halt, and I hear the gravity dampeners engage. My fingers are clamped on to the edge of the cockpit, knuckles locked so hard that it takes a second or two to get them to relax. I hear myself breathing noisily. The craft has stopped in the middle of nowhere, high enough off the ground that a fall might kill me.

From inside the cockpit comes Benicio's disembodied voice.

"Climb aboard."

I'm too startled to move at first. Has he set up some sort of voice-relay? How am I hearing his voice up here?

His voice repeats: "Climb aboard. You have ten seconds to turn off the auto-destruct. Nine. Eight. Seven."

There's no time to wonder what's going on: I scramble up the side of the craft and tumble in. In the pilot seat, I hit a flashing light on the control panel.

"I lied," Benicio says, with a laugh. "I'd drop you first. Then I'd auto-destruct."

"What the hell do you want?" I yell, at no one.

"This is Crazy Benicio," says the voice. "Touch 'play' to continue."

"Touch play to continue..." I mutter, as realization hits me. "This is a recording?!"

There's no answer. Of course not.

Hurriedly, I pull my visor back into position. The list of autopilot programmes is there, with a big play button over CRAZY BENICIO.

The recording continues. "Prepare to play with the professionals, buddy. I've called in some boys from the Mexican Air Force."

I grapple with what this can possibly mean. Benicio called the Mexican Air Force? When? Is he totally insane?

My muscles are so tense that my fingers have almost locked around the steering wheel. I breathe slowly, go through one of the calming exercises I've been shown. Almost immediately, my whole body eases.

"It's only death," comes Benicio's voice. He sounds absurdly cheerful. "You can't live for ever."

My fingers touch an invisible button in the air. The cockpit begins to close. I notice then that the cord attached to my waist is fastened with a sturdy metal clip, like the type climbers use. The other end goes into a socket on the dashboard.

Benicio must have clipped it on to my belt when I pushed past him on my way out of the cockpit.

The Muwan begins to rise slowly. After the first few seconds it accelerates. Muscles clamp tight in my stomach as the machine zooms high – fifteen-thousand metres in ten seconds.

What follows is a descent into insanity. Abruptly, the craft drops about a hundred metres, and then bolts ahead at a thousand kilometres per hour. A few seconds later, the plane begins to corkscrew. It straightens out after another breath-stopping minute.

A holographic radar map of the sky ahead appears inside my visor. It's clear, with occasional commercial airliners showing up over a thousand metres below. Commercial aircraft show up as blue. Anything else – military or UFOs – usually show up red. In the far distance over Campeche I spot a triangle of jets in formation.

"Military ahead," announces Benicio's voice calmly. "Select evasive manoeuvre. And whatever you do, don't get tempted to use the ion volley. . ."

I hold my breath, heart pumping. A list of pre-programmed manoeuvres scrolls before my eyes. Within a minute, I'm dizzy. My concentration flags; sweat gushes from under my arms.

I had no idea it would be so hard to stay calm.

There's something crushing about being alone in that machine for the first time in my life, totally responsible for my own life and a priceless bit of engineering. On the radar, I watch the triangle of military craft turning around. They are more than ten klicks away, but they're definitely heading for my position.

I steady my breathing and concentrate on the list of manoeuvres. Campeche Run, Orizaba Swirl, Stratosphere Dive. . .

I hit the last one: Bermuda Mask. It's risky because I'll be going out over the Gulf of Mexico, where there tends to be loads of air traffic. But the good news is that if you fly low, near the Bermuda Triangle, people are less likely to believe anyone who films your flight. The other bonus? Fires from gas and oil wells – they show up on infrared cameras and look a lot like a Muwan in flight. A great place to mask your appearance and to lose a tail.

But instead of changing course for the Gulf of Mexico, the Muwan turns in the opposite direction, until I've completed a one-eighty and find myself heading back the way I came.

I stare from the control panel to the holographic flight map, stunned, baffled, scared.

What did I do wrong?

Then Benicio's voice sounds again, slightly louder, animated by a slight crackle.

"OK, dude, that's not a good choice." He sighs. It's very confusing. Is this still the recording? Or is this Benicio's voice from the ground, watching me? "I'm bringing you in," he continues. "Man! You really have no clue when you're out of your depth!"

My mouth opens but nothing comes out. I gaze at the control panel, the holographic flight map, struggling to comprehend what I'm seeing.

The radar field is empty now. No sign of military aircraft, anywhere. The "Mexican Air Force guys" have vanished.

"In case you hadn't realized, Josh, you failed the test." There's another irritated sound from my cousin. "You did the escape bit OK, that was good. And you were scared, right? Yet you kept your cool. But Bermuda Mask is too, too risky, cousin. If three Mexican Air Force guys really had sighted you, you'd have to be ice-cold under intense pressure to beat them on that territory."

It takes me an embarrassing amount of time to process what Benicio is telling me. "You . . . you staged all this? The recording, the . . . the Mexican Air Force? The whole chase?"

"Fake, fake and, uh, fake. That's right, cousin. Crazy Benicio is the final test. I can't pass you without it. Without Crazy Benicio under your belt, you're nothing but a taxi driver."

Chapter 4

Ixchel reads my blog while I change into shorts and a T-shirt. She chuckles quite a bit and tilts her head towards me, saying, quizzically, "The Doomsday Manifesto?"

"Yeah. I thought I should have a manifesto. Like in that film you got so obsessed with when you were working as a waitress in Veracruz. You know? The one with those two Mexican guys, the ones whose photos you have on your wall."

She nods in approval. "Ah – I see. Point Seven of your manifesto: Get involved. I like it."

"Hmmm."

"How are you going to 'get involved'?"

"Not sure yet."

Ixchel waits for me to continue, but I don't. When she sees my expression, she comes over to where I'm sitting, a bit mournful, on the side of the bed.

"Don't be sad."

"But I was useless."

"How long did it take you to get good at your capoeira?"

I groan. "Years."

"You weren't doing all those somersaults and spinning kicks from day one?"

"Well, no."

"So don't complain," she says with an affectionate stab to my chest. "Benicio has been flying for five years – since he was fourteen, in fact. It takes time."

"I guess."

Ixchel begins to giggle. "You really believed he was a spy...?"

"Not even! That's what got me riled, to be honest. I knew something was going on. I wonder how long he worked on his Scary Hijacker routine."

"You're angry because Benicio made you believe some stupid lie?"

"That's just it, I didn't really believe it. Deep down I knew he had to be joking but . . . but. . ."

"Ah – he confused you?"

"Yes."

"And scared you?"

"A bit, yeah."

Ixchel hesitates for just long enough for me to guess where she's going with this. "But isn't that exactly what you'd feel if you really did have some dangerous enemy breathing down your neck, chasing you down in the Muwan, making it impossible to escape?"

I look at her, feeling a bit of an idiot. She's right.

"Did Benicio ever tell you what made him write that flight programme?"

"No."

"It was when your father was captured by the National Reconnaissance Office, the NRO. Benicio thinks that must be how they got him: the NRO pilots cornered him, pinned him down."

My eyes fix on hers. She's telling the truth. "Benicio told you this? When?"

"Just before, while you were taking a shower and writing your blog."

"That's . . . wow. I wonder why he didn't tell me."

"You know Benicio – everything's a joke with him."

"But he can be serious with you."

"Once in a while. He was upset about what happened to your father. He was against leaving your dad to fly that Muwan, with so little training. Benicio told me that he'd offered to fly your dad to where he needed to go."

Miserably I say, "I wish he had."

"There didn't seem to be any danger. Back then, no one in Ek Naab knew that the NRO had stolen our technology. No idea that they were a threat."

"I didn't realize that Benicio felt bad about what happened to my dad."

Tenderly she says, "Of course, Josh. Everyone in Ek Naab did. I still remember how sad and alone you looked the day of his funeral."

"Do you remember what you told me that day?" I murmur.

She squeezes my hand, just as she did that horrible day. "I said you'd get through it. And you did."

"Thanks to you," I say, very quietly. "Thanks to Benicio. But no thanks to Montoyo." Ixchel remains silent. She knows well enough the problem I have with Carlos Montoyo. She gives me a long, considered look. "Maybe it's time you talked to Carlos about all this."

"Talk to him? I see the guy almost every day."

"I mean really talk. You haven't let him know that you're angry about them not including you in the plans for 2012, have you?"

Ixchel's trying to help, I know. But it seems incredible to me that Montoyo wouldn't know. After everything I've done so far to help the scientists in Ek Naab stop the galactic superwave – how could he not realize I'd want to at least be on the team?

"Montoyo knows."

"You haven't actually said anything, though, have you? I bet you glower at him over the breakfast table, but he probably assumes that's because you don't like seeing him with your mother."

"No – he knows I'm OK with that."

Ixchel laughs. "Really?"

"Seriously, we had this proper man-to-man talk where he told me that he was obsessed with my mum and I was, like, Yeah, OK, and he made me promise to take care of her if anything ever happened to him and I was all, you know, Same. So, yes, he knows I'm OK with him seeing Mum."

"But wasn't that in a different timeline? The timeline where the Ix Codex had been stolen in the Mayan past? The timeline we changed when we travelled back into the past?"

"Oh," I say. "Yes, it was. It's hard to keep two different histories straight sometimes. It's like having feelings and memories from a dream."

"Maybe in this reality, Montoyo and you never had that conversation."

"You could be right," I admit. "I hadn't thought of that. We don't really communicate much. It's all 'How are your studies going?' and 'You still seeing that pretty girl you're supposed to marry?'"

"That would be me," she says with a grin.

"Blatantly," I say, gazing into her eyes.

"Good. So you'll talk to him?"

I slide an arm around her waist. "Sure. Remind me what about, again?"

Ixchel touches a finger to the tip of my nose. "Josh. Stop it."

She watches me go off in the direction of Montoyo's office. It's not somewhere I've ever been, because Montoyo and I tend to avoid each other during the day. So he's understandably surprised to see me.

24

As I stare around the room, Montoyo shuffles in his chair and stands up. The walls are covered in old maps, reproductions of the famous Frederick Catherwood illustrations of the Mayan ruins in the nineteenth century, and a frame containing book jackets of the first few editions of John Lloyd Stephens' book Incidents of Travel in Central America, Chiapas and Yucatan. It's not difficult to see what attracted my mother to the guy – his office is decorated almost exactly like my own father's study. Archaeology and discovery. It's the office of a university professor, not the behind-the-scenes ruler of a tiny, hidden world.

For a moment I wonder which is the real Montoyo – the part he plays as his "cover" in the outside world, a professor at the University of Yucatan? Or the Montoyo that I know – the wily, strategic operator?

Montoyo snaps his laptop computer closed and removes his reading glasses. He's dressed the same as always: a dark, long-sleeved shirt with a silky sheen and black jeans, his shoulder-length, salt-and-pepper hair tied back in a tight ponytail. Montoyo the campus guru, the hippie academic.

"Josh," he begins, clearly at a loss for words. "This is . . . well, I'm not certain what it is. How did your flying lesson go?"

"We did Crazy Benicio. I failed the test," I say, without expression.

His face falls, but it seems more for effect than sincere. "I see. I'm sure you'll improve."

I nod. It's hard to know how to begin. There's no easy way to bring the subject up.

Bluntly he asks, "So, why are you here?"

Good. He's cutting straight to the chase. I prefer that.

"How are things going?" I blurt. "With the 2012 plan. Is everything on schedule?"

Montoyo blinks. I ask him the same things at home, at least once a week. The answer is always the same. Everything's fine.

"Well, Josh, as I believe I've told you before. . ."

25

"You've told me nothing," I interrupt. "But I can work out for myself that something is wrong."

Now I've got his attention.

"You've instructed Benicio to tell me nothing, I know that. Every time I mention the 2012 plan, he shuts right up. And there's this atmosphere. Between you and me. Something you're not telling me. Something you don't feel right about keeping from me. It wasn't always like this; don't think I've forgotten."

Montoyo replies thoughtfully, "I see."

"The 2012 plan, it's all about bringing together the elements of the instructions in the Ix Codex. Right? Me and Ixchel actually wrote out part of the original Ix Codex – at least we copied out the translations that Itzamna had already made – so don't forget: I actually know some of what is in the Ix Codex. Enough to know there's a lot you aren't telling me."

"We've all heard about how you and Ixchel helped Itzamna to transcribe the ancient Erinsi inscriptions," Montoyo says, a touch sardonic. "And of course we're all very grateful for everything you've done."

"Men of destiny. Men of action. That's what you told me once. You said that's what we are, you and me."

In a level voice, Montoyo says, "Did I?"

"Was it all an act, Carlos? To get me to do something for you? Go on another deadly mission?"

His mouth tightens. It could be my imagination but he seems to turn a little paler. "Relax. There will be no more missions."

"I want missions! I've earned the right to be treated properly and asked to do stuff and told the risks!"

"What you've earned is the right to be left alone to enjoy what is left of your childhood."

"My childhood was over years ago!"

Montoyo gives a reluctant nod. "Maybe. Yes, that's probably true."

"Give me a straight answer for once. Is everything OK with the 2012 plan? Are we going to be able to stop the galactic superwave?"

My question hangs in the air for a few seconds, seems to freeze and glaze over with ice.

And whatever Montoyo was thinking of saying . . . he stops. Mid-sentence, mid-thought, even. He looks at me with unmistakable anxiety and mutters, "What is imperative, Josh, is that you say nothing. . ."

I stare.

"And you cannot take any action . . . Josh. You have to promise me."

"Is the plan on track?"

Montoyo goes to the door, which I'd left open. He closes it. He indicates the chair in front of his desk. But I shake my head. Adrenaline floods through me as I wait to hear what he's about to say.

His voice becomes conspiratorial. "You can't repeat this to anyone. Not your cousin, not your mother, no one."

"I'd have to tell Ixchel," I demand.

Montoyo hesitates. He has the look of a cornered animal, desperate to find some way out. "Yes, I imagine that's inevitable," he mumbles, almost to himself. "And you consider she can be trusted?"

I glare. "Yeah, sure."

Montoyo's hands spread on the desk in front of him; he gazes at them for the longest time, seemingly lost in the pattern they make amongst the neat, shallow piles of paper. Finally he looks up at me. There's a melancholy, wise, accepting expression on his face, as though this is a day he's seen coming and dreaded, but now that it's arrived it's not as bad as he thought.

"There is a problem with the 2012 plan. And for once, Josh, I can only think of one solution. A solution that goes against everything I've fought against for so many years. Against all the efforts we've made throughout the centuries to keep ourselves separate from the outside world. And even that solution is far – very far – from being certain."

Flinching, I ask, "Does it involve me . . . again?"

Montoyo smiles sadly. "No. This time, it doesn't. But I can be sure of one thing: you won't like it."

Chapter 5

By the time Benicio catches up with me I'm staring into the still, deep waters of the black cenote for which Ek Naab is named. It's a good place to go when you need to think; the mirror of water gazes right back at you until you feel like you're staring the answer in the face.

"Ixchel said you're not happy with what happened today."

It takes me a full five seconds to work out that he's talking about the flying lesson. He hands me my Muwan flight jacket. "Look what you left in the hangar bay." Then he grins, but not unkindly. "Don't feel too bad. It's normal to fail Crazy Benicio the first time."

I take the jacket and tuck it under my arm.

"Oh, that. Yeah. I mean no, I wasn't happy, but that's not your fault."

He gives me a quizzical look. "Something wrong? What did Montoyo say?"

My eyes widen, I turn red, but I manage to stay silent. Is there anything Ixchel doesn't tell her ex-boyfriend? But as I watch Benicio I realize that for once, he isn't joking around or teasing. He's anxious.

"Come on, Josh, what did Montoyo tell you about the 2012 plan?"

"You don't know?"

"No – and quit gloating. Only the ruling Executive know the truth. And everyone else. . ."

". . .has been ordered to keep silent."

Benicio nods. "Right." When I don't say anything, he sighs and gives a sarcastic smile. "Oh, I get it. And you too."

"Benicio. I can't."

"They send me on missions, you know, and I'm never allowed to see the full picture. But I'm not blind. I know that something is wrong. And this time it's serious, yes? Because we have the Ix Codex; we have all the knowledge we should need to protect the world from the superwave. This time, it's not as simple as sending good ol' Josh Garcia to hunt for the codex."

I look right into his eyes. I want to tell him what I know . . . but I promised.

Benicio gazes back at me until he sees enough to realize that I'm not going to talk.

"OK," he says after a moment. "Let's do this. I'll tell you what I suspect. If I'm right, you say nothing. If I'm wrong, Josh, then you have to try to change the subject. That way you've actually told me nothing."

My eyes plead with him. "Ben . . . don't . . . I promised. . ."

"Come on – we both know most of this anyway, from what happened to you when you went into the Mayan past and met Bosch, your crazy time traveller from the twenty-second century, the guy who persuaded the ancient Mayans he was a one of their gods."

"He didn't have to try very hard. . ." I mutter, remembering the Bosch's wild energy, his intensity. "Those Mayans were fully smitten."

But Benicio won't be thrown from the scent. "You wouldn't be giving away anything. It's just me here, theorizing."

"I don't. . ."

"Josh, why do you think I want to know? For the same reason as you. Haven't I been there for you every time you needed me, at least whenever I possibly could? Scooping up your sorry butt in Oxford, Switzerland, Mexico, Brazil. . . And half the time, cousin, I broke rules. Remember when we rescued Ixchel and your mom from the Sect? We went against Montoyo then, right?"

"Yeah, but. . ."

"I don't know about you, dude, but I'm done with the ruling Executive. They're tearing themselves apart right about now, through inaction. Somewhere along the line, we've hit a problem. The 2012 plan has stalled. There's a chance, just a chance, that someone in the outside world can help. But the ruling Executive is so stuck on keeping all our technology secret, they won't talk. Don't say anything, Josh; if I'm right, just let me keep talking."

I gulp and force myself to meet his eyes.

"The Sect of Huracan and the National Reconnaissance Office both have a piece of what we need, don't they? They each control one of the Revival Chambers. And we control one, too. The ancient Erinsi left the best and wisest people of their civilization in those chambers, in deep hibernation. Over history, they've been revived. Sometimes on purpose, sometimes by mistake. Now, their time has come. The galactic superwave is on its way. And only the Erinsi knew how to stop it. They put a machine somewhere – what in the Ix Codex they call the moon machine. Some kind of device to create a counter-wave or something, to protect the Earth. I'm just talking, Josh, theorizing; this is still just old Benicio, talking a blue streak, is all."

He pauses. I remain silent.

"The moon machine is on the moon, presumably. That's why we have the Muwans, I'm guessing. But so far as I know, there hasn't been a single mission to the moon, not yet. The superwave will hit the solar system in December. That gives us less than six months. We should be running test missions to the moon by now. So what I'm thinking is this: we don't know the exact location of the moon machine."

Calmly, I blink at him.

"OK, here's my wild guess. Are you ready? Here goes. I'm guessing that the dirty little secret is this: the precise location of the moon machine is secret; not written anywhere. It's the Erinsi survivors themselves who know. And . . . there are no ancient Erinsi survivors left. It's not just our own Revival Chamber, here in Mexico: all those Revival Chambers are empty. . ."

I cough, trying to think of a way to change the subject just as Benicio suggested, so he will understand that he's on the wrong track. "Seen anything good on YouTube?"

He frowns. ". . .the chambers aren't empty. . .?" I raise my eyebrows, trying to urge him to keep guessing. "Or . . . maybe not all of them?" he continues. "Is that it? Maybe we don't know where they are . . . or can't get into them." I give a tiny, almost imperceptible nod. Despite himself, Benicio flashes a grin, more relief than triumph. "Without the ancient Erinsi, we can't operate the moon machine. You need a specific number of Erinsi survivors, I'm guessing five, one from each chamber. . ."

I rub a hand across one eye. He's on the wrong track: I need to change the subject again. "The air's a bit rubbish today, isn't it? I don't think the filters are working properly."

Benicio stops. "Maybe not five. Maybe more . . . maybe less? Four. Three?"

I shrug and say nothing, hoping he'll pick up the signal that he's right.

Urgently now, he says, "Three Erinsi are required to locate and operate this moon machine. And we don't have a single one! So our only hope to get out of this nightmare, to recover all the careful planning of the genius Erinsi who put all the efforts of their dying civilization to save our future . . . is to trust our enemies. And that's why there's so much tension in the ruling Executive. Can you ever trust an enemy?"

I just smile.

"I'm guessing they're not thinking about asking the Sect of Huracan. The Sect is counting on the superwave. It's going to destroy the existing world order. The Sect will leap right into the vacuum. Those twisted sickos want billions to die so they can start their own, perfect society."

He pauses, giving me a chance to interrupt. I return his stony gaze.

"So if we're thinking of cooperation, it must be the National Reconnaissance Office. We know for a fact that they control one of the Revival Chambers – the one in Iraq. Yeah. The NRO may work for the government of the 'leader of the free world', but they're as bad as anyone else when it comes to grabbing power and technology. We work with them and we help ensure the continuation of the status quo. While adding a few priceless technologies to their arsenal."

Benicio's eyes have become cold, hard, grim. "For weeks now, the ruling Executive has been trying to make up its mind. Shall we sell out? Join forces with the NRO? "

Struggling to stay calm, I manage to limit myself to, "The NRO. They might as well have murdered my dad."

Into the long silence that follows, Benicio merely sighs. "Do you wish Montoyo had never told you?"

"No. I asked him, didn't I? I wanted the truth; I want to help. But I can't see how, this time."

"You could come on a mission with me. Probably a waste of time but you never can tell. At least you'd feel like you're doing something."

"Montoyo has been ordered not to send me on missions again."

"Ordered?"

"By my mother."

Benicio looks genuinely surprised.

"I'm serious. She knows enough of what's really going on to know that there's nothing that only I can do. So she told Montoyo to keep me out of it."

"Well, that makes sense. Montoyo's crazy about your mom. She's the boss of him, for sure."

"She's the boss of me too. I guess I've risked my neck one too many times."

"Naturally. You gotta understand your mom, Josh. Why should she allow her son to be endangered, over and over? If the world is going to hell, then at least she should have her only child with her."

"Montoyo would risk me, even so. He told me that once – that's why he protects me. So that I'll be there when he needs me to get the Ix Codex."

"Yes, as a time-travelling superstar you have your uses. As an ordinary soldier, however ... you're more use to Montoyo as the studious son of the woman he plans to marry."

"Yeah, maybe. But I'm almost sixteen. I should be able to choose my own life. What's all this flight training for if I can't fly on the moon mission? What's all my experience of fighting the Sect for if we can't use it?"

"For once, buddy, I'm a hundred per cent agreed. You're not a little kid any more. God knows, you've earned your place here."

"Right!"

"So, come on a mission with me. We won't tell Montoyo. You and me, just like the old days."

"The old days, last year?" I laugh.

"Yeah, those. Let's hit the road."

We've had our ups and downs, Benicio and me. But I think, at that moment, that I may actually love my cousin.

Chapter 6

We go directly to the garage where all the road vehicles in Ek Naab are stored. Most of them are pickup trucks designed to be used on the ranches. There are eight motorbikes. Benicio's Harley is there. Gently, he prises it free of the stand and pushes it out. Then he waves me on to the passenger seat.

"Huh? Don't I get my own?"

"You don't have a motorcycle licence yet, so, no. If we're stopped, the last thing we need is to draw attention to ourselves. You got your fake papers, yes? Your student card from Yucatan University?"

My hand goes to the Muwan flight jacket. There's a pocket in which you're supposed to keep some kind of identification that will work in the outside world, just in case of trouble. I check the pocket – the ID is there. I pull the jacket on over my white T-shirt, baggy shorts and trainers. It's not ideal attire for a motorbike ride, but it'll do. On the other hand, Benicio is wearing blue jeans, black boots and his leather biker jacket, which is a kind of madness in this scorching weather.

Benicio passes me a silver Shoei helmet and waits as I fasten it on. I ask, "What's the plan?"

He pulls on his own, identical helmet, climbs on the driver seat in front of me. He plants his right foot firmly on the ground to steady the bike and turns his head slightly so that I can hear him.

"OK. Whilst the Powers That Be of our city argue about talking with the enemy, while we wonder if between us and the NRO we can scrape together enough Erinsi survivors to activate the moon machine. . ." He takes a deep breath.

Before I can stop myself, I interject, "Assuming we can even find it. . ."

I can hear the smile in Benicio's voice. "Assuming, yes. . . So the Big Guys are focused on that. But little old me, I'm still worried about the Sect of Huracan. I think we've taken our eye off the ball. You don't hear so much about the Sect these days; they've gone pretty quiet."

"Big mistake," I say. "The Sect is in this for the very long term. We shouldn't let up on them at all."

"Exactly my view. Which is why that's the focus of my work. And I think you can help. Since it isn't Montoyo asking for your help this time, he's in the clear with your mom."

"Yeah, but if she finds out. . ." I say.

Benicio chuckles. "She's only my aunt. What's she gonna do, ground me?"

"Right," I say, forcing a laugh, but my stomach lurches a bit with the idea that Mum might actually ground me. The humiliation would be pretty severe.

"So. When you were time travelling, at one point you landed by Lake Bacalar, yes?"

"That's right."

"And you were using the time-travel bracelet that belonged to one of the leaders of the Sect of Huracan, yes? You were using Marius Martineau's device."

"Yeah."

"Well, the way you and Ixchel describe it, seems that the time-travel Bracelet always returns the user to the last place he was."

"In default mode, yes. But you go back to ten minutes before you left. That's the safety thing, see; it assumes you were safe ten minutes before whatever danger made you need to escape."

36

"You return to where you were, but displaced by ten minutes?"

"Right."

"OK. You were using the Bracelet belonging to Marius Martineau, and it defaulted, so you travelled in time and arrived at the exact location he'd left. Which was beside a house on Lake Bacalar. Therefore, the Sect has a house at Lake Bacalar."

"Exactly!" I say, triumphant. "The number of times I tried to tell Montoyo about that. The house was rented to that scientist woman from the Sect, Melissa DiCanio. I'm pretty sure she's one of their leaders. She was with Martineau's idiot son, Simon Madison. Finally, finally someone's taking me seriously."

"Oh, they've taken this seriously for a long time. But without you, Josh, to identify the house. . ." Benicio shrugs. "Well, I've searched a few. But we haven't found it."

"And you couldn't ask me to help," I say, bitterly, "because Montoyo promised my mother that he'd leave me out of this from now on."

"You got it, cuz. I'm down to the last few candidates. Just need you to confirm my suspicion. See how there's no danger? You just have to make a visual confirmation. That's all."

I'm actually a bit disappointed, but then Benicio does something that jolts me back into adrenaline mode. He grins and pulls back his jacket slightly, to reveal what he's wearing underneath. When I glance down I spot the edge of a holster containing a pistol tucked tightly under his left armpit.

"A gun. . .?"

"Right."

"You know how to use one of those?"

Benicio nods. Suddenly I catch a sense of the risk he's taking. Out on a secret mission with me, and he's packing a gun.

"You're not coming into the house with me," he warns. "The gun is just an insurance policy."

I'm silent, thinking through the possible outcomes. Worst case scenario – someone gets badly hurt. Even if nothing super-bad happens, if my mother finds out about this, I can see my flight lessons being cancelled. But it's a little late to lose face with Benicio. And I really do want to help him find that house on Bacalar.

"You still want to come?" he says, shortly.

I shrug. "Of course."

"OK, Josh. We're gonna find the house, take a look around. Anything we can find about the Sect could be useful."

We leave Ek Naab via the innocent-looking banana plantation that belongs to the city. Benicio swipes his security pass at the electronic gate. This gate is unmanned most of the time, but there's a CCTV that is monitored inside the city. Luckily the helmet makes it impossible for them to see that I'm the guy sitting behind Benicio.

The ride to Lake Bacalar takes just over two hours, all along tiny little roads that Benicio zips around, me riding pillion, holding on around his waist. It's good to see the outside world again. The hot-tar smell of roads. Sleepy Mexican villages with straw-topped houses. Roadside vendors wearing cowboy hats and selling plastic bags of sliced mango, coconuts hacked open with a handy straw, cans of fizzy drinks sitting in barrels of giant chunks of ice. My mouth waters each time we ride past one but Benicio doesn't stop.

But even better is the feeling that once again, I'm doing something about 2012. I'm getting involved. Nine months of solid studying and I feel as though I've been stuffed in a box. Riding with Benicio is like being sprung, jack-in-the-box style. Wild, unpredictable, thrilling.

When we reach Lake Bacalar, Benicio finds somewhere cool to park the Harley. He applies a massive lock to the wheel. There's almost no one around, only the occasional car driving past. Across the road, appearing in chinks of intense blue between the lakeside properties, the turquoise lake stretches in every direction.

I stare across the potholed lakeside street, beyond a semi-constructed villa that's already overgrown with raggedy weeds. The lake water is just as I remember it, a sharp, dazzling blue, improbably bright.

With the helmets under our arms we stroll down the lakeside road to a restaurant set in a neatly clipped lawn with flower beds. Accordion rhythms of Mexican norteño music play over loudspeakers. The restaurant is almost deserted – the lunchtime rush won't start for another hour or so. We veer past the bar, where two long-haired women in bikinis sit sipping beer from frosty glasses. At the edge of the lake a long wooden pier reaches out into the water. A glass-bottomed boat is moored about halfway up, waiting for the next batch of visitors. The water sports centre is before that; nothing more than a collection of slightly shabby-looking jet skis.

Seeing us approach, a skinny, very tanned boy about my age and wearing only a pair of bright yellow shorts lopes over, squinting in the sunlight. He shows us to where he's already set up two scratched-up Kawasakis for us. Benicio hands him a bundle of Mexican peso notes and gives him a friendly pat on the shoulder. "OK, pal," he says in Spanish. "We'll see you later!"

We both slide into position on the jet skis and rev up. Then we're moving out beyond the stacks of parked jet skis and into the water, giving a wide berth to the swimmers near the pier. At Benicio's signal I ratchet up the speed until we're both skimming the water, slapping the vehicles along an occasional small wave. Benicio edges ahead, indicating that I should follow. He swerves towards the edge of the lake and then slows down. I do the same, until we're both at a standstill.

Bobbing up and down on his Kawasaki, Benicio lifts up his visor. "So?" he yells. "Does this one look familiar?"

I follow his finger to a house on the bank. It's a modern white villa built in the old Spanish style, with a terracotta-tiled roof. Doesn't look remotely familiar. With a quick nod he flips the visor into place and we're back on the water. About ten minutes later we stop by another house. This one is almost impossible to see behind a thick forest of tall reeds. There are arched windows and the building is white, but instead of the tidy lawn I remember from the dream, there's a wide patch of gleaming white gravel.

I shake my head slowly. Benicio looks disappointed. "I was afraid of that," he said. "There's one more house that matches your description; lakeside, white, modern, arches, lots of glass. It's another five hundred metres from here. But it's been unoccupied for months. The realtor said the renters moved their stuff out but that they won't let it go on the market. Their rent keeps arriving, every month."

"It looks sort of familiar. . ."

Benicio nods, thoughtful. "It was one of the first houses I checked. But it was empty. I assumed that it wasn't the right place, so I didn't search it."

"All these houses kind of look the same. I'd need to see it close up to be sure. I mean . . . I really wish you'd asked me months ago. Maybe it's too late for us. To find anything, I mean."

"Don't be so sure," Benicio says. "There has to be a reason they're still paying the rent."

A moment later we reach the place and I'm standing right in front of the house. Seeing it gives me a shot of déjà vu. I push strands of damp hair out of my eyes.

"Yep. This is it."

Chapter 7

We park the jet skis among reeds alongside a clean pinewood jetty. There's only one mooring so we tie the machines together with the same rope.

At the back of the house a large French window opens on to a paved terrace. The second-floor balcony hangs over, creating a covered outdoor area. The back garden isn't overlooked by anyone except from the water. There's not much traffic on the lake, though. It's a quiet spot; a perfect spot for a comfortable, accessible hideout.

Benicio unholsters his gun, pulls the sleeve of his jacket down over the muzzle and whips it hard against a pane of glass next to the lock. The glass breaks noisily. We wait for a few tense seconds. But there's no reaction from anyone inside the house – if anyone's there.

Still holding the gun, Benicio unlocks and then steps through the door. I follow. Benicio stops and pushes a hand into my chest. He hisses, "Where are you going. . .?"

"I'm not letting you go in there alone," I whisper.

"Don't sweat it. I've got the gun."

"You're not going in there without at least a lookout."

Benicio moves away. "I'm telling you to stay outside."

"Got it," I tell him calmly. "But I'm coming in anyway cos you're a crazy boy with a gun. And some people I know will be upset if I don't have your back."

"Ditto," he says. But this time, he doesn't stop me.

The house is totally white, totally empty. Almost as I remember it: a house of grey and white marble floors, white furniture, muted abstract art and glass. Now, though, it looks faintly drab, dusty and forgotten.

We examine all the rooms downstairs. There's no furniture. Benicio motions to me that he's going to start on the stairs. I follow, stepping quietly, but I'm disappointed. There's nothing left here. If people were coming to the house, there'd be a sign of it in the kitchen. A fridge, at least, for snacks.

Upstairs immediately feels more concrete, familiar. We make a quick check - it's empty, every room.

"Oh, man."

"What is it?"

"This really is the place. I've seen this. That was a bedroom," I say, pointing. "That was Melissa DiCanio's office." Benicio steps inside and I follow.

He whispers, with deep satisfaction, "Goooooal."

There's a telephone on the desk, and a laptop computer. Benicio nods at me to get to the computer while he guards the door. I glance at what's open on the desktop – a Web browser looking at YouTube. I start unplugging the laptop when Benicio hisses at me.

"Just pull the contact database! You want to advertise that we dropped by?" He takes a memory stick from his pocket and tosses it through the air at me. I grab it out of the air just before it clatters against the desk, flashing Benicio an angry glance.

I open the email program and rapidly export the contacts database on to the memory stick.

"OK; done. Anything else. . .?"

Benicio opens his mouth to speak. Before a sound leaves his lips, from behind him, there's a noise. A door opens. The sound comes from inside the empty bedroom. We glance at each other, utterly astonished. Benicio pulls backs, gun at the ready. He slides behind the door, concealing himself.

There's nowhere in the room for me to hide. I grab the handle of the balcony door. It turns – I push the door open and close it behind me. There's a tiny part of the balcony that is hidden from view. Breathing rapidly, I press myself into the space, against the outside wall.

There's silence. I'm outside, holding my breath, straining to reconstruct a picture from every tiny sound that I'm hearing inside the room. Somewhere on the same floor, a second door opens. Another silence. Whoever opened the door must be looking into another room. Where did he come from? When we checked, the door to the bedroom was open and the room was empty; so was the ensuite bathroom. The guy must have been crouched behind the opened bathroom door, I realize with a sinking heart.

Crouching on the toilet.

Then there's the sound of footsteps. Someone's stepped into the room with the balcony. I can hear slow pacing. The sounds get closer to the windows. Why hasn't Benicio tackled the guy? I'm dying to sneak a peek at what's going on but if I budge an inch I'll risk being seen.

A little thing would give us up now. Just open the balcony door and I'm standing right there. . .

The balcony door handle turns. There's movement. A guns fires. There's return fire, two shots, then an agonized yell.

I can't stop myself from looking. I lean forward, stare through the glass. Benicio lies groaning, his gun on the floor, centimetres from his fingers. Blood is spattered on the wall behind him. He's been shot, but I can't tell where. Standing over him holding a gun there's a guy with his back to me. All I can see is that he's got a lithe build and long, black, curly hair.

"Don't move," the shooter advises Benicio, speaking Spanish. "Not one centimetre. Or I'll kill you, see?" He looks and sounds Mexican. "Who sent you? What are you doing here?"

Outside on the balcony I lean back, hiding again. Inside, the shooter is cursing, furious that he hasn't got anything with which to tie up Benicio. His fury erupts into violence – swearing as he kicks him. Benicio just manages to say "No, don't. . ." when the guy lands a hard blow. Benicio yells, then groans loudly in agony. I blink slowly, twice.

This is only going to get worse. Benicio is totally at his mercy. I could get away now, no doubt, swing over the balcony, escape on one of the Kawasakis. If I leave Benicio here, though, the Sect will probably torture him. Under that pressure, will he reveal the secret of the gateway to Ek Naab? Maybe, maybe not. Either way, I doubt that they'll leave him alive.

"Shut up and let me think!" the shooter screams at Benicio. He leans over Benicio and reaches for the gun that's lying at his feet. As he does so, Benicio's left foot slams into the shooter's groin. The guy yells, enraged, and whips Benicio across the face with his pistol. Benicio's arms go up, fending off the blows. It's instantly clear to me that this is going to end with Benicio being beaten to death.

The element of surprise – that's all; the only possible advantage I can get.

Bring the house down.

I leap on to the edge of the balcony, drop into a handstand, facing the house. With a slight dip to build momentum, I swing hard into the window, feet first. I crash through, plunging into the room in a noisy cloud of shattered glass. When I land a second later, the guy has turned round and already fired off a bullet. But he's way off target, distracted by flying shards of glass.

My next move kicks the gun clean out of his hand. I follow up with a second kick to his ribs. He staggers, winded for a second. By this time Benicio has recovered his own gun and dragged himself to his feet. He leans against the desk, clutching his own weapon. Blood spills from his right leg on to the parquet floor.

"Get his gun," Benicio mutters, his voice icy. I do it, glancing at the closed door to the corridor. Only silence from the rest of the house.

The shooter gazes at me in sudden recognition. "I know you."

Benicio glances at me. "You ever saw this guy?"

Blood drains from my face. I shake my head. The Sect must still be on the lookout for me. Ever since Melissa DiCanio used me as a human guinea pig for her genetic experiments, they've wanted to get hold of me. I still don't know exactly what for, but it has to do with the genetic abilities they introduced into me when they turned my eyes from brown to blue.

"Why are you here?" Benicio asks the guy, his voice trembling. "What are you guarding?"

He doesn't answer.

Benicio's breathing goes into overdrive when he sees his own blood. The shooter looks at me again for a second, then back at Benicio.

"Buddy," Benicio gasps at me, not taking his eyes off his attacker. "Leave. Now."

I stare at the growing pool of blood at Benicio's feet. I glance at his face. He's deathly white.

"Let's both go," I reply.

"I need to finish this guy. Not gonna kill him in front of you."

But there are tears in his eyes. Benicio's never killed anyone before.

"Why kill him at all? We have both the weapons."

"He's right," the shooter says, now speaking in English with a heavy accent. "What am I gonna do?"

Benicio frowns. He raises his arm, aiming the gun. His hand shakes.

The pool of Benicio's blood starts to trickle towards me.

"Let's go," I repeat.

There's a long, tense pause. Benicio breathes out, long and slow.

"OK." Then to the shooter he says, "Turn around."

The guy hesitates. I watch, rigid, appalled.

Shooting a guy in the back. . .?

"No te voy a matar, menso. . ." Benicio spits: I'm not gonna kill you, moron. He steps forward, hooks a foot around the guy's knees, forcing him to turn. As the shooter's back is exposed, Benicio whacks his pistol across the back of his head. The guy crumples to the ground.

By the time Benicio turns to me, the fire in his eyes is already going out. "Come on," he stutters, nodding towards the staircase.

He stumbles with every step; trails blood all the way down the shiny white marble stairs.

Chapter 8

On the lawn, Benicio staggers, recovers, staggers again. This time he stops, doubles over. His whole body trembles. The gun drops out of his hand. He throws up, violently, on to the grass. I reach him, pick up the gun and get my right shoulder under his arm, supporting him.

Whispering deadly curses under his breath, Benicio wipes his mouth with the back of his wrist. I try to be sympathetic. "I know. I got shot once. It's bad."

"I'm losing a lot of blood," he breathes. Benicio's left trouser leg is almost completely soaked. "If he hit an artery . . . I could bleed to death."

Is there an artery in the leg? I'm vague on the details of anatomy but I can see plainly that he's losing blood pretty fast.

"You need to make a tourniquet," Benicio says, fading. "Do it now. Fix it good. Use my bandana."

I find the bandana inside Benicio's jacket. I don't look too closely but the wound looks bad – a nasty, ragged exit from which blood pumps out. I tie the cloth above and pull it hard. Benicio flinches, and I pretend not to notice.

He leans against me, making me take most of his weight. As I look towards the jet skis I realize that he's not strong enough to ride alone. Moving slowly, I guide Benicio to the jetty, help him climb aboard and then slide in front of him, standing up at the controls. Every time anything touches his leg, he screams. When he's finally settled into the seat he seems to breathe a tiny sigh of relief. But he must know he's not in the clear, not yet.

"You were pretty crazy in there," Benicio says, struggling to chuckle. "Breaking the windows. . .? You couldn't use the door?"

"I was going for the distraction," I mutter, untying the jet ski from its mooring. "You were the mental one. Why did you have to bring a gun? That's why he shot you."

"I know . . . I know. Better drop them both now," Benicio says and drops his forehead on to my shoulders. "In the water." He groans. The weapons slip into the lake.

I start the engine. "Josh," Benicio says. "You have to get me to a hospital."

"Huh? We should call Montoyo. Get someone to pick us up in a Muwan."

"No!" His voice rises for just a second, then drops. "No . . . you gotta do what I say. Take me to a hospital. I have my papers, everything. It'll be fine. Just drop me in front of a hospital and disappear. You can't be questioned. "

"What. . .? So – not tell Montoyo?"

There's a painful pause. "That depends, doesn't it? If you want to be grounded, then tell Montoyo I'm here."

I don't reply. We speed away from the lakeside. After just a moment I have to slow down. The hard bounce of the waves is too agonizing for Benicio. We keep going at a bearable speed until we're back at the water sports centre. I shunt the Kawasaki roughly into position alongside the pier and grab Benicio's arm. All colour has drained from his face, but when I look down at his right leg, I don't see any more blood leaking. At least the bandana seems to be doing its job, holding back the bleeding. I help Benicio across the garden of the restaurant, ignoring the curious glances of the tourists.

One of the bikini-clad women at the bar offers to drive us to the hospital. "Your friend looks terrible," she tells me, wide-eyed. "Was he in an accident?"

I'm about to accept when Benicio hisses in my ear, "No! We can't involve anyone. Just get me to the Harley."

We arrive at the Harley. I reach into Benicio's jacket to get the keys.

"Head for Chetumal. Drop me on the pavement in front of the hospital. Get back to Ek Naab. Can you do all that, Josh?" Benicio says, breathing hard.

"Mate, no problem."

Then we're on our way to Chetumal, the nearest city. Benicio is totally silent on the twenty-minute ride. I wonder how much blood he lost before I bandaged his wound. I'd guess a litre at least. It feels heartless to just dump him on the pavement outside the hospital.

When we arrive, I ease Benicio off the bike and help him to the door of the hospital. We spot an abandoned wheelchair and I grab it. I'm about to wheel him into the reception area when Benicio grabs my wrist. "No. Get back. And take this – you'll need it to sneak back into the city."

He hands me his security swipe card. I can only stare at it, open-mouthed.

"You absolutely sure about this?"

"Yes. You've got the contacts database. You and Ixchel, get working on that. Get some new leads on the Sect. Who's their new leader, do they have any other bases apart from in Switzerland, what are they doing? They're planning to run a broken world starting from December, Josh. That takes major planning. And we're almost completely in the dark."

"I guess everyone in Ek Naab is counting on us stopping the superwave. . ."

He grimaces. "Let's not count any chickens."

I grasp Benicio's security pass between my fingers and nod. "I'm totally on it."

"You're my deputy on this, OK? We're just covering the bases, Josh. Nothing too dangerous, promise me? Don't go planning any raids on the Sect. . ."

"Basic detective work only," I grin.

"If Montoyo finds out, you acted alone, yes?" Benicio groans and clutches his right leg. "Who am I kidding? He'll guess right away that I helped you."

"He won't find out," I say. "Not until I've found something pretty major."

"That's it," he says with effort, but still joking. "You find the Sect's secret weapon and how to neutralize it. And then tell Montoyo. He'll have no complaints."

We both grin. He grabs my hand. I squeeze back. "Thanks for this, mate."

"Are you kidding? If you hadn't been with me I'd be as good as dead."

"I'll check in with you," I promise. "In a few hours, see how you're doing."

Benicio nods. He places both hands on the wheels of the chair and starts to roll towards the hospital's emergency reception area.

"Take care of my Harley, Josh."

As I mount the bike, I'm already in action mode. How am I going to get back into the city? They'll be expecting two riders, or at the very least, Benicio. I'm meant to be passing myself off as him. I check my watch. It'll be dusk by the time I get back to the city. With a helmet and my navy blue flight jacket, there's a chance that I'll pass for Benicio. But the bright white trainers on my feet and the long shorts will have to go. I drive to the giant covered market of Chetumal, where I met Ixchel once upon a time in a parallel reality. There are stalls with jeans and stalls with boots. I pick up the cheapest items I can find that will make me look like Benicio, at a distance. Inside a roadside service station, I change. Then I'm back on the road, back to Ek Naab.

It takes me over three hours to get back to the ranch on the surface of Ek Naab. With Benicio's words rattling around my brain, I lose my way about five times on those tiny dust tracks through the jungle of Campeche. Too bad we're strictly forbidden to ever programme any Ek Naab location into the satnav.

Luckily, the outside security gate is still unmanned. It's only the gateway to a huge banana plantation; once you're inside you still need to know the correct route to enter the city. And there are always ranch workers – some of them armed – wandering around. But I'm a familiar face. Once Benicio's swipe card has got me in, everyone I see either ignores me or gives me a friendly nod. I keep my helmet on, just in case.

After I've stashed the bike I call Ixchel on my mobile phone and arrange to meet at the library. It has the fastest Internet access in Ek Naab, and any Web searches won't be traced to my apartment. Not that I suspect Montoyo of tracking my Web searches . . . but it's best not to take unnecessary risks.

Ixchel has already found us a nice quiet research booth when I arrive. She pulls me into a hug and as I'm holding her, I whisper some more information about Benicio. I reckon he's probably going to be OK, but they may need to operate. When I release her I notice that she's pale, almost shaking.

"I'd forgotten what it felt like . . . doing these kind of things. . ."

"I know." I watch her closely. "We can stop, if you like."

"No, you're right. Even if the city is on the brink of some kind of stupid alliance, it's a mistake to ignore the Sect of Huracan. I can't believe the ruling Executive sometimes."

Eyebrows raised, I say, "Don't question the grown-ups."

We sit down and venture together, into a wide world of names, dates, and as-yet-unnoticed links.

Very late that night, we hit pay dirt. A name crops up; a name we don't recognize – a guy called Jonas Kitrick. He's been leaving mean comments on an astrophysics research site, targeting a scientist called Dr Banerjee. By the looks of things, he's picked up a trick or two from my old adversaries in the Sect of Huracan.

BLOG ENTRY: SIGNS OF RENEWED ACTIVITY FROM SUPERMASSIVE BLACK HOLE AT CENTRE OF THE MILKY WAY

OK, so, I've found something and I think it needs to be shared with the world.

This is about some astrophysics research by Dr Banerjee. The work can't be published because a key, influential scientist strongly recommended that it be blocked. That's how scientific research works; other scientists get to decide if your work gets published.

It's the same with archaeology. My dad was often asked to decide if other archaeologists should publish their work, and they made decisions on his.

It works, so long as the researchers don't have it in for each other!

But sometimes, they do.

At the end of this post I'll link to Dr Banerjee's research here so that it gets the widest possible coverage. Feel free to publicize!

The guy who is trying to block this research – Professor Jonas Kitrick – is a fraud. He shouldn't be allowed to call himself a scientist. He works for one of the most evil organizations ever – the Sect of Huracan.

I have the list of major contacts in the Sect of Huracan, which I pulled from the computer at the lake house. They plan to reorganize the planet after a global catastrophe in December 2012. They're counting on all the computer networks going down, and a massive wave of chaos in the aftermath. Then they'll take over.

The last thing the Sect wants is for anyone to stop what's coming in December.

The second-to-last thing they want is for anyone to know about what's coming.

We started researching the members of the Sect. One of them, Jonas Kitrick, just recently posted his referee report on an astrophysics site. What could possibly make someone in the Sect of Huracan really want to block a piece of astrophysics research?

Which led us to Dr Banerjee. We looked her up – she works on a telescope in the hilly desert of Chile. She's been observing the centre of our galaxy. And now she's found something pretty bizarre. She's found the first sign, real scientific evidence that a gigantic wave of electromagnetic energy is on its way from the centre of the galaxy

The Sect of Huracan don't want Dr Banerjee's work to be published in an official, respected science journal. So they used one of their own, Professor Jonas Kitrick, to block its publication.

Here's the proof: the comment from Kitrick that appeared on a pre-publication website where astrophysicists put their up-and-coming research articles.

Re: submitted for publication; Banerjee, R.M. et al. Signs of Renewed Activity from Supermassive Black Hole at Centre of Milky Way

I must object in the strongest terms to this outrageous piece of sensationalism. This research is flawed in a number of ways. If this paper is not immediately retracted, not only from consideration by the journal but indeed, from the Internet, then I must warn that grave consequences will follow for Dr Banerjee's continued work.

Sounds like pretty threatening language for one scientist to use to another. . .

Then there's a massive long report that I guess is his entire argument, written in technical language that I struggled to follow. You can read Dr Banerjee's article here.

Believe it, world! The superwave is on its way.

Chapter 9

Within half an hour of posting the article on my blog, an email pops into my inbox. It's from Dr Banerjee. There's something horribly familiar about the scenario she describes. A scientist being warned off their research – just like the Sect tried to do to my father.

Dear Mr Josh Garcia,

The notification of your blog post rather surprised me. Obviously I was upset that Professor Kitrick had such a negative reaction to my research. I must admit, his response is extremely disappointing, because the work is a result of years of careful observations.

Moreover, some other rather odd things have started to happen. Until I read your blog post, I assumed that I was just being paranoid.

I'm not at all sure yet that it's a good idea for you to link to my research on the Web. I suspect that you and I are somewhat out of our depth. But I thank you very much for your kind interest and your offer to link to my work.

Regards,

R.M. Banerjee

P.S. You don't mention where you work. I can't find you in the abstracts database. Are you an astrophysicist?

Ixchel sees it too. "This doesn't remind you of anything?"

"It totally does. When my father went looking for the Ix Codex, I found nasty emails to him from Marius Martineau. One of the leaders of the Sect of Huracan warning my dad against investigating; suppressing the search for the Ix Codex."

"Well, Kitrick's name is in that contact database. Looks like the Sect is up to their old tricks."

"No wonder the Sect recruits all those top scientists and researchers . . . Melissa DiCanio, Marius Martineau, now this Kitrick guy. They have people at the top of every relevant field! And if they want someone silenced, they bully them, threaten their work."

Ixchel looks at me. "What can we do?"

"I dunno. I wish we could talk to Dr Banerjee. She might know more than she's letting on."

"About the superwave?"

"That . . . and about Kitrick. They're both astrophysicists. I bet she's met him."

"I've done a Web search. There's a bit about Kitrick there, his faculty page and things."

"It tells us nothing. Don't you think there's something . . . I dunno . . . dismissive about her email to me? Almost as though she wants to brush me off . . . because she's afraid?"

Ixchel frowns. "Afraid . . . of having all her research blocked, not just this?"

"Not sure. It feels like there's more here. Look at what she says: 'a conspiracy to silence me'. People want to shut her up. Which people?"

"It's true," Ixchel admits. Her tone becomes pensive. "Have you noticed she doesn't comment on what you're saying about the Sect, or about 2012?"

"I know. She either thinks it's too bizarre to mention or . . . or like I say, she knows more than she's letting on. I wish we knew."

"Well . . . why not send her an email, see if she'll let you call her?"

"On the phone? The minute she hears me she'll tell me to get lost."

"Why? Your voice is pretty deep."

"Yeah, but I still sound young. And I'm not a scientist. One wrong word and she'll hang up."

"If you were in the same room as her, she couldn't hang up."

"If I was in the same room. . .? How's that gonna happen?"

Ixchel picks up Benicio's security card from where I've left it on the desk in our library research booth. "This is Benicio's card, yes? It can get you out of the city."

I begin to grasp the audacity of what Ixchel is suggesting.

"Dr Banerjee is in Chile. South America, that Chile."

Ixchel grins and waves the card under my nose. "Yeah, so?"

"A Muwan. . ." I manage to say. "You're suggesting that I use Benicio's swipe card to nick a Muwan. . .?"

"It'll get you into the Muwan hangar, won't it?"

"Yeah but. . ." I swallow. "A Muwan!"

"You're a good pilot, aren't you?"

"Dunno about that . . . I can fly."

"You can be a taxi driver, yes? Just to this telescope place in Chile and back."

"A taxi driver. . .?"

"With one well-behaved passenger."

"Oh . . . oh, hang on." Despite myself, I grin. "You're such a con artist."

Ixchel gives me a sweet smile. Trying to look innocent. "What's that?"

"You want to go on an adventure! It's been nine months since you left the city, too."

Ixchel swallows. "Ha ha, OK. I admit it; I'd like to get out too. Even just to a desert in Chile."

My arms go around her waist. This is the girl I went crazy for – the escape artiste who ran away from the city at the age of fourteen to avoid our arranged marriage. Who lived alone in the outside world, paying her way as a waitress. Who goaded me until I did mad things, daring escapades. She's still doing it now.

"Email Dr Banerjee," Ixchel whispers. "Tell her you'll be in the vicinity tomorrow morning. Ask to meet for half an hour."

I gasp. "The vicinity?! In the middle of the desert in Chile?!"

"She can only say no."

Deliberately, I remove Benicio's security card from her fingers. "You're mad."

"Come on! I want to see you fly a Muwan."

"I should pass the pilot exam in a couple of months or so – you can see me then."

Ixchel looks disappointed. I turn the security card around in the palm of my hand. "Still . . . I'm not easily going to get another opportunity to leave the city. . ."

"That's right – Montoyo will be on to you soon. The minute it's noticed that Benicio is missing. . ."

"It's got to be a couple of days, at least, would be my guess. We can call to ask."

"When he gets back, Benicio is going to need his card to get into the city."

I hesitate. "It's just a little trip down to Chile, really."

"Exactly."

"In a couple of months I'll be doing errands like this all the time. . ." My fingers close around the swipe card. I gaze at Ixchel in disbelief at the words that are about to leave my mouth. "Let's do it."

She pretends to be horrified. "What, steal a Muwan?"

"Hey, not so loud!" A grin spreads across my face and my voice drops to a whisper. "Borrow a Muwan."

"Who's to know?"

"Benicio isn't telling anyone he's in hospital in Chetumal. If his security card keeps being used then people will assume he's still around."

"If they miss anyone, it will be you."

"We should maybe . . . arrange a sleepover. One of your friends, someone my mum doesn't really know. We tell them that we're going to sleep in really late tomorrow. With any luck, none of our parents will start wondering where we are until tomorrow lunchtime."

Ixchel nods. "I know exactly who to call."

Chapter 10

We're about to close all the windows down on the library computer when a chat window pops up. When I see that it's my old friend from Oxford, Tyler, I can't resist sitting down for a few more moments.

Ty! What's up?

Oii! Mariposa! *Tudo bem*?

Tudo bem, EddyG.

So cool how chatting to Tyler can put a smile on my face. We've taken to greeting each other in Brazilian Portuguese, and our capoeira nicknames.

I type: You're up early.

It's all going on. Got a GCSE exam today. And capoeira practice before that.

Capoeira?

Another tournament coming up, after exams. In Amsterdam.

Sweet!

How's you? And Ixchel?

She's great. We're taking a little trip. Don't tell. Pilot = ME!

Sick! Don't crash.

DON'T crash? K, I'll try to remember that.

I only give sound advice, my bro.

LOL. OK. I need to sleep. You need to revise.

Tres bien. Allons-y.

Let me guess, you've got French GCSE.

You KNOW you miss it.
I really DON'T.

Ixchel taps my shoulder and makes a face. "We need to go."

"What . . . now?"

"The sooner the better, don't you think? Who knows when Benicio will be missed?"

"You're right. We need to get as much use out of his security card as we can."

As late as it is, we're not the last people in the library. A couple of curious pairs of eyes follow us out. When we leave we head directly for the Muwan hangar bay, past the black *cenote*. It's after midnight so there's almost no one around, apart from a few late night couples at the café right in front of the library. I grab hold of Ixchel's hand and pull her close to my side.

"Walk slowly," I whisper into her ear. "Make it look like we're going for a romantic midnight stroll."

Ixchel follows my lead and wraps an arm around me. "Don't worry, I know one of those girls over there. She'll get the picture – you and I want to be alone. She'll cover for us, if anyone asks."

With a little kiss to her cheek, I murmur, "Excellent work, Robin. At this rate you'll soon be driving the Batmobile yourself."

She digs me in the ribs. "How come you're always Batman?"

We reach the hangar bay and I slide Benicio's card into the reader. Then we're inside. The lights are on, but at the low power setting. We gaze at the hulking masses of the city's Muwan fleet. Silently, I count them. They're all here. Our timing is good – not even a routine Sky Guardian patrol to worry about. The first shift starts at two in the morning, so we have a little while yet.

I use Benicio's card to open the equipment storage cupboard. I grab the remote for the Muwan we used earlier today. Leading Ixchel over to the craft, I open it up, watching the blue external lights flicker into action. When I check the storage underbelly I notice that the motorbike is still inside.

A fully equipped Muwan – the ideal getaway vehicle.

Ixchel climbs inside and drops into the co-pilot seat. I shuffle into place next to her, begin to run through the system checks.

System checks, all on my own. It's the first time that it occurs to me that this may be more dangerous than I've let on. Normally an engineer would check too. I know what I'm doing, but without anyone to double-check I'm well and truly on my own.

The nervousness I'm feeling must show, because Ixchel notices my hand tremble slightly as I tap buttons on the control panel.

"Hey," she says soothingly, touching my fingers. "You can do this."

"The maiden flight of Josh Garcia," I say, trying to chivvy myself along.

"Captain on deck!"

As I sink deeper into my flight preparations, my anxiety begins to melt away. There are checklists and protocols to follow. Soon enough my thoughts are fully occupied. Headset and visor are in place, earpiece attached for the radio; I'm wearing flight gloves with sensors attached. The antigravity generator starts. I give it a minute or two to power up, and then we begin to rise. Ixchel hits the remote control to open the outside hangar-bay doors. The Muwan floats through the air and out of the underground base.

Outside there's only starlight, so I use the lowest running lights to stop the Muwan being too visible. Collisions are unlikely, but you don't want to take a chance. Even if it means someone is about to sight yet another UFO. . .

El Tololo Observatory in Chile is in the middle of the desert somewhere. The Muwan's on-board computer pulls satellite data, throws up a holographic map of the observatory and surroundings. Behind the eyepiece of my visor, the route appears. It's low enough that I need to be vigilant, but it's designed to avoid any military bases or low-flying commercial jets.

Kick back, pop on some tunes. My fingers can find the Muse playlist without any help from my eyes.

"Uprising". Ideal.

Looking across at Ixchel, I grin. Just taking a relaxing ride with Ek Naab's newest pilot.

I don't chat; I prefer to concentrate on the systems, watching the feedback reports about windspeed, upcurrents, nearby traffic. An Aeroméxico 757 flies directly overhead, about twenty-five thousand feet above. If the captain looked out of his left window he might see us flash beneath, a trail of quicksilver.

The trip to Chile takes five hours. At first, we don't really belt along; flying faster than the sound barrier can draw unwelcome attention. Also, I can't see anyone being in Dr Banerjee's research office at the telescope too early in the morning. But when I mention this to Ixchel, she reminds me of a very obvious fact that I've overlooked.

"What – have you lost your mind? Astronomers work AT NIGHT!"

The penny drops. "Cos they need it to be dark. The morning is when she finishes her day!"

After that little comment, we speed up.

As we get closer, the terrain becomes bleak, devoid of vegetation, brick-red dust coating wrinkled lines of mountains. Around two hundred kilometres from the hilltop observatory I start planning the landing. No cloud cover. Then again, no one to see us. The chances of the telescopes being pointed at our portion of the sky are small. No harm narrowing the odds, though: I drop us in to skim the ground at a height of a hundred metres.

I land the craft on a smooth patch of desert, about twenty metres square, underneath the low foothill. The observatory perches above, five white, domed telescopes arranged like a crown. A faint mist rises near the ground, burning away in the rays of the rising sun. The silver dome of the largest telescope glows a pale pink, reflecting the dawn sky.

Just after five in the morning, we leave the Muwan. I clip my visor on to the wall next to the pilot seat and swap it for a pair of aviator sunglasses. Ixchel and I start the walk to the El Tololo Observatory, on top of the hill.

It's colder than I'd expected. Ixchel and I hold hands for a few minutes as we pick our way along the rocks. It reminds me of the time we climbed the volcano Mount Orizaba. What a day that was. . .

Only one telescope appears to have the observatory window open – the largest one, which, according to the Web page we checked on the way here, has a four-metre-diameter reflector.

We approach the telescope, which has a silver dome. Standing close to it we're dwarfed in its shadow. The featureless desert makes it look almost like a toy, but standing up close, it's impressively huge. Two white metal doors are the only way into the facility. They're locked. No doorbell, either.

I blow on my hands. "How do people get into these places?!"

Dryly, Ixchel says, "I'm guessing that if you're allowed to be here, you get a key."

"Well . . . we're going to have to wait until she leaves."

"Hmm. Could be a couple of hours."

"Let's hope she's dying to get home."

So we wait. As the cold starts to bite, I turn to Ixchel and hug her tightly; we cling together, trying to stay warm. Thirty minutes go by.

Finally, the metal doors open. A petite woman appears, long, straight, jet-black hair falling loosely over her shoulders. She's wearing jeans and a low-cut, exotic print blouse, with a hiking jacket thrown over her shoulders – quite a bit more casually dressed than I'd expected. I don't suppose astronomers need to wear lab coats, but I sort of assumed.

She takes only a few paces before noticing us and stopping, rigidly, in her tracks.

"Can I help you?" Behind narrow glasses, her dark eyes blink.

"Um . . .are you Dr Banerjee?"

"Are you one of my students or something. . .?" Dr Banerjee stares at us, more bewildered by the second. "What's going on?"

"Dr Banerjee, we need to speak to you. Really badly."

"Ah . . . OK. I don't know you. How did you get past the gate?" She starts to edge back towards the dome, opening a door as she retreats. I step forward.

"The gate. . .?" Ixchel and I glance at each other. I'd hoped that Dr Banerjee wouldn't be suspicious at first; after all, the Muwan had dropped us right into the observatory grounds, well past security.

Pressing on, I say, "Please, Dr Banerjee, can we just talk for a minute? We know about your paper, the one about the supermassive black hole. The one that Jonas Kitrick rejected. There's something really important we need to tell you about that."

A pained expression sparks in the astronomer's eyes when we mention Kitrick. Her tone grows cold. "Kitrick. . .? How do you know about that?"

"Can we talk inside?"

"Who are you? Oh wait . . . not possible. . ." She gasps, amazed. "You're not that guy with the blog, Josh Garcia?!"

"Yeah, that's right. It's me. And this is Ixchel, my girlfriend."

She stares at me, eyes boggling. "Jeez, man, you're Garcia? Seriously – I'm getting old. You look about twelve! Are you some kind of child prodigy? How come I haven't heard of you?"

I shrug, a bit disappointed. Somehow I thought that the Muwan flight jacket and aviator sunglasses might make me look much older than my almost-sixteen years. I give her what I hope is a disarming smile.

"Please, Dr Banerjee, how about we talk inside? Me and my girlfriend, we'd love to look into a telescope. We've never seen one like this. Maybe you could show us a real black hole."

She frowns, obviously taken aback. "A black hole? Right. You're not an astrophysicist . . . are you?"

"No, miss. I just read stuff on the Internet. You'd be amazed what turns up."

I take off my sunglasses and try to look as young as possible. The child prodigy idea seems to have amused Dr Banerjee; at the very least, she's puzzled. There's a pause, then she says, "You can't see black holes. Not actually."

"So what's with the swirling void of blackness, swallowing everything in its wake and all that?"

For the first time, a hint of a wry grin appears at the corner of her mouth.

"You're really Josh Garcia? Man, I've been scratching my head about you for hours. Ever since your blog post popped up with my name on it. You should have told me that you were here in Chile!" Then she stands back, critically, sizing us up. "Kids, you'd better come in. Seems to me like you've got a lot of explaining to do."

Chapter 11

We leave the rose-gold light of morning behind as we disappear into the darkness of the telescope facility. Dr Banerjee leads us to a lift, one of those old-fashioned metal cages. She pulls the doors open with a grumble about how stiff they get. A concrete wall zips by as we ascend. She opens the cage; we spill out and follow her into a control room from which an array of flat-screen monitors blink their multicoloured streams of data, computer graphics cycle through mathematical models, and everywhere there are dazzling images taken by the telescope. For a few moments I can't move; I'm mesmerized.

"Whoa . . . so cool . . . so seriously cool. . ."

Ixchel also seems to be blown away, gazing at each screen in turn. There are so many, all around the room, one stacked above another.

Dr Banerjee drops into a swivel chair in front of the panel and points at a couple of empty chairs. "Take a pew. Now, children . . . did you actually understand my research paper?"

Ixchel glances at me while I hide my embarrassment with a grin. "Sure! Well, mostly."

The astronomer nods. "I see."

"We got the gist," I say, unconvincingly.

She casts us a sceptical look. "You got the gist. . ." she mutters, "even though you didn't know that a telescope can't 'see' a black hole."

"Oh," I say. Ixchel shakes her head and sighs. "I guess we're rumbled," I admit.

"Maybe it's easier if I show you." Dr Banerjee types a few commands. All the lower plasma screens instantly flick over to the same display.

It looks nothing remotely like a black hole – just a series of images of stars and dust clouds with numbers floating over some of them.

"I've been watching the centre of the galaxy for about five years. I noticed a weird reading from some radio telescope data so I started doing some observations here, collecting images, along with my other projects. About six months ago I thought I was spotting a pattern, so I looked back at even older data. Images from ten years ago. And when you compare something from ten years ago and now. . ."

As she speaks, the two images alternate, then align on the screen. And even I can see that there's a difference. Some of the numbers next to the image are higher and some stars look more intense.

"So like I said, you can't see black holes. Instead, we look for their effect on the surroundings stars. I looked at the galactic centre with infrared, saw lots of dust and cloud. The overall luminosity – it's getting brighter. That's because there are more X-rays, returning as the black hole's 'blazar' jet moves closer. It begins to paint a picture of a wave of energy. And it's pointing towards us."

"X-rays – like you get when they look at your bones?"

"Those are images taken by passing X-rays through your body. Stars, pulsars; lots of things in space give off X-rays."

Ixchel frowns. "How come no other scientists have seen this?"

"It's not an obvious thing to look for. I only saw it by chance, really. Some weird radio telescope data got me curious. I doubt that anyone else is even looking."

"But it will become obvious?"

Dr Banerjee shrugs. "Eventually, I guess other astronomers will start to get strange data too. They won't necessarily put the whole picture together."

"Especially if your research can't be published."

"You got that about right, yeah." She turns from Ixchel and fixes me with a determined glare. "So, Josh. Why don't you tell me what the heck you meant by that blog post?"

"Here's the thing. I've been investigating this secret organization. The Sect of Huracan. They're very well-connected, rich and powerful. Loads of important scientists are in it. Like Jonas Kitrick."

She smirks. "You've been investigating? So who am I dealing with here; Fox Mulder?"

Ixchel says, "Who?"

"The guy from that TV show, The X-Files," I tell her.

"Oh, that's why your blog is called The Joshua Files. . .?"

Astonished, I say, "You didn't know?"

Ixchel shrugs. "Josh, I keep telling you . . . I don't watch TV."

"Kids, I hate to interrupt such an adorable relationship, but I need answers. What is this 'Sect of Huracan'?"

"The Sect is real," I tell her. "But you won't find anything on the Internet about it."

Dr Banerjee chuckles nervously. "Secret organization. Right. Next you'll be telling me that they want to take over the world?"

Calmly, Ixchel replies, "Yes."

"Gee, actually that was a joke."

"By the end of this year it won't be so funny."

"The world's kind of messed up," Dr Banerjee says, somewhat dismissive. "Who in their right mind would want to take over?"

"Look, Dr Banerjee, Ixchel is telling the truth. We don't have proof here, but we know that Kitrick is trying to silence you."

"Ain't that the truth. . ."

I say, "In your email, you said that there were other things going on, apart from Kitrick blocking that research paper. What did you mean?"

"Oh. Just a small matter of all my research proposals being turned down, is all."

"So someone is already trying to stop you doing any more research?"

"Your cute boyfriend has it right, Ixchel. Is that, like, a Mexican name or something?"

"Mayan," Ixchel nods.

Dr Banerjee reaches across her desk for a can of Coca Cola, pulls the tab and takes a sip. "You kids are pretty odd, you know that? Feel like I got Mulder and Scully here."

"Scully. . . " Ixchel murmurs, "had better not be the sidekick."

"Hah. If this isn't the strangest conversation I ever had with a couple of teenagers. . ."

I interrupt, "Don't you want to know why?"

Dr Banerjee stops talking. She puts her Coke down. For the first time, I glimpse a chink in the astronomer's easy confidence and apparent scepticism.

"Why you're here? Why my research is blocked? Why Kitrick has a problem with my paper? You think I don't want to know? Of course I want to know! But knowing isn't the same as being able to do anything about it."

There's a brief silence. Ixchel edges her chair closer to mine.

Dr Banerjee's voice softens. "Look, kids. I understand the implications of my paper. God knows I've had time to think it through. There's a chance . . . if I'm right, and I hope I'm not . . . that towards the end of December, a gigantic wave of electromagnetic energy is going to pulse through our atmosphere. I guess Kitrick thinks I'm wrong, and he doesn't want to instil panic. . ."

"Kitrick knows you're right," I insist. "That's the point. He – and the rest of the Sect – they're waiting for the world as we know it to end. And then they rebuild. The whole world, from scratch. With them in charge."

She gazes at us. "Uh huh." Dr Banerjee seems to hunt carefully for her next words. "So, the Sect is – what – some secret government agency?"

"No way. Governments are their enemy."

"Then who's in charge?"

"Well . . . we're not sure. The Sect seems to have at least two leaders. One is a scientist called Melissa DiCanio. She used to be in charge of this pharmaceutical company in Switzerland called Chaldexx. Then she faked her death. I know that cos I read about it in a newspaper, but a few weeks later, I actually met her! So she's not dead at all. And the other guy who seemed to be in charge, his name was Marius Martineau." I stall at the memory of Martineau's gruesome death.

"His name 'was' Marius Martineau. . .? Did he fake his death too?"

I gulp slightly. "Nope. He's dead all right."

Not that anyone will have found Martineau's body – since he died whilst time travelling to the Mayan past.

"So, you think Kitrick has taken over from this Martineau?"

"Maybe. Or maybe DiCanio was in charge all along."

"And you, Josh. . . Ixchel. Where do you come into it?" She points at the insignia on my flight jacket. It's embroidered in the Ek Naab code. "What's with the kooky paramilitary get-up?"

I take a deep breath. "We're with the guys who are trying to save the world. When this galactic superwave hits the earth's atmosphere, it will bring an electromagnetic pulse so powerful that it will erase the data on every hard drive on the planet. Computer networks will fail. Banking systems will crash; aircraft will fall out of the sky."

She stares back at me. For a few seconds all I can hear are the electronic blips from the machines nearby. And my own breathing.

Dr Banerjee begins to speak, haltingly. As if she doesn't dare to hear the words spoken out loud. "Kid, listen . . . if I'm right. . . it's gonna be a whole lot worse than that. Dangerous criminals and zoo animals will escape. Vaults containing deadly diseases will be unsecure. People will die. From injuries. From disease, because drugs can't be supplied. From hunger because supermarkets can't get deliveries. Most of all, from violence.

"Because when you are starving, when your children are starving, you will do anything to survive. I've had this data for a while. For a few months now, it's all I've thought about."

She shakes her head. "Have to admit, I assumed that Kitrick was so desperate to persuade folks to fund his Futurology Institute, he didn't want anything to scare off his investors. . . and that's why he hexed my paper."

"Futurology Institute. . ." Ixchel and I glance at each other. "What are you talking about?"

"Kitrick's latest project. That's his thing now. He spoke about it at the last conference we attended. A think tank made up of scientists and other academics, dedicated to futurology."

"Futurology. . .?"

"The study of the way we will live in the future. He wants to put it in England somewhere. Oxford or Cambridge. Sounds a little off-the-wall, by the standards of 'Oxbridge'. But who knows, these days." She swings around, clicks on a Web browser on the nearest computer screen and brings up a website. "There's not much here yet, to be honest. In fact, Kitrick's name isn't even on the site. That's kind of weird, considering how much he was giving it the hard sell at the conference."

Ixchel and I lean in and start reading the text of the Futurology Institute website. There's mention of funding from various investors, including Chaldexx BioPharmaceuticals.

Melissa DiCanio's company, the place where I was taken when the Sect kidnapped me and changed my DNA.

I leap out of my chair. "Dr Banerjee! That's the Sect of Huracan! Oh no. That's what they're going to do. They're already starting... This Futurology Institute ... it's going to be the headquarters of the Sect's new world order!"

Chapter 12

But Dr Banerjee doesn't budge. Instead, a smile spreads across her face. She takes a long swallow from her Coke. "We're with the guys who are trying to save the world. I can't believe you actually said that, Mulder and Scully."

Ixchel stands up. "You think this is a joke. . .? In that case, we'll just go."

"Hey, relax! I am in fact trying to get my head around the fact that it can't be a joke. Being logical: if you got past security, then you must either be pretty darn good at sneaking around, or you have some high-level clearance. So what are you, some new kind of division of the secret service? Are they recruiting children now?"

"We're not spies or anything like that. We're not from any government. I can't tell you who we're with . . . and anyway, you wouldn't believe me."

She takes another sip. "Let me guess, you're from the future and you're trying to save the world from the giant electromagnetic pulse in December 2012."

I consider this statement for a moment. Then, to my and Ixchel's surprise, I reply, "Yes. Time travellers. That's what we are."

The smile on Dr Banerjee's face completely vanishes. With mild disbelief, she asks, "Seriously?"

Behind my back, I seek out Ixchel's hand. "Yes, totally right. You've been very helpful, Dr Banerjee. And now it's time for us to get on with our mission. 2012 and all that."

"No wait . . . you're telling me that you kids are actually time travellers, time travel is real, you're for real on some sort of mission to stop the giant EMP?"

"Yeah," I tell her, backing away. Dr Banerjee seems friendly and all, but she's getting a bit close to the truth for comfort. One phone call to the wrong people and things could suddenly get tricky for us. "What you said. All of that. And now we have to go."

"Oh . . . oh, OK, I get it. You can't say too much." Dr Banerjee sounds dazed. "I guess that might change the course of history in ways you didn't plan. . .." She looks at us, a touch disappointed. "You could always erase my memory, though, afterwards. . ."

"We can't," I say firmly, as Ixchel and I reach the door. "Not today. Forgot to bring our amnesia thingummy."

As we leave, from above, a mechanism begins to grind; a panel in the dome slides into place. Dr Banerjee follows cautiously, at a discreet distance. We rush out and down the emergency stairs.

Time travel. Close enough to the truth, even if we're not actually time travelling right now.

Outside, the sunlight is becoming sharp, clear through a cloudless mauve sky. The low mist has burned away, and the crisp russet of the desert is startling, every crinkle in the terrain visible. I put on my sunglasses and stand for a moment, gazing out over the vast, mountainous desert. It's how I imagine another planet might look, or the moon.

Ixchel murmurs, "I think we may have scared her just a little. . ."

We both slide down the loose, dusty surface of the hill underneath the observatory. "She's just a bit disoriented," I say. "It does seem to weird adults out when they realize they're talking to kids about stuff like this. Remember that archaeologist woman at the museum, the one who bought our golden Mayan bracelets?"

The Muwan nestles in the shade at the base of the hill. The sunlight is touching the tip of the craft's nose, but the brushed matt surface stops it from glinting too harshly. When we're in range I lift my arm and hit the remote control for the Muwan. The cockpit window opens.

"Come on," I say, holding out my hand to Ixchel. "I'm a bit worried about Dr Banerjee. I think we need to get out of here, quick, before she starts wondering if she should report that she's seen us."

"You think? No; she'll be too confused. Time travel isn't something you go reporting to people, not unless you want attention. And Kitrick seems to have scared her off. . ."

We reach the Muwan and I step aside to let Ixchel climb aboard. Glancing back at the observatory, I spot Dr Banerjee at the crest of the hill. She followed. Her hand is raised to her forehead and she's peering at us. In the distance, I see her other hand reach inside her jacket. She takes out a phone, raising it.

I follow Ixchel into the cockpit and hurriedly run through the system checks.

"I have a bad feeling about this."

"Seriously, Josh – why?"

"Take a look! She's videoing us. Better hope no one believes her."

"She's won't tell. She liked you."

"Hmm. Don't know about that."

I'm itching to leave right away, but force myself to take time to scan the satellite data for updates. It records radar station readings from all over the world, so I can see a map of anything that's been flying in the vicinity within the last five minutes. I don't spot anything on my first sweep, but when I look again there's something at the extreme northern periphery that looks unusual: a single aircraft moving very fast, headed directly on a course for El Tololo. I look back over the past five minutes. It's definitely moving faster than anything commercial or private. Has to be military. But its point of origin is in Paraguay. Not a country whose military I've ever encountered.

Ixchel notices that I'm stalling over the satellite data. "Problem?"

Within a second I'm prickling with sweat. "Not sure. I'm trying to cover all the bases. . ."

Paraguayan military . . . and there's just one of them. How much trouble could they be?

"You think Dr Banerjee liked me?" I mutter. "Babe, I hope you're right."

I take the Muwan up medium fast, which is enough to make us both catch our breath. My mouth is already dry when I check the satellite map again. The radar data is coming in now too.

The aircraft I've been tracking is almost on top of us.

With a shiver, I switch to manual and shoot up to Mach 2, on a dummy course heading for the Mexican military base in Chiapas. It's one of the Sky Guardians' standard manoeuvres to fool observers into thinking we're a military aeroplane.

We shoot past the aircraft, seven thousand feet under it. I check the radar again, breathless.

It changes course immediately. And follows us.

Urgency enters Ixchel's voice. "Josh. What's wrong?"

Deep breath. "There's something on our tail. Approaching from Paraguay."

"Paraguayan?"

"I can't tell. But it's moving like a military jet."

"Can you lose it?"

I don't answer, but flick through the list of possible evasive manoeuvres, feeling a twinge of embarrassment when Bermuda Mask flashes past. Before I pick one, I check the radar data one more time.

What I see almost makes me vomit.

Two more aircraft have appeared from nowhere, both closing in on our position from directly east.

I swear under my breath but Ixchel catches it.

"What's wrong now?"

"Two more of them."

"WHAT?"

My voice remains calm but I'm shaking. "Coming in at eleven o'clock."

"Oh no. . ." groans Ixchel, staring through the window behind her. "That looks like a Muwan!"

I check my readings. "A Mark I! I bet the other two are as well. . .!"

"Josh . . . it's the NRO!"

I say nothing, muscles rigid, forcing myself to hold a firm line of descent.

Three National Reconnaissance Office Muwans.

The only escape move that will get me out of this is the one I watched Benicio pull when he rescued me from the island in the middle of Lake Catemaco.

Stratosphere Dive.

Problem is, that move is even more insane than Bermuda Mask.

"Gotta do a Stratosphere Dive. . ."

I glance at the radar. All three are altering course again. They're coming in on different angles.

A burst of light flares in the sky ahead for the tiniest fraction of a second. Then the whole craft shakes, rattling like an old can. There's a change of pitch in the sound of the engine.

Ixchel whispers in horror, "What was that?"

"They hit us," I say, grim as death.

"With what?!"

"Some kind of beam weapon. We have to land."

"Are you kidding?"

"No. If we shoot at them they'll destroy us. And another hit like that and we'll be down."

"Can't we eject?"

"Ixchel, we're above a desert. . ."

"But . . . but we have survival supplies, don't we?"

I've pulled out of the dive, gently, and we're sweeping along a few hundred metres above the dusty ground. I can see two of the Muwans through the window now; they've dropped to the same altitude as us.

"Three NRO Muwans, Josh. How could this happen?"

"They must have seen us coming."

"Yes, but how?!"

"No idea. It's too soon for it to have been Banerjee. . ."

Ixchel watches with increasing disbelief as I let the two Muwans guide me to a landing area. "Josh . . . no. You're going to surrender to the NRO? After what they did to your father? After everything we've all been through to stop them getting our technology?"

Grimly, I say, "I'm not surrendering. Just chill for a minute, if you can. I've got an idea."

All three Mark Is are now visible in the sky, less than a mile away. Stealthily, I stretch out an arm and flip open the catch I noticed in the dashboard. I push a fingertip inside and find the metal hook, pulling it out slowly. The taut static rope follows. I pull it level with my waist and then open the hook, snap closed over my belt.

I give Ixchel a quick glance. She's breathing rapidly. With a sigh, I settle back into my seat.

OK, Benicio. Let's see who's crazy now.

BLOG ENTRY: CRAZY JOSH
(PASSWORD PROTECTED)

Benicio, I've called the hospital and your mobile phone but still can't get through to you. The hospital says you're still sedated, so I guess that's why you're not answering the phone.

OK so this is what happened since we last saw you.

Ixchel and I found out about a Sect scientist called Jonas Kitrick. He is blocking the research of an astrophysicist called Dr Banerjee. She's got proof from telescope research that the galactic superwave is on its way. We decided to take a little trip to Chile, to visit Dr Banerjee. We sort of borrowed your Muwan . . . and it's all got a bit tricky.

As we left Chile, three NRO Muwans turned up. I still don't know how they got on to us. They forced me to land the Muwan.

We landed, they landed. The NRO had four agents on the ground by then, standing next to their Muwan Mark Is. Two of them were aiming at us with rifles. I jammed the radio so they couldn't talk to us but they just yelled across the empty wasteland: GET OUT!

Ixchel climbed out first, then me. I had the line attached to my belt. Just the way you did to me in the Crazy Benicio routine. . .

I stuffed the Muwan remote into my back pocket. I touched the control panel and initiated Crazy Benicio. As I stepped outside, I put an arm around Ixchel. All the time, in my head, I was counting. How many seconds to go? Surely Crazy Benicio had to start any moment now?

There was a small rock in my path; I made a big show of tripping over on it. The NRO agents weren't fooled. They immediately started yelling at me: "Don't move!" "Get your hands where we can see them!" and such.

But they were too late. Our craft was already lifting off the ground. I felt a swift tug at my waist. I grabbed hold of Ixchel, tightly.

Then we were in the air.

When it happened in training, I was almost paralysed with fear. This time it was the bullets that terrified me. The NRO agents didn't shoot at us at first – I guess what they were seeing was too surprising. Unless you could see the line, it looked as though we were floating away. One second later the pulley mechanism kicked in and dragged us to the Muwan. Then the shots began.

On the ground, I heard shouting, arguing. A man's voice ordering them not to shoot. Then I slammed against the cockpit, right against my kidneys, and Ixchel thudded hard against my ribs.

Pure adrenaline must have pushed me through it because I remember feeling like I couldn't breathe. I guess I was winded. I could feel Ixchel's hands grabbing for the edge of the cockpit. It was a mess; we were in a complete panic, trying to get in. Next thing I remember, I was inside, Ixchel was inside, although upside down, with her head jammed against the floor.

I sealed the craft. Outside, we could hear them scrambling for their own aeroplanes. I grabbed the headset as Ixchel was strapping herself in. We didn't say a word to each other, but we were both shaking like leaves just before a hurricane.

The sensor data started feeding me holographic images right away. Two of the NRO Muwans were rising off the ground. There wasn't a second to spare.

Stratosphere Dive. I knew I could make it work. And when I beat them on the descent, I'd do just what you did, Benicio, that first time we escaped from the NRO.

I headed for the stratosphere. Those two NRO Muwans were trying to get on my six. But they started to ascend too early. Flying on the hypotenuse, trying to intercept. But basic geometry proves that can't be done – unless you can fly faster.

And I was hitting a vertical rise approaching maximum speed. The pressure in my sinuses was like putting my face in a vice. But that's what training does for you; I didn't care. When I hit the stratosphere I cut the engines, flipped the craft on the drop. I passed the Mark Is on my way down. They were trying to brake, but it was too late, I was already falling too fast. I knew I'd pull out of the dive before they'd even course-corrected. The Mark I is really no match for the Mark II when it comes to manoeuvrability.

They didn't get closer than five klicks behind me all the way back to Mexico.

Then, Benicio, I used your old trick of hiding. You know what I'm talking about. In the tunnels. . .

The best hiding place within a thousand kilometres of Ek Naab.

I landed the Muwan inside the mouth of a cave. Just like that time when you rescued me from Catemaco, when I first located the Ix Codex. And that's where we are, Benicio.

With three of those NRO Muwans swooping around looking for us.

So we're stuck. Until we dream up some way to get out of here.

Chapter 13

The nearby volcano Mount Tacana is extinct, but there's always been a hint of sulphur to the air when I've been there. The sun is too high to penetrate directly into the cavern. It's pretty dingy inside. The air tastes of hot stones.

Ixchel asks, "Do you think they know we're in here?"

"I've turned off all the flight systems, so they shouldn't be able to pick up anything electronic. The rock is pretty thick above us – I doubt they'll get any heat readings on infrared, either." I pass Ixchel an energy bar. "We're OK in here. But it's hundreds of kilometres to Ek Naab. I don't think I could lose them again between here and home."

"So we're stuck. . .?"

I peel open the wrapper of another bar. "That's what I've just been telling Benicio. Posted to my blog from my phone."

"He's still not answering?"

"I left a message with the hospital reception. His operation is happening round about now."

"You're using the Ek Naab phone? Can't the NRO trace that? If they know how to use that Muwan Mark I properly, they can trace any of our technology."

"Already thought of that. I'm using my ordinary phone."

Ixchel looks doubtful. "I don't know too much about cell phones and everything, but I'm pretty sure any cell phone can be traced. It just takes a high enough security clearance. And the NRO probably have one of the highest you can get. After all – they're the National Reconnaissance Office!"

I blink, confounded. Ixchel reaches across and plucks my phone out of my hand. With a wry grin, she turns it off. "Time for a bit of radio silence."

Now we're completely cut off. From Ek Naab; from the NRO; from the world.

"Well . . . if it comes to getting out of here . . . there's always the bike. This Muwan is fully equipped: bike, survival kit, everything."

She wrinkles her nose. "Ride a motorbike all the way back home?"

"We can be like Che Guevara in that film, Motorcycle Diaries. I really love that film."

"Me too," she says, approvingly.

"Hmm. Yeah," I remark. "Another film with that bloke you like."

"Sweetie, you're twice as cute as him."

We both have a smile about that, because it blatantly isn't true. "Seriously. Here to Ek Naab. We could do it in, like, a day. We'd go across Chiapas State and into Campeche from Villahermosa. It's got to be less than fifteen hours."

"We could go and look up Bosch on the way, in San Cristobal de las Casas. See if he ever did retire there, like he told us."

"If he actually survived life with the ancient Mayans, you mean! Still, it's not a bad idea." I take a bite of the cereal bar. "We could see how he feels about giving me his time-jump bracelet early."

"What do you mean, early?"

"Remember? Bosch and his retirement plans. San Cristobal de las Casas, late twentieth century. He said he'd leave me the Bracelet of Itzamna in his will. Maybe if he's there, he'll give it to me now."

86

"It would certainly make things easier."

"That bracelet?" I laugh. "Since when did it make anything easier. . .?!"

"No one knows where the moon machine is. We don't know what the Sect has planned with their Futurology Institute. But you could get the answers to those questions."

"If I had the Bracelet. . ." I'm beginning to understand Ixchel's suggestion. "If I time travelled . . . into the future."

"If we time travelled. . ."

"You don't want to go through all that again, do you?"

"No, Josh," she says softly. "If you go, I go. That's the deal. I don't want to wind up being separated from you."

"But that wouldn't happen. I can always use the default to get back to my starting point. And if I only travel forward, to the future, there's no danger of changing the past."

Ixchel sighs. "I don't know, Josh. All that time-travel causality business confuses me. But I bet it's possible to mess things up, somehow."

I become insistent. "But if all I do is to go into the future, snoop about a bit, gather some intelligence, then jaunt back . . . that's not so dangerous."

The idea is beginning to grow on me.

"Josh . . . what if we go into the future and find that the Sect has won? Then we'll know that there's no point changing things, because we've seen our own future. We'll know that we're doomed to fail."

I gaze at Ixchel. "But also, what if we go into the future and everything is fine? Then we can find out how that happened, how we defeat the Sect, the location of the moon machine, everything! And you know what else? If we go into the future and everything is fine, that's like a sign, isn't it – a sign that maybe we're meant to travel to the future, that it's all part of how things work out in our timeline."

A shadow of doubt crosses her face. "I don't know. There's a reason the people who made the time-jump bracelet didn't use it. I don't think we understand enough about how to use it. Or how it really works."

"I'm not saying it couldn't use a manual," I admit. "But anyway, without some kind of instructions I couldn't use it. Bosch would have to show me. And he probably wouldn't agree to that."

"He's probably a grumpy old man by now," agrees Ixchel, "if he's even still alive. . ."

"Bosch?" I smile. "That crazy time traveller? I can't imagine him not being alive. Bosch is indestructible!"

Ixchel unscrews a metal bottle of chilled water. I open a packet of beef jerky and offer it to her before taking a couple of strips of dried meat and putting them in my cheeks, where the salty flavour begins to seep through.

I say, "We should definitely swing by San Cristobal and look him up. He'd want to know that there's a problem with the 2012 plan. Who knows; maybe he can even tell us the location of the moon machine."

Ixchel chews the beef jerky thoughtfully. "Can't see how that's possible. Bosch didn't seem to understand much of what he was writing when he copied out those ancient Erinsi inscriptions into the Books of Itzamna. He may have studied the Erinsi civilization, but I don't think he had much clue about their technology."

"That was when we met him. But he'd be a lot older now. Who knows what ideas have occurred to Bosch since then?"

"I think maybe you're being a little too kind to his memory, Josh. Have you forgotten how he was about to trick you out of your time-travel bracelet and use it to escape from the past?"

I shrug. "Bosch could be a bit of a lad. But he made it good, didn't he? He helped us to trick Martineau, got his warriors to save us, and gave us our own time-travel bracelet back."

She chuckles. "You can be very forgiving. Why aren't you that way about the NRO?"

"Bosch was panicking. He just wanted to write those books and then get out of there. He was scared. When we turned up, he saw a chance to escape." I swallow. It's not easy to keep my voice even. "It's completely different with the NRO. That was all premeditated. They chased my dad . . . hunted him down . . . threw him in an underground jail and left him there without letting anyone know. And to make sure no one came looking, they faked his death! So, you tell me: what's to like about the NRO?"

"They did all that, true. But at least they're on the same side as us. They want to stop the superwave."

"We don't even know that for sure. All we know is that they want as much of the ancients' technology as they can grab. Can you imagine what kind of technology this moon machine must be, if it can stop a cosmic event like the galactic superwave? It's got to be mega. The NRO want that for themselves. That's one heck of a power imbalance in the world."

"Doesn't mean it would be used for evil purposes, though."

"Depends on whether you think nukes should ever be used, doesn't it?"

Ixchel sighs and takes another piece of jerky. "But surely a point comes when you have to make a deal, even with someone you don't like."

"Deal with the NRO?" I mutter darkly, leaning back against the dry volcanic rock of the cavern. "Maybe. When hell freezes over."

Chapter 14

Sky Guardians are required to wear wristwatches, something that I don't often do. The watches are equipped with torches too, but I'm already in survival mode; no point wearing out the battery. I check the time: 07:08.

It's going to be a very long day.

Ixchel and I start hauling out everything we're going to need from the Muwan.

I put two emergency packs into the inside pockets of my flight jacket. Two hard plastic cases, each about the size and thickness of a paperback book. The supplies inside are identical: medicines, bandages, a syringe and needles, currency worth one thousand US dollars in bills of, Mexican pesos, US dollars, euros, UK pounds and Chinese yuan. A Gerber Octane multi-tool. A foil thermal blanket, folded up into a tiny wedge. Water purification tablets, cotton wool, waterproof matches.

The motorbike – Benicio's Harley Davidson – has loads more stuff in its packs: a tent and proper outdoor survival gear. The flight jacket packs are just a supplement if a pilot is forced to eject from the Muwan.

We could survive for a few weeks on what's inside the Muwan.

It's a hazy morning, with almost total cloud cover. In the valley below, a warm mist has settled. Patches of washed-out foliage poke through it; trees and cacti are scattered across the terrain. The cave is halfway up a mild slope in the Tacana mountain range.

Ixchel takes a pair of binoculars and surveys the area. "There's a road to the east, a few kilometres. But I'm pretty sure that's Guatemala. Mount Tacana is right on the Mexican border; just about everything to the east is Guatemala. I don't know if we can risk being there without passports. Would make getting back into Mexico pretty difficult."

"So we stay on the Mexican side."

Hopefully I sound more confident than I feel. Ixchel is right; we're fairly isolated. I really want to be able to tell someone our location but until the last second when I had the Muwan radar operating, those NRO craft were still hovering. They know roughly where we are, I'd bet, down to fifty kilometres. We need to put distance between us and the Muwan before they start a ground search. I dread to think how good their satellite images are. Chances are they'll be tracking us pretty soon after we're in the open.

"OK," she says. "There has to be a trailhead somewhere; this is hiking country. We just need to head south to the nearest town, keep our eyes open. But Josh, it might be impossible to get a motorbike down the trail."

I hand Ixchel the spare helmet. "It's going to be OK. It can't be too hard to find, so long as we keep heading for the nearest town."

"You're right," she agrees. "Hikers only have one way to arrive there . . . so that's where the trail must start."

The next hour is tricky going. The terrain is dusty, lots of crumbly volcanic rock. We have to ride slowly, watching out for sudden dips or needle-sharp cacti. We lose count of how many times our elbows and knees catch the pointy end of some fierce-looking plant.

It's slow going without being able to risk using our phones to find a map on the Internet. But eventually we locate the trail. Miraculously, at first there's no sign that we're being tracked. I guess the NRO have realized that even if they land a Muwan they won't be able to catch us while we're on the move. The Mark I Muwans don't have much storage space, certainly not enough for a motorbike. Those pilots are stuck once they've landed.

Even so, I guess that they're hatching a plan. We're on the only machine moving for kilometres in every direction. How hard must it be to spot us from a satellite?

It takes us an hour to finally reach the meagre road at the nearest town, Chiquihuite. It's a huge relief. Ixchel's arms are loose around my waist but as we hit the tarmac, she squeezes. I turn on the satnav. Within a few seconds it's calculated a route to the plantation entrance of Ek Naab. Just over one thousand kilometres, roughly thirteen hours of riding. As I'd hoped, the route takes us right through the central highlands of the state of Chiapas, and the town of San Cristobal de las Casas.

By nine in the morning the heat is already uncomfortable. We strip down to sleeveless T-shirts and shorts, and smear sunblock over our shoulders and arms.

I'm uncomfortably aware, every moment, of the fact that the NRO might still be tracking me. Plus, I don't even have a motorcycle licence. But the reality is that once we hit Highway 200 a few kilometres out of the miniscule village of Chiquihuite, it would be hard to identify us from the sky. The motorbike is a fairly new model, bigger than you'd normally see being ridden by a guy my age. I make sure not to ride too fast. Ixchel reminds me not to take my helmet off anywhere where people can see us with the bike.

With water and food on board, we decide not to stop anywhere public, apart from refuelling. When we do, I don't remove my helmet and Ixchel pays for the gasoline, so that no one sees my face. Altogether, the whole escape goes well. By the time we ride into San Cristobal I'm hopeful that we've outwitted the NRO.

When we roll up at the edge of town, my watch says it's four-fifteen in the afternoon. Tourist buses are arriving, lining up at the coach parks on the outskirts. I keep riding, helmet visor lowered, until we reach the colourful *zocalo* – the central plaza.

The town is prettier than most I've seen, even by the standards of cute old colonial towns. Low red-tiled roofs, cobbled alleyways. Buildings painted in sugar-frosting colours, sunflower yellow with cinnamon red, peach and white, eggshell blue. Terracotta pots filled with flowers. Palm trees with white-painted trunks.

But unlike any place in Mexico that I've ever been – except Ek Naab – the town seems mainly to be populated with indigenous Mexicans wearing items of brightly coloured traditional dress. Women carrying babies in shawls wrapped tight around their chest. Crowds of people wearing traditional Mayan clothes, quite a bit like Ek Naab.

And tourists. Absolutely loads of pale-skinned faces, mostly young, studenty types. Seeing so many of them actually jars. Nine months since I've seen such a variety of non-Mexicans!

I stop for a moment, just leaning on the bike, to marvel at the sight. A proper big town, seething with the energy of people from all over the world. And unless things change, the lively bustle of this place and most others like it will be destroyed.

I don't have the energy to face this right now. Exhaustion is beginning to hit me. I've been on the move for almost two days. Ixchel doesn't say anything but she's got to be tired too. I'm desperate for a proper meal and a rest.

We lock up the bike in a secure-looking motorbike parking area, then start to wander across the square, a park of brilliant green flowering shrubs. Footpaths cross the garden, shaded by heavy palm trees. The square is surrounded by a red and white colonnaded arcade on one side and the grand, vanilla-ice-cream city hall on another.

Shoe-shiners buffing the leather uppers of old guys who sit high up on their stalls, reading the newspaper. Kids buying fancy covers for their mobile phones; a stall laid out with a different kinds of sweets. I take out one of the hundred-peso notes I've stashed in my trouser pockets and buy a Snickers bar, and some round cakes of peanut marzipan – Ixchel's absolute favourite. She gives a tiny scream of delight when I hand them over. For a moment I just watch her open the wrapper and bite into the soft, powdery sweet. It's so good to see her smile, to have a small break from the feeling of vague, omnipresent fear.

"So this is where Bosch chose to spend his final days," I say.

"Wonder how he adjusted to being plain old 'Zsolt Bosch' again," Ixchel says, "after years of living amongst the ancient Mayan as Itzamna."

"From what we saw of Bosch, I'm sure he missed being thought of as the living incarnation of one of the Mayan gods."

"I'm not so sure," she muses. "Being a living legend might be a bit of a chore." She gives me a sidelong glance. "After all, you're the Bakab Ix. And you know, once in a while, Josh, even you complain!"

Chapter 15

Clutching the coins I got in the change for the sweets, I hunt for a payphone that doesn't have a queue. This isn't the kind of town where everyone has a mobile phone, I guess. But it's the only way to get hold of Benicio without turning on our own mobile phones and risking being traced by the NRO.

I have to call directory enquiries to get the number of the hospital. My call is transferred from the main desk to the ward sister. Eventually, they put me through to Benicio.

"Josh, buddy! What's going on?"

"How's the leg?"

"They got the bullet out, pinned the bone, stitched me up. Another stupid scar, I guess."

"Sorry," I mumble. "At least it wasn't worse."

He sighs. "Yeah. I'm feeling pretty lousy now. I just called Montoyo, trying to get a lift home. But no answer. Do you know where he is?"

"Benicio . . . look, mate . . . I can't really talk. Not properly."

His tone alters immediately; tension enters his voice. "Josh . . . did something happen?"

"Ixchel and I found a name in that contact database. An astrophysicist called Kitrick. He was getting all weird with this other scientist, who's made a massive discovery. She's only gone and found the first signs of the galactic superwave!"

"The Sect won't like that."

"Too right – they don't! We went out to Chile. To see Dr Banerjee, the scientist woman."

I hear his gasp. "Chile. . .? Josh, don't tell me you took a Muwan. . .?"

I lick my lips. "We might have. . . "

There's a disbelieving silence. "You're finished, you know that? With the Sky Guardians – that's over. Take a Muwan before you're licensed and that is the end."

"No – they don't know it was me. We used your security access card."

Benicio groans. "I get it . . . you want me to take the rap."

"Buy us some time, OK? The NRO chased us down – I hid in Tacana. Have you seen my blog yet? I know you know the password."

"No . . . I just woke up like thirty minutes ago."

"Well – read it. Look, we'll be home tomorrow. We've stopped on the way to get some rest. Just cover for me, mate."

Exasperated, he says, "What do I tell the chief, Josh? I'm supposed to fly a shift today."

"Even better – you'd have to get out of flying anyway, with your bad leg. Tell the chief you took the plane out early. Unless they check the CCTV footage they won't know any different."

"Sure, it's OK for me to go down too, lying to cover your sorry butt."

"One more day! Look, it's worth it – we've got some intel about what the Sect might be up to next."

"Josh . . . what aren't you telling me? Why is it taking you so long to get home. . .?"

I pause. "Listen. The Muwan – we had to leave it. It's in Tacana, in one of those caverns you showed me. Problem is, the NRO know it's there."

"Oh God, not a Mark II." His voice sounds hollow. "Josh, tell me you didn't leave a Mark II somewhere the NRO might find it. . . "

"Benicio, I'm gonna sort this out. Really. There's a plan. But I need you to cover for me."

It's too late. My coins run out just in time to hear Benicio's wail of anxiety turn into a tirade of the spiciest Mexican curse words I've heard for a while.

Slightly shaken, I return to where Ixchel is admiring some oil paintings being displayed by the artist.

"What did Benicio say?"

"Oh. . ." I can't meet her eye. "He's pretty annoyed."

"How is he?"

"Bit upset about us leaving the Muwan in the cave . . . kind of obvious, really, that he would be." My voice trails off.

Ixchel continues to fix me with a steady gaze. "And what did you tell him?"

"I told him . . . that we've got a plan."

"Which is. . . ?"

There's no way I can stop myself looking helpless. "Well, I more sort of don't have a plan."

Ixchel is speechless, but she doesn't actually look too surprised.

"Apart from yours, of course," I add, hastily.

"My plan? Which one?"

"Getting Bosch's time-travel bracelet and going to the future. Then we find out how to fix everything and come back as heroes."

She bursts into laughter. "You think that's my plan? I was joking, Josh. Talking hypothetically. There's a reason Montoyo locked away your time-travel bracelet. That thing is dangerous!"

She tries to move away but I grab her hand. "What? If you didn't want me to get another Bracelet, then why did you agree to search for Bosch?"

"Because we're passing through the town anyway. It makes sense to see if he's here. Realistically though - what are the chances? Josh, wouldn't he have contacted you?"

"You think he's dead?"

"If Bosch is dead and he actually kept his word, left you his own Bracelet, then why didn't his lawyers contact you? Isn't that what happens when someone dies?"

I release her hand. "You – you want me to go and find out that Bosch isn't here, is that it? To realise that there's no chance of getting the bracelet? Were you just messing with my mind?"

There's a note of irritation in her voice. "Don't be ridiculous. I was simply saying 'what if?' That's what people do, isn't it? I was thinking aloud."

I step away, shaking my head. "No. I'm right, aren't I?"

There's a hint of panic in her eyes now. "Josh, please . . . you can't seriously be thinking of time travelling again."

I begin to walk away. It feels as though I've been slapped in the face with a cold towel. Ixchel follows me into the colonnades.

"We should find the central records office or whatever," I mumble, vaguely. "Find out where Bosch lives. Or lived." I'm simply going through the motions. Truth is, I haven't a clue what to make of Ixchel's sudden objection. Her idea was a good one, I thought. Risky, but then look at the stakes – it's the end of the world we're talking about!

We walk in silence through the town, stopping only to ask the occasional street vendor to point us towards the town hall. A frosty distance grows between us; by the time we reach the building I can hardly look at Ixchel. My mind is a jumble of all the thoughts and feelings that I can't put into words, but that all start with the sense of betrayal that gets worse with every step we take.

Eventually I stop in the middle of the pavement on a side street. "Why would you string me along like this?"

"Like what?"

"Say you'll time travel with me and then turn round and say that it's a stupid idea. . ."

"Josh, can't I say anything to you that isn't strictly true? I have my own imagination, after all."

"But don't you understand anything about me?"

Ixchel looks puzzled. "What do you mean?"

"Ixchel . . . like it or not, I'm a time traveller. A time traveller. You know? You can't go putting ideas in my head. Because – once the idea is there – it's there for good."

"But it's just an idea. . .?"

"If I have the idea to time travel, and it feels right, then – you know what? It can happen."

Ixchel shrugs but says nothing. I detect a sharpening in her interest.

I stick both hands in the pockets of my jacket. "When you move your leg, it's because before you moved it, you had the idea of moving. Like - when you get into university, it's because you first had the idea to apply. See? Me and time travel: other people can dream about it – and nothing comes of it."

"But you," she says eventually and with a trace of bitterness. "You can actually do it."

"Right. Even having the idea makes me wonder – is this it? Am I meant to time travel? Will some crucial event in history turn out to depend on me deciding to jump in time, right now?"

We stare at each other. "You think I'm crazy, don't you?" I say, quietly.

"No." She swallows and I notice tears in her eyes. "You're not crazy. You're right. Ever since I opened my mouth to say that stupid thing I've been regretting it."

"Things happen for a reason, Ixchel."

"But you don't know the reason, do you?"

I shake my head and reach for her. "No."

"How can you trust . . . if you don't know the reason?"

I shrug. "Sometimes you have to go with your gut."

Slowly, Ixchel's arms go around me. I reach up to wipe away her tears. A couple of bystanders give us a glance but no more. We hold each other loosely, me stroking her hair with one hand and wondering what to say.

But finally, I know what she's afraid of. The reason for me to time travel again; the truth of what I might become: Arcadio.

The name that's haunted us both since we first saw his name on a letter to me. The mysterious time traveller who seems to be following me around in space and time. Arcadio is the reason that I even had a time-travel bracelet in the first place – his cryptic postcards led me to my lost father, who gave me the Bracelet of Itzamna.

Arcadio – who fell in love with an American nurse, Susannah St John, only to abandon her for one last, fateful time-jump. Then he disappeared without a trace. That was 1962.

Arcadio, who my father dreaded I might become. Ixchel's worst fear about my future – that one day I'll time travel, lose my memory and never return.

I don't want to become Arcadio.

But what if things can only work out if I do?

Chapter 16

Zsolt Bosch is dead. Died before either of us was born, in fact.

"Which explains why he didn't come looking for you," Ixchel says.

We find out after queuing up at the records office, where they send us to the registry of deaths. And there's his name, on the list of deaths in 1992: "Don" Zsolt Bosch.

"He got to be a 'Don'," I say, impressed. "I guess people round here must have respected him."

It turns out that there's a memorial museum at the house that used to belong to Bosch. He donated it in his will, to be an exhibition centre dedicated to the local Lacandon people, descendants of the Maya who live in separate communities in the nearby rainforest. According to the pamphlet we pick up about the museum, Bosch lived among a local tribe of Lacandones for many years.

"Of course he did." I can't help smiling. "Bosch the famous anthropologist, living with the indigenous Mexicans. I bet he couldn't resist."

It's hard to tell if Ixchel's relieved to find out that Bosch is dead or not. Maybe it means that we'll never get hold of Bosch's time-travel bracelet. Perhaps it's buried with him.

I've already made my own mind up: it's no coincidence that we're passing through San Cristobal. Part of my subconscious mind – or Ixchel's – knew that if we came here, we'd look for any sign of Bosch. He promised us that when he was done with time-travelling, he'd retire to San Cristobal, in the twentieth century. He promised me that he'd leave me his bracelet.

I can't let go of the idea that Bosch would only do that for a reason. He knew how dangerous time travel can be. He wouldn't invite me to take another trip, not unless he knew that it was destined.

All these years I've felt like a pawn being moved in some kind of chess game, but I never knew whose hand moved me. For a long time I suspected that it was Montoyo. Then Arcadio, or even Blanco Vigores, Ek Naab's mysterious blind guy who always seemed to me like a kind of prophet.

The 2012 plan has absorbed the lives of several individuals. But there's never been any doubt about its main architect: Zsolt Bosch. The man who broke the plan and then tried to fix it.

Could it be that my puppet-master is Bosch?

I don't admit it to Ixchel; I barely admit it to myself. Yet, as we stroll through the bustling late afternoon streets of this old town, I can sense it. I'm giving myself over to whatever we find. If Bosch's Bracelet is there, then I know I'm going to use it.

The house is a few streets away from the main plaza, in a quiet alley lined with houses painted in a series of shades of orange, interrupted with the odd one in blue. There's a big double wooden door, heavy dark wood with fading varnish. A single door is cut into the main entrance, and a little Mayan girl, maybe nine years old, sits there.

"Entry is free," she says, looking up at us with wide eyes. For a second she looks a tiny bit like Ixchel and I wonder about all those years when Ixchel was growing up, years when I didn't know her and Benicio did.

We both give her a friendly smile and step over the threshold. The door leads to a small, neatly kept patio with a tiled fountain. Three walls are brilliant white; the fourth is a deep blue, the kind that little kids pick when they crayon the sky. The edges of the courtyard are lined with blue-and-white glazed pots filled with red geraniums.

"The geraniums," Ixchel murmurs. "Who do they remind me of. . .?"

"Susannah St John," I whisper. "The one from the parallel reality, where there was a nuclear war."

When Bosch changed the timeline by writing the Books of Itzamna, he erased that future. Now only Ixchel and I can even remember the Susannah of that reality. Maybe that's all existence really is – to exist in the minds of other people?

There's a door marked "Office", just off the entrance to the main part of the house. Through the doorway I can see a room, white walls hung with paintings of abstract art, tapestries and the occasional free-standing sculpture.

We can hear voices and footsteps from the room beyond, which sounds like a group of visitors. I knock on the door of the office and after a minute it opens. A slim, smooth-shaven young guy wearing trendy glasses opens it, holding a thin paperback between his finger and thumb.

In Spanish he asks, "Can I help you?"

"I need to speak to someone about Zsolt Bosch."

He looks me up and down for a second. "Are you family?"

I think for a second. In a way, I am. Bosch's son was the first Bakab Ix, and I'm descended from him, even though it was almost two thousand years ago.

"Yes."

The guy looks doubtful. "What's your name?"

"Joshua Garcia."

He's definitely taken aback. "You are Joshua Garcia? Born in Oxford, England?"

"Why not?"

He looks at Ixchel. "And you – are you family too?"

"No," she replies calmly. He stares at her for a minute until he realizes that Ixchel's not going to volunteer anything else.

Then back at me: "You can prove this? You have a passport, something?"

"I have a student ID card."

The guy seems a bit nonplussed.

"Why shouldn't I be Joshua Garcia?"

"Well, friend, you look about sixteen, agreed?"

"I'm eighteen," I lie. That's what it says on my fake ID.

"Even so. Zsolt Bosch died in 1992. He mentioned Joshua Garcia in his will. His condition was – the object had to be collected in person. By someone who didn't have to wait to be invited."

My heart pounds heavily for a few seconds; I have to take a deep breath. "Right, well, that's me."

"Hmm." He peers suspiciously into my eyes. "Mr Bosch couldn't have known of your existence."

"Obviously, he did."

"We expected an older gentleman."

It's a struggle to contain my excitement. Bosch did it! He actually left me something. Could it be the Bracelet?

"Look, I'm Joshua Garcia. I'm here to collect what Bosch left me."

The guy holds the door open a little more. There's barely enough room to get past him into the tiny office. He invites us to take a seat. With an officious air, he rifles through a filing cabinet, pulls out a file and sits down opposite me with the file in his hands. He coughs, almost ceremoniously, and opens the file. Inside is an envelope, with my name handwritten on the front. There's also another envelope. It's not labelled, and is already open.

"There are some questions," he says.

"Go for it."

"Question one: what are the names of the four books?"

I assume Bosch is talking about his four books of inscriptions copied from the walls of a buried Erinsi temple; the Books of Itzamna. "They are Ix, Kan, Muluc and Cuauc."

The guy's eyes narrow but he says nothing. He clears his throat. "Question two: who were the first Bakabs?"

Drat. I should remember this. Bosch introduced me to them all, four young boys, the last day that I saw him. This one is going to be harder.

"Leaf Storm," I begin, starting with Bosch's own son. "Sky Wind, Swift Light, Fire Son."

Almost triumphantly, he closes the file. "Wrong. You can leave now."

I bite my tongue. How can I admit that I met Bosch himself nine months ago, if this guy reckons he's been dead for almost twenty years?

"It's Swift Wind," I say firmly, focusing. "Sky . . . Sky Son. And Fire Light."

The guy seems disappointed. He opens the file again. "Final question: who died helping me to reach San Cristobal?"

"Josh. . ." Ixchel reminds me, "think carefully . . . what would Bosch say?"

That's a tricky one. To reach San Cristobal, Bosch needed the Bracelet of Itzamna. His warriors killed Marius Martineau, a leader of the Sect of Huracan who'd travelled in time to try to murder Bosch. And Bosch took Martineau's Bracelet.

"Marius Martineau," I say.

The guy lays down the file. Slowly, he holds out his hand. "Your ID card."

After he's looked it over and taken a photocopy, the guy picks up the envelope inscribed with my name. He looks faintly queasy. "Take it. Although I cannot understand how it can be you."

"Bosch was a time traveller," I tell him, very calmly. "And we met a while back." I open the envelope and remove the only contents – a key. "Bosch left me his time-travel machine."

The museum guy scowls. "There's no need to be disrespectful."

I hold up the key, grinning. "What does this open?"

"A safety deposit box at the bank on Insurgentes Street."

We leave right away. The guy seemed so disappointed to be handing over the precious envelope, I half suspect he'll change his mind. There's just time to get to the bank before it closes.

The bank is in the centre of town, a fancy, ornate building. The safety deposit security check is a bit dodgy because they make me open my survival packs and get all worried when they find the Gerber multi-tool with all the sharp pointy bits. In the end they only let me through if I leave my jacket and everything I'm carrying with Ixchel.

Finally I'm on my own in a room with the safety deposit box. I open it to find another envelope containing a sheet of handwritten instructions, plus a short letter from Bosch. But the object that sets my heart pumping right away is the Bracelet of Itzamna. Trembling slightly, I push the Bracelet on to my arm and fasten it. I roll my sleeve down to cover the object, and pick up the letter.

I walk out of the room, feeling suddenly powerful and scarily conspicuous. As though it must be written all over my face.

Ixchel gives me a searching look and then whispers, "Bosch did it, didn't he?"

Without a word, I take her hand and lead her towards the doors. By the time we leave the bank my skin is fizzing, tingling underneath the strange, arcane metallic surface of the relic. Reacting with some mysterious secretion of my own flesh, the Bracelet of Itzamna recognizes one of its owners.

Chapter 17

It's just past five in the afternoon but after over thirty-six hours on the go we're ready to drop. We check into the first hotel we find and make straight for the room. We don't even have the energy to eat in the restaurant, so we order club sandwiches, fries, pizza and Caesar salad to be brought to the room.

The hotel is a grand old Spanish building with a jungle-style garden in the central courtyard, and terracotta tiled floors. Our room is huge; there's light wooden flooring and arched walls painted with a red trim. There are two beds covered in pristine white sheets; we kick off our shoes, throw ourselves on to the beds and lie there sighing with relief.

"I've been awake for nearly two days," I groan. "And my legs ache like mad from riding the bike. . ."

"Think you're the only one in pain? My muscles are going into shock."

I roll over on to my side and look at Ixchel. "I'm glad you came. I hope you are too. Even though I've messed up."

She smiles, very sweetly. "Of course I'm glad. It's you and me against the world, isn't that right?"

I reach across the gap between the beds and touch Ixchel's fingers. "If I do it, Ixchel, if I use the Bracelet, I do want you to come with me. Don't think I can do it alone."

Ixchel's gazes at me with her deep brown, almond-shaped eyes. Her fingers intertwine with mine. She tugs until I'm almost rolling off the edge of my bed. "You're not alone, Josh. Never."

"Do you mean it this time? Please don't just be saying it."

Ixchel shakes her head. "I've decided. You don't get away from me that easy, Josh, Arcadio, or whoever you are."

I'm about to slide off the bed to kiss her but there's a knock at the door. It's the food, presented with fancy stainless steel cover plates. We're too hungry to do anything but attack the food solidly for several minutes.

Outside, it begins to rain, lightly at first, and then settles into the hard summer rain that keeps everything around here so dazzlingly green.

A helicopter flies low overhead, noisily shattering the medley of voices and traffic sounds. Ixchel and I poke our heads through the open window, glance up to see a black bubble of a helicopter above the *zocalo* – the town square. It circles a couple of times and then cruises off.

For one ghastly moment, the thought that it might be the NRO crosses my mind. But I keep the thought to myself. Ixchel and I are managing to calm down quite nicely; I don't want to risk another row.

But after a while, munching fries and drinking Mountain Dew, I get to thinking again and starting wondering: is Bosch my puppet-master?

"Did you ever think that Bosch could be Arcadio? He had the blue eyes, like Susannah said."

Ixchel frowns. "Bosch didn't mention travelling to the twentieth century. I got the impression that he'd only been to the Mayan past."

"He must have gone afterwards."

"Bosch was already in his forties when we met him; too old to be Arcadio. Susannah described a younger man."

Then Ixchel goes quiet. Tentatively I say, "You still think Arcadio is me."

"Can you think of another answer?"

"Yes – how about Blanco Vigores? He's all enigmatic about his past. No one knows for sure where he came from. No one remembers him being young. And Martineau got a time-travel bracelet from someone. Blanco's missing. We know he went to that club that Marius Martineau was a member of, in New York. So, who else but Blanco?"

"It's possible, I guess."

"And he's still missing from Ek Naab. He could be anywhere. Or anytime."

Ixchel thinks for a moment. "Blanco Vigores knows about your life, that's true. But how did he first learn about your life?"

"If he's a time traveller, we might be meeting each other out of order. Maybe he first meets me when I'm grown up. Maybe I tell him stuff. Or maybe he meets my dad?"

"Stop, you're giving me a headache. I told you, it's not natural to play with time like this. We're supposed to live and grow a day older each day."

I grin. "We do – just that us time travellers don't live life in order."

"Listen to you. Us time travellers."

I roll up my sleeve to reveal the Bracelet of Itzamna. "Look at it. Shiny new Crystal Key too, by the look of it. I reckon old Bosch might have sorted the technology out, finally."

"You think he's fixed it so it doesn't cause amnesia, or so that the crystal doesn't burn out and trap you in the past?"

"Yes," I say brightly. "Maybe!"

Ixchel puts down her knife and fork and dabs her mouth with a napkin. She places both hands on her knees. "Well, Josh . . . aren't you going to open the letter from Bosch?"

I sit up, take the letter from the envelope and spread it on my bed. Three pages of handwritten instructions for using the Bracelet of Itzamna. There's a brief memo on top of the three pages.

Josh Garcia, as I live and breathe! Except that obviously I don't breathe any longer, not if you're reading this. No worries – it hasn't happened yet.

Kid, I've no idea what would bring you to town, looking for the Bracelet of Itzamna. Maybe you make a mistake and want to put it right? Or maybe you want to do the one thing I've never dared to do – to venture into your future!

I don't know how far into the future you could go. I've thought about the physics of this and . . . well, bottom line is, I'm not a physicist. In theory the Bracelet goes both ways – into the past, into the future. In theory! I haven't tested it enough.

All I know, tjommie, is that you and I will meet again. Can't tell you when and where, but we do.

So – I figure maybe you're going to need the Bracelet. Hey, it's not as if I know anyone else that can use it. Not now that Marius Madman is dead!

Good luck, Josh Garcia. Hope you're still with that girl, Ixchel. You make a cute couple.

Yours in anticipation, Zsolt Bosch

San Cristobal de Las Casas, December 22nd, 1990

Reading Bosch's letter, a tingle enters my body through my fingertips and sweeps through me within seconds. Something happens to Ixchel too because I feel her grip tightening on my arm.

Bosch's meaning couldn't be clearer. All doubt leaves my mind.

I'm going to use the Bracelet to time travel again.

Silently, I wrap my arms around Ixchel and embrace her tightly. She's clinging on to me, trembling all the way through.

Remember to breathe.

"Don't be afraid," I whisper against her ear.

Ixchel hugs me even harder. "I hate that you have to do this stuff. Was it too much to hope to fall in love with a normal boy?"

"I know, I'm sorry. What can I do to help?"

"Not go. . . ?" she mumbles, hopefully.

"What else can I do to help?"

Ixchel's sigh is muffled against my jacket. Then quietly she says, "Sing me something. Like you did on the beach that time."

"I don't have my guitar. . ."

"Please. Just . . . anything."

I try to sing part of "Last Night On Earth" by Green Day. But it's no good. There's a knot of air moving through my chest. I just can't get through the song.

We hold on to each other for the longest time, as though we're being buffeted in a storm. I think about the millions of couples who are hugging each other, right this very minute, or holding their child, how all of that happiness will be smashed to pieces when the superwave hits the Earth. The stupidity of the entire world's power play and how idiotic it is that even in a situation like this, you have to ask yourself who can be trusted. The insanity of the Sect, who want to see billions of lives ended just so that they can have their own version of heaven on Earth. Compared to all of that, the warmth that flows between Ixchel and me seems like a trickle, even though the sensation is strong enough to make me dizzy. Compared to all of that, Bosch's letter stands out as a shining beacon, the only way forward.

The 2012 plan has reached a stalemate. It's time for us to break it.

Chapter 18

We make our way through the streets of San Cristobal. The sound of my blood pulses in my ears. The air is still cool at this altitude. It's eight in the morning and the town centre is already getting busy with people ambling to work. We pass a corner where a street vendor sells hot tamales wrapped in banana leaves, which he takes out of a large aluminium steamer that sits on top of a brazier. The air smells of steamed maize and chillies.

The Bracelet of Itzamna on my arm is primed – Ixchel and I used Bosch's instructions to work out how to set it. Six symbols need to line up. We want to travel to the same geographical destination, so that was easy – one touch sets the symbols to auto-locate to the current position. Next, the destination date. That was easy too, for Ixchel; she reads Erinsi script fluently now.

And that's it. The Bracelet will calculate the rest: how to compensate for the movement of the Earth through space.

"One year may not be enough," Ixchel pointed out, when I suggested 2013. "If things do go wrong . . . it might take a while for the world to get organized again."

So in the end we settled on June 2014.

We spent all night planning (arguing, more like) and decided that we need all the help we've got on this mission. That means finding a way to still have access to the motorbike and the Muwan, two years from now. We're going to ride out to an isolated spot, hide the motorbike, then jaunt into the future. And hope that the Muwan is still in the cave in Juny 2014.

"Then we use the Muwan to check out Ek Naab," I say. "That's the simplest thing. Ask them what happened in December 2012."

Plan B is to pay a surprise visit to the Sect of Huracan. The Bracelet can manage short teleport jumps within the same time so long as you can get a visual lock on where you want to go. Bosch's instructions mention that he's tested this but finds it the most dangerous version of Bracelet travel. His comments actually remind me of what Blanco Vigores told me about the first time Blanco used the Bracelet – he nearly ended up inside a rock.

We decide to try other ways of getting inside any Sect building before risking a Bracelet jump.

We have a printout of the Web page that Dr Banerjee showed us, with the location where this Futurology Institute is being built in Oxford. I'm still guessing that it's the Sect of Huracan's new headquarters.

"If you're wrong. . .?"

"Then we try Chaldexx in Switzerland. Even if that isn't where the Sect is mainly based, that's where Melissa DiCanio hangs out. So she'll have key intel on her computer."

"Which we're going to take?"

"I've still got the memory stick that Benicio gave me, the one I used to copy the Sect's contact database. We'll copy their emails, all their documents. All we need is ten minutes with one of their computers. Whatever we do, we'll arrive in the middle of the night: fewer people around to see the Muwan landing, or to notice us snooping around."

I'm pretty excited at the thought of my first solo flight across the Atlantic. In contrast, Ixchel looks pale and seems subdued. She didn't eat any breakfast, hardly slept either. We were up pretty late, learning how to operate the Bracelet settings; time and place. But she's still worried that we've made a mistake.

I guess we can't know for certain, until we use it.

We continue on the way to the small parking section at one corner of the *zocalo* where we left the motorbike. As we're drawing closer, a voice calls, in English, "Hey, you there!"

I stop and turn my head. All I see is a row of newspapers spread in front of three guys having their shoes shined. I glance around to see who else the voice could have been talking to. The voice sounded casual and friendly, spoken in English but with a Mexican accent. All the same, I'm too paranoid now to let even a tiny sign of danger pass by. Immediately I'm tense, watchful.

"Did you see who said that?" I whisper to Ixchel.

She grips my hand tightly, the other hand clutching our motorbike bag.

For the next few seconds we just watch the streets, searching. A mother walking hand-in-hand with a little girl, each carrying a straw shopping bag laden with fruit. Two women setting out their bright, stripy woven wares on a grey blanket. The ice-cream man wiping down the creamy white surface of his mobile cooler. The shoeshine boys and the squat, shirt-sleeved man who seems to be running them. Backpackers arranged over one of the green-painted metal park benches, reading tourist guides and smoking. Another obvious foreigner dressed in green and yellow Lycra cycling gear, wraparound sunglasses and a cycling helmet – he stops near the motorbikes to tie a lace on his running shoes. A party of female tourists, quite a few nuns among them, begins to cross the centre of the plaza.

Nothing suspicious. Yet no one has owned up to the "Hey you." I'm tempted to check the faces of the guys behind the newspapers. But I decide to press on. The sooner we're out of here the better.

Something is wrong. Definitely. But I have no idea what. The motorbike is parked less than twenty metres away. I put the phone back in my pocket. We break into a jog.

Out of the corner of my eye, I see the cyclist standing up, taking off at a jog. His path is about to cross ours. Ixchel, looking in the same direction, utters a sharp cry that seems to get lodged in her throat.

At the very last second the cyclist swerves and throws his shoulder round hard, bumps into me less than three metres from the bike. I'm braced enough not to fall hard, but I land awkwardly. Ixchel's swung away from me; out of the corner of my eye I spot her on the pavement. Then I hear her voice, a warning.

I'm standing up when the cyclist's fist flies through the air. It connects hard with my right cheekbone. The pain explodes inside my eye socket, and I reel for a second. With a burst of adrenaline, my capoeira training kicks in. I drop low, feint right, then roll in the opposite direction, dodging the next blow. Low to the ground, I switch legs with a *troca* and swipe at his legs with a *corta capim*.

He falls backwards. Not a capoeira fighter, at least. But Sect – most definitely he's with the Sect.

I don't stay to fight, but leap over him and towards the motorbike. Ixchel's already there, taken up pillion position, urging me onwards. I reach into my jacket pocket for the bike key. Before I can unlock the bike, the cyclist is coming at us again, trying to shove Ixchel off the bike.

She struggles with him for a moment, then tries to punch him in the face, but he grabs her fist. I wallop my elbow into his ribs, and follow up with a backwards punch. While he's temporarily distracted, Ixchel sinks her teeth into his shoulder. He yells, lashes out with a fist and catches Ixchel on the ear. I twist around and give him a heavy shove. As he staggers backwards I stare into his face – wraparound sunglasses under a white cyclist's helmet. He smells of sweat and hair gel. But even from the little I see, this close up, I know him.

Simon Madison.

Madison staggers for just long enough to give me time to turn the key in the lock. Ixchel takes the heavy chain lock from the handlebars; she swings it into Madison's advance. That buys us another second. I twist the throttle. The bike jerks into movement, pulls away with Madison's fingers clutching empty air.

Our fight has alerted the cops now; two patrolmen in beige and khaki uniforms have dashed over to Madison. One motorbike cop enters the *zocalo*. The witnesses must have told them that Madison started the fight, because the cops are piling towards him. But the motorbike cop yells out to me: "You! Stop!"

I turn, briefly, twist the throttle and speed around the corner. The motorbike cop responds by zipping across the pedestrianized section in the middle of the square and cutting off our escape route.

For a second we face each other, about three metres apart. The cop dares me to challenge him, eyes peeping out from beneath the peak of a silver-and-blue badged helmet.

There are shouts from the other side of the square. Madison is on his feet and one of the two patrolmen is on the ground. The second is holding a gun on Madison, yelling at him to get on to the ground.

A background hum of whirring blades from a helicopter suddenly explodes into a riot of noise. I glance up – it looks like the black helicopter that we spotted last night. For a second I freeze.

The black helicopter swoops into view, low above the square. There's the sound of two shots being fired, followed by a woman's scream. Then a hysterical stampede away from the centre of the square, to the colonnades.

The helicopter's appearance is a jolt to Ixchel, too. She can't tear her eyes away from it.

"Simon Madison followed us to San Cristobal, Josh! How?!"

Madison arrived in the helicopter. He's here, with others from the Sect of Huracan. I stare at the helicopter just in time to see a rifle being pulled back inside the cockpit.

A sniper. No wonder Madison wasn't carrying a gun. He has all the air cover he could need.

Both patrolmen are on the ground. The motorbike cop opposite me seems to take a moment to process what has happened. Two of his fellow officers have been shot from the air. The woman who saw the shootings up close can't seem to stop screaming. No wonder. I've seen someone killed by a bullet at close quarters – it's a chilling sight.

In confusion, the motorbike cop looks across the square from Madison to me. Madison's mouth is tightly closed, jaw clenched. He's walking towards our motorbike; then he breaks into a run.

I rev up my bike. "Get out of here," I say to the cop. "Hurry!"

He throws a nervous glance at Madison. I turn the wheel, feel the motorbike drag. In another second I'm on my way out of the square. I hear Madison yell at the cop, hear two more shots fired from the looming helicopter, hear the loud rev of the cop's motorbike.

And I don't even look around, don't need to. I can already sense it; Madison is chasing us. With a helicopter in tow.

Chapter 19

We're navigating the streets of the old colonial town as fast as I dare take the bike. The head start we gained won't last long – that police motorbike looked pretty hefty, more powerful than my Honda. On his stolen vehicle, Simon Madison is gaining fast.

Falling into the hands of the Sect – especially with the Bracelet of Itzamna – is simply not an option.

Our only way out is the Bracelet. Is it safe to use it while moving? Bosch's instructions said you should be stationary, but he didn't say how dangerous it might be to risk a time-jump while you're actually moving pretty fast.

But how are we going to buy enough distance and time to be able to use it?

There's wild electricity to riding at this speed without a helmet. Death might be seconds away and yet it's unimaginable.

Madison sticks behind us, only fifty metres away and closing. If we stop, he'll be on top of us in a second. I begin to take bigger risks, the kind that Benicio might take. Squeezing between a yellow school bus and delivery truck, speeding up to sixty to get through a traffic light before it turns red. I feel the icy touch of sweat rolling down my back.

Madison is just as reckless – he runs two red lights and catches up with me. The helicopter trails along less than thirty metres above the road, somewhere between Madison and me. Ixchel grips my waist so tightly that it's difficult to breathe. I sense her fear but also her trust as she leans against my back.

The town thins out. There's less traffic. I use the space to speed up to seventy. We're rocketing down the main exit road. Madison is still in relentless pursuit. In the distance, police sirens.

Things pass in a blur. Every decision has deadly potential. We swerve past coaches bringing in another load of day trippers. The road begins to climb, the green hills and forests of the countryside lie ahead.

The moment we hit the country road, I speed up yet again. I've never ridden the bike this fast, not even when I raced against Benicio. It's exhilarating, yet terrifying. The covering of trees thickens at the edges of the road. Soon we're riding through a pine forest. I glance over my shoulder.

Madison is no more than ten metres behind.

He accelerates again. He's almost alongside. I slam on the brakes and watch Madison sail past. I swerve off the road, into the woods. Our tyres skid on the damp forest floor of pine needles. We double back and head in the opposite direction, zigzagging deeper into the woods. Madison's motorbike roars as it enters the woods, seconds behind. He leaps over a heap of logs and crashes down ahead of us. We barely stop in time. The Harley slides and topples. Ixchel is thrown free of the bike, to my left, but I'm trapped under the bike.

Madison is already off his bike and diving through the air. He throws himself at Ixchel, lands right on top of her and rolls her over, until they're both facing upwards, Madison with one arm in a tight lock around Ixchel's neck. With his other arm he's pinned both her arms to her sides.

"Wanna hear me break her neck?"

119

Cautiously, I slide out from under the bike, bruised and grazed but nothing worse.

"Don't come any closer or I swear, I'll kill her!"

Less than two metres from Madison, I hold out my empty palms to him.

"Let her go. I'm not armed. I can't hurt you."

Madison is panting fiercely, his eyes fixed on mine. Ixchel gulps down each breath, fighting for air.

"What do you want?"

Madison barks out, "Where is Marius?"

How ironic; Madison asking me about his missing father.

"I don't know. . ." I reply, carefully. Technically, I don't know where Marius Martineau's body is buried, so it's not exactly a lie.

He sounds furious. "You know something, you and your moronic friends in that place. . ."

Ixchel's eyes are glazing over. Maybe Madison is out of control. He's definitely hurting her.

"Let go of her, Simon; this is between you and me."

He manages to snort out a laugh. "I'm holding on until the others get here with the helicopter. I know you wouldn't abandon your new girlfriend. She's easier to hold on to than you would be. A lot nicer too," he adds, with a disgusting grin. My eyes flash to Ixchel's and I hold her gaze for a second, trying to find some way to reassure her. But my own fear must be visible, because I can't stop myself from trembling.

The clatter of helicopter blades comes closer, until it's almost directly above our heads. I gaze at Madison, squirming amongst the pine needles, struggling to keep Ixchel in position.

Still shaking, I find myself moving my right hand, reaching for my left arm, under the sleeve. Ixchel sees the movement of my hand and her eyes widen, just for a second. I see her acceptance. My fingers find the sharp edges at the heart of the Bracelet of Itzamna. I press down on the Crystal Key, feel the moving parts of the Bracelet of Itzamna engage, metal slithering over metal.

The countdown starts.

Then I'm on the ground, punching Madison, loosening his grip. It's like an iron bar around Ixchel's neck. Fists fly, legs kick, the three us wrestle for a second. I open my arms, trying to get a hold on Ixchel, but Madison wedges his feet against her stomach and shoves hard. Ixchel is sent flying backwards, mouth open in a cry of shock and despair.

I launch myself into a full-on cartwheel to build up momentum, and spring out of it into a handstand twist – the au cortado. My kick falls just shy of Madison's shoulder as he dodges, gasping. I drop backwards into a queda de quarto, flip over and slam his knees with a scorpion kick, then pivot and scissor his legs with mine for a takedown. As Madison falls, he throws a weighty punch, which catches me in the side of the head. For a second or two I'm wobbling, ear ringing with pain.

We're both breathing hard as we face each other. There's a calculating glint in his eye.

Madison throws himself at me, hands open like a butterfly's wings, grabbing for my head. A fire of rage lights his eyes. The tough plastic of his cycle helmet smashes against my forehead. I see a dizzying array of stars.

Then the Bracelet rips time and space open and we go hurtling through. Trees and the blue chinks of sky are ripped out of my field of vision. The world around us explodes, reassembles into patterns of green and brown.

A subtle shift, the same position as before. But suddenly, there is silence. It's noticeably darker, too. Almost dusk.

The helicopter is gone.
The police sirens have gone.

Ixchel is gone.

Simon Madison collapses beside me. He rolls on to his side, shaking violently, groaning. He vomits.

My head pounds with the impact of his headbutt, and when I stand I'm shaky, almost as unsteady as Madison. On all fours now, Madison lifts his head for a second. He stares past me, bleary with confusion. Another retch heaves through his body. I turn in the direction of Madison's gaze: the motorbike. There's only one in sight – I don't know what's happened to the one that Madison was riding.

But the motorcycle is still where I remember.

Madison struggles, starts to get to his feet.

Instantly, I understand what he's doing; he's going for the bike.

I spin around, vault across the distance between us and the motorbike. By the time I've dragged the bike into a standing position Madison is already upon me. We're both still groggy, me from his head-butt, him from the time-jump, so for a few seconds we stagger as if in slow motion, like two drunks in a pub brawl. But I have the advantage; I'm already on the bike, shoving a foot in his chest, fumbling with the throttle, jolting the motorbike into life. The machine and I leap forward, unsteady at first, until I regain my balance.

Then I'm away. Tearing through the pine forest, the rumble of the motor like a fire in my belly, every vibration going straight to my bones. Madison, left behind, calling uselessly, his voice reduced to nothing more than a faint whimper in the woods.

And the undeniable, the riveting thrill of time travel. Energy coursing through me, the residue of an unimaginable journey through the space-time continuum. I'm learning to recognize this feeling for what it is: overwhelming, alluring.

Totally addictive.

Chapter 20

The urge to return to my own time is pretty acute for the first half hour. It would be so easy: zap back to the woods and return to Ixchel. Madison would be out of the way. And then?

Then I'd have Ixchel urging me to try again, to bring her with me this time. But every single usage of the Bracelet carries a risk of being stuck in time, of getting hit with amnesia. As well as being flooded with adrenaline, I'm almost overwhelmed with relief.

I got away with it – again.

Somehow, the fact that it isn't working out how we planned makes it feels as though this was meant to be. I wanted to bring Ixchel, and yet she isn't here and I am. Deep down, I'm afraid to tempt fate again. What if there's a reason for me being alone on this mission?

I retrace our steps, heading back for the Muwan. It's closer than Ek Naab but also – I feel too vulnerable on the motorbike. Thoughts of Ixchel keep threatening to break my concentration. I keep telling myself that now that I'm in another time, everything is suspended. Ixchel is still back in those woods, alone. But for her, hopefully, only a minute will pass before she sees me again. The real worry is this – how much will I have changed by the time we meet again?

The silence all around me is my first clue that something is wrong. Even in the pine forest of the state of Chiapas, you don't get silence, not on a road, not during the day. It's a while before the silence registers, however, because the roar of the Harley dominates the landscape. Only when I slow dramatically to take a hairpin bend do I realize just how relatively quiet it is.

People talk of the romance of the open road, but the thought that you might really be all alone isn't as romantic as you might imagine.

The second clue is the fact that the motorbike's satnav doesn't work. It turns on and then just sits there trying to connect to the satellite grid. The network is down. Either it's just very bad luck or else . . . the 2012 plan failed.

I check both my mobile phones – Ek Naab and my old UK phone. Neither of them work either.

NO SIGNAL.

It doesn't take me long to come across my first casualty. A huge delivery truck for a supermarket, rear doors gaping open. And by the doors, something gleams white. I catch my breath when I see it's a collection of human skeletons, their bones picked clean.

Someone held up that delivery truck, forced the employees to open it and surrender the contents, and then killed them in cold blood.

After the initial instinct to bolt passes I simply stand, motionless and silent, watching the road around me. I begin to suspect there won't be any other cars on the road, probably none between here and the Muwan.

If the Muwan has been found, then I'm out of options. I'll be forced to return to my own time.

Something stops me getting too close to those human bones by the truck; I don't want to know exactly how those people were killed. There must be something primitive in your brain which makes you fear a sight like that. It's as though a sixth sense is triggered.

The fear of being hunted.

I'm suddenly hyper-aware of the smells around me, the combination of grasses and pine, the faint scent of spilled diesel and oil on the asphalt. I sniff the air for a trace of anything that might be alive. Once I'm aware of it, the smell of my own sweat seems like a loud announcement of my presence. I steer around the supermarket truck without getting off the bike. I take a decision not to stop until I reach the Muwan. Something tells me that if I were to become separated from the Harley, there wouldn't be much chance for me.

Every ten minutes or so I come across another abandoned vehicle. One of them is a motorbike, rusting badly, slung on its side by the edge of the road. I stop my own bike, lean over and unscrew the petrol cover. Even with my nose close to the opening, I can't detect any petrol fumes – they must have run out of gas. And then what? Walked away?

What if there is no fuel – anywhere?

Hastily, I check my own bike's petrol gauge – almost full. If I hadn't refuelled just before Ixchel and I entered San Cristobal, at one of those cheap edge-of-town petrol stations, things could be getting bad right now. At any rate, there should be enough to get me back to the Muwan, near Mount Tacana.

But a new fear has just been added to my list: in a world where people have abandoned their cars and motorbikes on the road because they're out of fuel, a full tank of petrol might get you killed.

I ride onwards, fully alert, watching the road ahead, listening out for sounds behind me.

The Honda eats up the road, cruising through the forest, into the valley, past roadside shacks and shrines and shops, not one with the tiniest sign of human occupation. Or even a loose chicken.

When I see signs for Comitán, the first town on the route, my knuckles tighten around the handlebars. If there are still people around, they're probably in the towns. And the people are almost certainly dangerous.

125

But when I reach the place, it dawns on me how totally wrong I am. The town is still there. But it's empty. A proper ghost town; broken-down doors in most houses, shattered windows. Shops are the worst; every single one has been cleaned out, that much is very obvious even from the road. I slow down as I pass through, filled with a combination of horror and fascination. Part of me wants to look around and see if there's anyone hiding. But the need to keep going is beginning to dominate my thoughts.

Comitán is done for. I don't know how long ago but it looks to me as though no one has lived here for a long while. Anything that could have been used, burned or eaten has been taken. There is a giant garbage pile on the other side of town, the size of a house. It doesn't even smell.

It's June 2014. The skies are still – not a single aeroplane has passed overhead since I left Madison vomiting in the woods. Everywhere I look – Armageddon.

The town of Tapachula is next, but I'm already anxious about what I'll find. I remember driving through a fairly big town in 2012. Will Tapachula have faced the same fate as Comitán? Or has everyone in the state moved to the biggest centre of civilization around?

I'm tempted to risk avoiding the town by going around the country roads. But without a satnav to guide me, it's dangerous, uncertain. Even though the roads are littered with abandoned vehicles, it still makes sense to get to my destination as fast as possible.

So I keep going. All the way to Union Juarez, where the highway runs out, to the tiny villages in the foothills near Mount Tacana. And not a person in sight.

They're all hiding, or they're all dead. Either possibility is enough to set my nerves on edge.

By the time I reach the village where the hiking trailhead starts, it's too dark to see the road. I've been reluctant to use my headlamps, because in the dark the beam is going to stand out for a long way. And even though I haven't actually seen anyone, the hairs on the back of my neck and arms, the gripe of my stomach and the tension in my throat make it impossible to forget: there are predators around.

But the predator I'm really scared of is the human.

What happened to everyone?

As I pull my bike off the path and find some meagre shelter under some trees, I open up the bike container that carries the tent and sleeping bags. Both are a bit of a surprise. They're not the standard-issue equipment that the Muwan carries, but a brand I don't recognize. I'm too tired to spend much time wondering about it, and once I've got the tent up, I crawl inside, zip the mosquito net closed and slide into the sleeping bag. I check both mobile phones one last time.

Nothing.

Images of the fractured roads, deserted, rusting vehicles, those grey vacant towns linger on, flicker behind my closed eyelids. The sense of solitude is overpowering.

The urge to chicken out and zap back to my own time begins to well up again. The future looks like a bad dream. I could make it just disappear, use the Bracelet and return to where I started. Rescue Ixchel, take the police bike.

But I resist. I've been given a glimpse into the future. Something catastrophic has happened. I've ridden for hours and seen no sign of human life. There are no satellite networks. I can't shake a pervading sense that this is just the tip of an iceberg.

It's going to get much worse.

This future awaits me and everyone I know – unless something is done to fix the 2012 plan. I need to find out exactly what went wrong. If I can get to Ek Naab, there's a chance I can do that. All I have to do is hang on here a little while longer. Then it's back to June 2012 with whatever intelligence I've found.

The secret path to a different outcome, a more optimistic timeline.

In the dark, I fumble in my pocket for an energy bar, tear the wrapper and stuff chunks of it into my mouth. I drink from one of my water bottles. My muscles start to relax, but I can't fall asleep. It might be dark in 2014 but it's less than eight hours since I woke up in 2012. I'm still wide awake and alert. With all the thoughts of what might have happened since December 2012, there seems little chance of dropping off.

How's a guy supposed to sleep with a mind full of films like I Am Legend and 28 Days Later?

I find myself mumbling a couple of Hail Marys and a very simple prayer:

Let it not be a zombie apocalypse.

Chapter 21

The night is pure torture. In the darkness every single sound seems to be magnified. I daren't even plug in my earphones and play my dad's iPod. As ominous as each wilderness noise may be, I need to remain alert. Dawn begins before I manage to sleep.

When I wake I'm drenched with sweat, starting to roast in the blaze of early afternoon heat. I emerge from the tent gasping for a bit of cool and drain all but the last drops of my water bottle.

Nothing to drink now until I reach the Muwan.

Apart from a few small-animal tracks near the Honda there's no sign that anything disturbed the camp. So if there are any crazed zombie vampires hanging around, they're probably not anywhere close. . .

I pack up my little camp, eat a few more strips of beef jerky and an energy bar, then hop on to the Honda. The next bit is going to be pretty difficult without satnav. But at least there's a compass in the survival kit. Even with that, it takes me an epic three hours to reach the hill underneath the cave where we left the Muwan. By then I'm so parched that water is all I can think about. I'm easily the thirstiest I've ever been in my life. It takes three days to die of thirst. I can't even begin to imagine what suffering you go through before that happens, if it feels this bad after three hours.

The slope towards the cave is pretty steep; I remember Ixchel and I came blasting down like a bullet from a pistol. When I reach the opening of the cave, I make the bike crawl along the rough track, preparing myself for what could be a crashing disappointment.

If the Muwan is gone then bang goes any chance I have of finding out what happened to create this timeline. Gone will be any hope of changing things when I return to 2012.

But as I creep closer to the craggy, shadowed shelter of the cave, I spot the smooth metallic surface of the Muwan, about twenty metres inside. I'm a little surprised to find the craft tucked quite so far into the cave, because I remember thinking that ten metres would be enough. I guess I overrode my first decision, after all.

The Muwan remote is still in my back pocket. When I try to use it, I get a seriously unpleasant surprise.

The Muwan doesn't respond. I press the button repeatedly. But nothing.

It seems impossible that this could be happening to me now, yet the remote batteries must be dead. I check in my survival pack for spares, change them using the Gerber multi-tool to open the remote casing. When I press the button, this time using fresh batteries, still nothing.

Inconceivable. Maybe the lock mechanism is jammed; maybe some dust or something got inside in the past two years. I position the motorbike underneath the wing and stand on the seat, then step on to the handlebars and launch myself at the wing. Once I'm there I crawl over the surface of the craft until I'm on top of the cockpit. I run my fingers all along the opening until I find the culprit.

It's not what I expected. The Muwan isn't closed. It's open, but lightly jammed into the closed position with a piece of folded paper.

Now I'm totally mystified. I unfurl the folded paper. It's a flyer, a simple black-on-white printed sheet of A5 paper, written in Spanish, inviting people to come to a health testing centre for genetic profiling.

Weird. Who'd leave a notice like that on something as strange as the Muwan?

Now it's a hundred per cent certain that someone has tampered with the Muwan. Kneeling on top of the craft, I close my eyes and prise the cockpit lid open. No booby trap. The window pops up, as fresh and well-oiled as if I had left it here yesterday and not two years ago.

I stare inside. There, on the co-pilot seat, is a second Muwan remote. Bewildered, I lower myself into the pilot seat and pick up the second remote.

If I press the button, will the whole thing blow up?

Ixchel could have done this, or even my future self – left the craft ready to be flown. But why a new remote control? It doesn't make sense.

Still, I can't risk everything on the hope that someone friendly did this. I climb out with the Muwan's own metal-fibre ladder, take the Honda to a safe distance, from where I activate the Muwan with the new remote.

It doesn't blow up. Instead, the running lights come alive, and the craft begins to purr.

Tentatively, I park the Honda against a wall of relatively smooth rock about ten metres from the Muwan. It's almost out of petrol anyway, and without a refuel the bike is just extra weight.

Back on board I find the head-visor in its resting position and put it on. In another minute I'm running through the pre-flight checks. Everything seems to be working fine. Only my remote was faulty.

Someone knew that mine wasn't working. Someone replaced it. Someone is helping me – or setting me up. Without some kind of hint, it's tricky to know which.

I manoeuvre the Muwan into a hover position, then fly out of the mouth of the cave. I programme the location into the navigation systems so that I can return for the motorbike. I try to pull up the Internet on the screen. The browser returns an error message. I try some other websites. It's the same story everywhere.

The whole Internet seems to be down.

I take a long look out of the window at the rugged green landscape that flashes beneath. From up here you'd never know there was trouble.

Within the hour, I'm almost back at Ek Naab. The ruins of Becan come into view, heavily overgrown. The stone temples are an ancient constant in changing times. I bring up the landing control menu. Suddenly an alarm blares across the radio – a channel used only by Muwans.

Unregistered aircraft, alert, abort landing mission, hangar is closed, repeat, Muwan hangar is closed. Do not approach! This is a quarantine zone. If you come any closer, you will be shot down.

The message repeats over and over. A recording. I circle the area for about five minutes, wondering what to do.

Ek Naab is there, all right. But whoever left that message doesn't want any visitors, doesn't even recognize my Muwan as a friendly vehicle. My fingers move mechanically to the landing menu and close it down. Then I find myself bringing up the course plotter.

OK, on to Plan B. This is a perfect opportunity to find out what the Sect have been up to. From what I've seen of the world, there's not much to stop them being on a path to having influence over most governments of the world in the twenty-second century.

That was Bosch's future. Will it be mine?

According to the website, the Futurology Institute was being built in Oxford University's science area, in the car park of the Radcliffe Science Library.

With a few clicks, I select Oxford, England. The Muwan soars to an altitude of around twenty-thousand metres and turns east. In another moment I'm over the Caribbean Sea.

I fly in silence, headphones in place as I scour the radio channels for any sign of communication. There's plenty of chatter on the lower wavelengths, but the craft is moving too fast to focus in on anything. Higher up the spectrum it's pretty quiet. The Muwan leaves Cuba far behind and heads for the middle of the Atlantic Ocean. Then there's almost total radio silence. The effect is nerve-jangling.

I plug in the iPod and play something calming, my dad's jazz playlist. "The Peacocks" played by Bill Evans. Real smooth.

No commercial airlines at all. The skies are eerily empty. My mouth goes dry as I begin to think about what this means.

Eighteen months after the galactic superwave has hit, and the airplanes still aren't flying.

Flying over Ireland, the radio kicks back into life. Plenty of short-wave chatter. And around 93.8 FM, a clear female voice breaks across the airwaves.

This announcement brought to you by the Emergency Government of the UK and Ireland. Food stamps still available for the families of citizens who have registered for the Healthy Rebirth Drive. Badlands residents are not eligible. Applicants must be under thirty years old and disease-free. Applicants must register with their nearest centre. Married couples must apply jointly. Please present yourself for genetic screening at your nearest EG Health Centre. Together we will build a better tomorrow for the best.

The broadcast is repeated twice, then there's a confident announcement: "Locations of the EG Health Centres are as follows: Greater London area: Northolt, Ealing, Shepherd's Bush, Kilburn. . . " and continues with a list of another six or seven places.

Badlands residents are not eligible.

133

What, or where, are the "badlands"?

It sounds as though these kinds of statements are run-of-the-mill. Her voice is calm, measured, soothing. Then she starts reading out locations of health centres in other counties. I listen carefully until I hear the announcer mention Oxfordshire. "Oxfordshire – Manor Hospital, Headington."

After the very long announcement, some classical orchestral music begins to play. I turn it down and lean back in my seat. Ireland passes by in a flash of green patchwork and spectacular cliffs. In another minute, mainland England fills the flight image recorder. Mesmerized, I gaze at twisting strips of grey concrete that cut through the land; empty motorways and roads. I sit up sharply when I see the occasional car trundle along, a little toy in a model village. Literally the first sign of life I've seen since Mexico. So there's still some activity, on the roads and in the airwaves. Interesting that here, the roads are mainly clear.

Maybe people in the UK didn't have to abandon their vehicles. Or else someone else has cleared the roads – the Emergency Government?

A better tomorrow for the best.

But who are "the best"?

Chapter 22

I decide to land under the cover of Wytham Woods. It's not too far from the centre of town, with nothing there but trees. It's seven o'clock in the evening. At this time of the year, sunset is still hours away. If someone saw the landing, they'll already be on their way.

I lower the craft into a tiny coppice, well away from any footpaths. I snap off some branches to camouflage the surface. There's been nothing but birds in the sky since I time travelled. But that doesn't mean that this "Emergency Government" don't have access to airplanes. Maybe they're just for emergencies.

Let's hope that to anyone who saw it, the Muwan is just another UFO.

No sign of any eyewitnesses yet. I've landed on the edge of a field on Wytham Hill. The Oxfordshire countryside stretches out below. The city of Oxford is on the other side of the wood, which will take about twenty minutes to cross, if I remember the route.

A cool breeze rustles the canopy; fresh new leaves move in unison as it passes through. They continue in every direction as far as the eye can see. Unspoilt, silent. If all the computer technology really has gone from the world, the trees don't miss it. I'm the only person around. And this wood is truly beautiful. All those years walking through it with my mum and dad, I never noticed the beauty.

It could be risky to be caught using electronic devices – could draw the wrong type of attention. I hide the Muwan remote and both my mobile phones in the hollow of a tree trunk close to the craft. Inside my jacket are the two survival packs, but my hands are empty. The Bracelet of Itzamna is hidden above my elbow. It really has to be a last resort.

If this mission fails then there's still a chance I'll find answers with the Sect in Switzerland.

The paths are overgrown but still just about recognizable. I manage to find my way across the woods, to the old car park. There used to be sheep in the nearby fields. Instead, the fields are filled with neat rows of bright green crops. From a distance I assumed it was tall grass but now that I'm closer, I see it's something else; everywhere I look, the fields are bursting with different shades of green. Rows of corn, as tall as me. Swaying very slightly in the breeze.

This land is organized, fertile.

"You! Get your hands in the air. Turn around."

The orders are barked out by someone behind me. He doesn't seem to be kidding. I turn around as casually as I dare. Standing ten metres away is a guy who looks barely older than me, with sandy blond hair that touches his shoulders. He's wearing jeans and a sleeveless blue T-shirt. At shoulder height, he carries a rifle. It's aimed at me.

Slowly, I raise my hands.

"Who are you?" The guy takes a couple of steps closer. "What are you doin' up here? I know all the teams assigned here. You're not on any of them." He comes right up to me, and I can't seem to take my eyes off the nose of his rifle. His eyes run along my right forearm.

"No chippenpin scar?"

I hesitate for just too long. He jams the rifle under my jaw and grabs hold of the front of my jacket. "Don't move. . ." he hisses. I can feel the hard metal cylinder pressing against my throat, almost blocking off my air. He unzips my flight jacket and reaches inside with one hand. When he sees the plastic casing of the survival pack, his eyes bulge.

"You dirty thief. . . Where'd you get this?"

It's the first aid kit; it pops open at the touch of a button. Sandy marvels at the contents as though they were emeralds. He laughs nervously, then thinks better of it. Slowly, not taking his eyes from mine or his finger from the trigger, he bends down and places the first survival pack on the ground. Then he's reaching inside for a second pack, the one with the Gerber multi-tool and survival supplies. There's a long silence.

Then: "Why don't you have a chippenpin?"

I swallow, try to stay calm.

He turns me round and marches me in front of him, down the country lane and towards the village of Wytham. On the way he talks briskly into a walkie-talkie.

"Found a runaway. Dunno if he's badlands, no. He looks all right, to be honest. No chippenpin scar, though. I know. That's what I'm doin'."

My hands are on my head but I'm on the verge of reaching across, pressing the Crystal Key on the Bracelet through my jacket sleeve. Would he try to shoot me first? The problem is the stupid countdown – I won't vanish immediately. If I get the timing wrong I'll be sending a corpse back to Ixchel.

I decide against it. This guy seems to be nothing more than a guard. It's clear that I'm being taken to someone with more authority. Maybe I can learn something before I leave.

As often as I can, I sneak surreptitious glances at Sandy. His clothes are dusty and he smells like he hasn't had a shower for several days. He's strong; I can see that in his arms and shoulders. Even so, with what I've learned about fighting, I could probably risk taking him on. If it wasn't for the rifle.

For now, I'm going to have to play things very carefully.

We reach the pub – I can't remember what it used to be called but I remember going there with my parents. The pub sign is gone; the garden is full of tomatoes, rows of vegetables and herbs. We stand in front of the conservatory doors and Sandy waits.

After a minute a woman appears: short, untidy blonde hair, tanned face, wearing dusty jeans and a loose T-shirt. She looks hard, like she's used to giving orders and being obeyed. The woman doesn't introduce herself, just takes a plastic wand like you see in the security checks at airports. She waves it over my arms and then starts talking, short, staccato statements.

"Name?"

Might as well buy some time. "Matt Murdock." The name is out before I have time to think up anything better.

"You don't have a chippenpin?"

"Err . . . no."

"Why not? You look healthy."

Sandy passes the woman my two survival packs. "Found 'em in his jacket."

She stares at them, baffled. Her eyes return to mine with something like fear, or a newfound respect.

"You stole these. . .?"

"They're mine."

Sandy interjects, "Have you seen his eyes. . .?"

"Shut it," the woman snaps, without taking her eyes from mine. "Matt Murdock, yeah? But you got no chippenpin, 'Matt'. Also, I do believe that's the name of a comic-book superhero. So, why don't you tell me your real name and how you got into the Controlled Zone? Are you one of the Caps?"

Chippenpin . . . Controlled Zone . . . Caps . . . there's so much that I don't understand that I simply shake my head, bewildered.

"I don't remember," I say.

"What were you doing in Wytham Woods? It's a sacred wood, you must know that."

I open my mouth and then close it. There's nothing I can say that won't sound suspicious.

Very precisely, the woman tells me, "Last chance. I'm going to call the EG office. We'll soon see if anyone's been reported missing."

The woman disappears into the house. Sandy raises the rifle, now aiming at my chest.

About three minutes later the woman comes out. Her face looks totally different. She's gone from looking bored, as though there'd been a routine infraction, to ashen-faced solemnity.

There's something terrifying about her nervousness, and Sandy's.

Under her breath I can just about make out what the woman is saying, almost to herself. "Piece of badlands trash; why don't they just respect the CZ? Then things like this wouldn't have to happen."

Sandy mumbles, "But how did he get in?"

"Don't know," she says between gritted teeth. "And don't care. My orders don't cover any of that."

"We've actually got to. . .?" Sandy whispers. He sounds shocked.

"Sandy, get him out of my sight! Why do badlanders even DO this? Do they think we like giving these orders?" The woman turns to me and I can see that her cheeks are flushed, her eyes cold with fear-tinged rage. "Why can't you just stay in the badlands and leave us alone?" she says, spitting the words. "You know what happens if you come into Controlled Zones!"

She gives Sandy an angry nod. "You know what to do."

His eyes are full of trepidation as he tells her, "You'll come too. . .?"

The woman nods, lowers her eyes. "I'll come too, I always do."

"I've never done one," Sandy says, very quiet.

"Be grateful that they're rarer than they were."

I look from one to the other. "Guys . . . what are you talking about?"

Sandy lifts the rifle and pokes it into my ribs. "Let's go, 'Matt'."

I follow the woman, winding down the lanes of Wytham village towards the fields across from Godstow, Sandy nudging me along with the end of his rifle. "Where are you taking me?" I keep asking. When they don't reply, my nerve starts to give way. A tense silence has fallen over Sandy and Boss Woman. Whatever is going on here, it's not good.

We pass through a band of oaks and beech trees, and then I see it.

A trench in the ground, two metres across, three metres wide, close to a large beech tree. The stench of decay is nauseating, makes me stop in my tracks. I don't need to get closer to realize that it's an open burial pit.

They're going to execute me.

Chapter 23

The horror of that moment is such a jolt that before I know what I'm doing, my hand is moving towards the Bracelet. Before I can press the Crystal Key, I've been walloped in the side by the rifle. The blow is like an explosion inside my ribs. The wind is knocked out of me; I fall to my knees gasping for breath. I'm dimly aware of Sandy and the woman exchanging heated remarks; did he not search me properly, what kind of idiot security guard . . . but the pain in my ribs keeps coming in waves and I'm almost sick. Sandy pins me to the ground with his rifle, which he shoves against my temple.

From the moment Boss Woman finished her phone call to the EG Centre, their attitudes to me completely changed. It's like finding out that I might be from these "badlands" makes them think that I'm not even human, that I'm some hideous, sick criminal – or worse.

There's nothing faint-hearted about Sandy now. "I'll blow your brains out, you lying badlands scum. We work hard for what we have. Diseased filth coming in here, nicking what's ours. . ."

Boss Woman sets to work on getting the Bracelet of Itzamna off my arm. When it's in her hands her eyes gleam. She turns to me, lips pulled into a thin, cruel smile.

"Where did you get this?"

The pain begins to focus my mind. This is actually happening; I'm going to be executed by this scruffy guy with a rifle.

She lands a sharp kick to my ribs. I fall over, groaning.

"You know what, filth, I think I might go back and ask for permission to interrogate you first, after all. You've been on the rob, obvious. Where'd you nick this bracelet from, one of them fancy houses in the country?"

I struggle back to my knees, Sandy's rifle bore hooked underneath my jaw.

"Go on, sis," he says. "I'll watch him. You're not gonna budge, are you, scumbag? Else I'll blow a hole in your guts and throw you in with the corpses to die all slow and lonely."

The woman he called "sis" backs away, a vengeful glitter in her eyes. She holds out the Bracelet of Itzamna and says, "Be right back. Then you can start hitting that again."

She turns and in a few seconds I lose sight of her in the trees. Sandy orders me to place my hands on the back of my head. I do as he says and turn slightly to catch a glimpse of his face. He looks angry, yet he's still guarding something: fear.

He's scared of me getting anywhere near him. As if my touch were deadly.

I'm swamped by fear too, but it's clear enough to me that Sandy doesn't want to shoot. He seems comfortable with the idea of hitting me, though.

"Why don't you put your gun down and kill me with your bare hands, like a man," I say, in a voice as cold and tough as I can muster.

"Touch you? Oh yeah, you'd like that, wouldn't you, germ sack?" Sandy cocks the rifle a bit higher. He seems unsure of himself. There's a sudden loud rustle in the trees somewhere to our right. We're both momentarily distracted.

The attack comes from the left. It's a sound I've heard once before: the swish of an arrow slicing through the air. Then another. When I look back at Sandy, he's staggering. The rifle falls from his fingers, his wrist skewered by one arrow. The second arrow has taken him in the upper chest. I'd guess that it's missed his heart, but even so, he's defeated.

A figure emerges from the thicket to our left; a kid, probably no more than twelve, lithe and slim, dressed in skinny jeans and a jade-green hoody. There's a bow slung over the kid's shoulder. The kid closes in and scoops up Sandy's rifle. I'm thrown a quick glance, then the kid beckons, waves at me to follow.

I hesitate. Boss Woman still has the Bracelet of Itzamna. Without that, I'm well and truly trapped.

When I don't move, the kid looks back. This time I catch sight of him under the green hood: short, spiky hair and a piercing gaze. The thought of Peter Pan comes into my mind. "Come on," hisses the kid. "We need to get out of here."

"That woman took something of mine. . ." I begin. Then to my astonishment, the kid pulls the Bracelet out of the pocket of the hoody.

"You mean this? Don't worry; I got it. And I got her."

"You killed that woman?!"

"Probably not. It's best if we don't kill them; they always insist on killing some of us if we do." The kid steps a little closer. "You came out of that spaceship. Didn't you? I saw it land."

I stare back in silence. Sandy moans softly, squirming in the dirt.

"They're wrong about you, aren't they? You're not badlands. And I know you're not one of the Caps." The kid backs off, then turns and starts to trot briskly away. I catch up and fall in beside him.

"I'm Harry," the kid says, casually. "What's your name?"

"Josh," I reply.

"All right, Josh, you need to come with me."

I notice that the arrows are carried in a small backpack. There was only one more. Lucky for me, this kid is a sharpshooter.

Harry doesn't offer the Bracelet back to me, but stashes it away, then tucks Sandy's rifle under a free arm. Since I've just been rescued it seems ungrateful to argue. Just the same, I'm already contemplating how I'm going to persuade this tough little kid to give it back. I keep trying to get a good look at Harry's face under the hoody but every time I make eye contact for even a second, the skinny kid glances away.

We start to jog over the field until we come to the Wolvercote bypass. For a couple of moments I just stand, listening to the silence. Somehow, even more than the relatively deserted, tiny village of Wytham and the empty skies, the silence of this road is the most disturbing thing I've seen so far.

Harry crosses the dual carriageway without even bothering to look. I find it impossible to do the same. We head towards Godstow and Port Meadow. The fields near the River Isis stand empty, ploughed into furrows, but around here, unlike the fields next to Wytham, there's nothing growing.

We enter Jericho through the allotments. Harry murmurs, "Walk where I walk. It's all booby traps around here."

I follow the instruction, wondering who laid the traps. I guess it must be Harry's group – who I'm guessing must be the Caps.

When we reach the primary school I'm transfixed by heaps of rotting garbage, supermarket bags piled high, split open and decomposing at the base, the flick of rats' tails as they crawl amongst the grime. The tarmac is stained with liquid runoff that dried long ago.

I pass between them, holding my breath. Then I notice the state of the buildings. Like the playground, they're badly overgrown. Metre-high saplings poke through the concrete. The grassy part of the playground has gone to seed, a knee-high meadow of wildflowers and weeds. As we approach the bridge over the canal, there's a metallic click. Less than ten metres away, emerging from behind bramble and elderberry bushes, a teenage boy stands, very precisely aiming a rifle at me. He can't be older than fourteen, a mop of greasy black hair flopping over his forehead.

"Oh, it's you," he says when he sees his friend. "A'ight, Harry. What you got there? We taking them prisoner now?"

"He's not a chippenpin, fool."

The teenager looks surprised. "What, then?"

"I dunno. Need to take him to see the chief."

The boy emits a low wolf whistle. "Nice-lookin' bit of kit there, Harry. You went all the way into the CZ to get another rifle?"

Harry keeps walking. "Better stay at your post, Zak."

Zak stays put, rifle slung across his shoulders as he watches Harry with undisguised admiration. I continue at Harry's side, into the new housing estate nearby, through deserted streets lined with wrecked cars, all the way to a crescent of tall townhouses. Two more teenagers stand guard by the door, rifles dangling from their shoulders. When they see me approaching with their friend behind, they perk up.

"You got one?" They sound impressed.

"Get the chief," is all Harry says.

One boy goes inside and comes out a couple of minutes later. He's followed by a tall, muscular Afro-Caribbean guy, light-brown skin, dressed in Adidas tracksuit bottoms and a yellow sleeveless Brazil T-shirt. His hair is bleached blond and cropped close to his skull. He's fully gangsta, mean-looking too.

Yet there's no mistaking the face of my old friend Tyler Marks.

Tyler's eyes look different, and I realize why. They're blue. I've finally got used to seeing my own face with strange blue eyes staring back at me. It's different when it's someone else's face.

A blue-eyed Tyler, all grown up.

Chapter 24

It's pretty obvious that Tyler recognizes me.

"Wait a minute, I know you. You're Josh Garcia."

I begin to grin with relief. But Tyler frowns. "Man, you haven't changed a bit since I last saw you, apart from the eyes. They must have you blue-bloods on some serious health regime."

Harry turns, incredulous. "He's a blue-blood. . .?"

"Josh Garcia, yeah, he's a blue-blood all right; he was made the same time as me."

Bewildered, Harry says, "But Ty, they were about to kill him. He doesn't have a chippenpin. I think you're mixing him up with someone else."

"What is a 'chippenpin'?" I ask, butting in.

"Oh, and I almost forgot, he was wearing this. That chippenpin leader seemed to think it was interesting." Harry pulls out the Bracelet of Itzamna. Tyler regards it blankly.

I shrug, trying to make light of it. Better that they don't realize I'm sweating at being separated from the Bracelet. Tyler saunters over to me. His eyes bore into mine.

"Jewellery, Josh. . .?" Tyler glances at Harry. "Where did you find him?"

"There was this aeroplane, Ty. But it was completely silent. Like a UFO. It landed in the woods! Then he comes walking out of the trees like nothing happened."

"Can I just ask, though, what is this 'chippenpin'. . .?"

Tyler shoots me an angry look. "D'I ask you to talk? No. See, Harry here is giving me this crazy story, yeah? So I got to listen. Now Josh, answer me this and nothin' else. Did you come out of a UFO?"

I hold steady under Tyler's suspicious gaze. "Not a UFO; a Muwan. You know, I told you about them."

He frowns. "A Muwan?"

"From Ek Naab, remember?"

"Bro, you're makin' no sense."

I pause as his words sink in. "You don't remember about the Ix Codex and 2012 and Ek Naab and all that?"

Tyler holds up a finger. "You're trying to play your blue-blood mind games. Just stop. I mean it."

Numb with shock, I close my mouth. Tyler doesn't remember any of it. He didn't recognize the Bracelet of Itzamna, even though I'm pretty sure I showed it to him.

This isn't the Tyler I knew, at all. And from there, it's a short step to the next bone-shaking realization.

This isn't my future. It's the future of an alternate reality.

I make myself focus back in on what Tyler is saying to Harry. "Then what happened?"

Harry replies, "Then the chippenpins were all over him. Like I said, they were about to kill him."

"Until Harry came along," I say.

Tyler looks downright murderous. "You talk when I tell you to and not unless, you get me?" He lifts his right arm to reveal a tiny scar in the middle. "See this scar? Everyone inside the Controlled Zone has one. You say you don't. But Josh Garcia was made a blue-blood, same as me; he's a chippenpin. All the blue-bloods are."

In my head, the sound of the word falls apart into three neat pieces. Chippenpin – chip and pin. Like the chips that get swiped in credit cards. I put my hand up tentatively and cough.

Tyler glares. "Blue-bloods can mess with people's minds, do weird stuff with their voice. So. Don't. Talk. Got that?"

Before the bemused eyes of Harry and the two rifle-toting teenage guards, Tyler grabs my arm and steers me into the house, through a narrow corridor and into a living room that extends into the kitchen. The house is tidy but there are signs of grime on the stripped pine wood floorboards and a black leather upholstered tub chair. There's a wooden dining table. Tyler backs on to it, sits on the table and indicates that I should sit in the tub chair.

"What's going on?"

"Oh, I can talk now, can I?"

Tyler looks scornful. "We're alone now. I ain't got no hip33. And you know blue-bloods can't affect other blue-bloods. . ."

"What's a blue-blood?"

His mouth stays open.

"I'm not who you think I am. I mean, I am Josh Garcia, but . . . I'm from. . ." I take a deep breath. "A different time. Like, you know, a time traveller. I'm Josh from the past, from before the 2012 thing. So I don't know what a blue-blood is. Or the Controlled Zone, or a chippenpin, or . . . what did you say . . . hip3?"

Tyler looks dumbstruck. "Hip33," he mumbles. "Proper name is hypnoticin . . . it's a drug. They inject blue-bloods with it, and it enhances some latent power of suggestion. Bottom line, it lets blue-bloods control people. . ." His voice trails off. With utter incredulity he adds, "Did you say . . . a time traveller?"

Hypnoticin, the drug Martineau injected into me to give me hypnotic powers over the warrior who was about to cut my throat with a knife; the Sect of Huracan's mind-control drug, developed by one of their leaders, Melissa DiCanio at Chaldexx BioPharmaceuticals.

"Oh," I say. "Right. That. Yeah. I know what hypnoticin is."

"S'right, hip33. You've used it?"

"Yes."

"I knew it, could tell by your eyes. They never look naturally blue. You got any here?"

"No."

Tyler seems disappointed. "Shame. We've run out. Next time the EG send a squadron into Jericho, there'll be nothing I can do to protect my boys."

"You and your boys, you're not in the Controlled Zone?"

He shakes his head. "Technically, yes, but we're not chippenpins. We're Resistance. Not that there's many of us left. Doubt they'll even bother. They think we're all boys. They won't bother us, just let us starve to death."

I'm confused. "You're not all boys. . .?"

"Harry is a girl; Harriet. And two others. They disguise it pretty well. But they, you know, man, they're growin' up. Soon enough we're gonna have to hide them away completely. And soon after that. . ." He breathes a heavy sigh. "Soon after, we're gonna run out of food."

"You can't grow stuff in the gardens?"

"Some, yeah. But we need protein, Josh. That means animals, fish and that."

"Or soy?"

"Ha, ha. Soy. You know how to grow that?"

"Why don't you join the chippenpins?"

He scowls. "I'm a blue-blood, right? So that means I get to be an overseer, makin' people do stuff they don't want to do. And all the rest . . . Harry and the other girls have to go to the baby farms, be baby-mothers. The boys got to work the fields all day long. Eat when they tell you to eat, what they tell you to eat, have kids with who they tell you to have kids with. And on top of that, all the weird religion stuff." Tyler sniggers contemptuously. "'Summer is a comin' in' . . . pffah!"

I can only shrug. "Weird religious stuff. . .?"

"Believe. But you! Listen, bro – seriously – time travel?"

"You think I'm lying?"

He laughs.

"But you said you're a blue-blood. So can't you make me tell the truth?"

"If you're Josh Garcia, I can't stop you foolin' with me."

"Why would I do that? I need your help."

"If you're working for the EG, maybe it's some new way to use hip33. Maybe you're testing me."

"Harry already told you, they were about to kill me."

Tyler hesitates. "She mentioned they was giving you abuse."

"It doesn't matter; you don't need to believe about the time-travel thing. I have proof."

"Proof? Now you're talking."

"Proof – and a way out of here for you and your mates. If you help me."

For a moment, Tyler peers into my eyes. "Continue. . ."

"Look. Why don't you pretend like I don't know anything that's happened here since 2012?"

"Right, right. So you don't know about the computers goin' down and the plague and . . . and the EG taking over and sending away all the people who was sick with the plague, and rounding up all the healthy people and putting RFID chips in everyone's arms."

"RFID chip?"

"Radio-frequency identification, on a computer chip. Your name and your number. On a chip, which they can scan. You're not allowed into the CZ without one. Chippenpin. Don't let the EG hear you callin' it that, even though everyone does. The official word is EGRI – Emergency Government Registration Identification."

I sit back in the tub chair, the weight of Tyler's words sinking in. "Wow. They've got it all sorted. The genetic engineering to make the blue-bloods. The mind-control drug. The chippenpin chips so they know who's part of their controlled, perfect world. Execution for badlanders caught in CZ territory."

Tyler's eyes widen. "Yeah, that's right. Sorted. And you know what, you're part of it. Or you will be, Josh Garcia. You're a blue-blood, aren't you? The Josh I knew had brown eyes – until he was made a blue-blood. Yours are blue."

My hands bunch into fists. "Tyler. Can you help me get into the EG's headquarters here in Oxford?"

He pauses, then laughs. "Now I know you messin'. Why would you do that?"

"I need to get in. If I can find out how they made all this happen, maybe I can go back in time and stop it."

The smile leaves his face. "What Harry saw in the woods – is that for real a time machine?"

"No." I stare into my old friend's face, trying to find the Tyler I once knew. But this guy's eyes are flat with the ache of loss, the burden of responsibility. I can't imagine how Tyler managed to keep a group of kids alive during whatever happened after 2012, but however he did it, the experience has hardened him. He's older too, eighteen years old.

But maybe I can still trust him?

"Harry . . . has the time-travel device," I tell him, haltingly. "That bracelet – it's not jewellery; it's technology. Created by a very ancient civilization. I can use it to get back to 2012. And if I go back with the right kind of information . . . maybe I can prevent all of this."

Tyler's lips curl into a smile that doesn't reach his eyes. "Ancient civilization. Well I neva. You can change time?"

"None of this will ever have happened. There's a plan to protect the earth from the electromagnetic pulse that comes along with the superwave."

"The superwave, that thing that happened in 2012?"

"Right."

"So . . . assuming you're not mad or lyin', that fixes things how?"

I stall. "For you? I don't know."

"Do I just disappear? Or lose all my memories and wake up as another Tyler?"

"Honestly, Ty, I don't know the answer to that."

He nods, gives a bitter chuckle, then slides off the table. "You got nothin' to offer me, bro."

Slowly, I stand. We're less than a metre away from each other.

"I do have something to offer you." I pause. "The thing that Harry saw in the woods."

"The UFO?"

"In Wytham Woods. I flew here in an aircraft. Very advanced; you've never seen anything like it. You could use it to fly out of here. Go somewhere sunny, warm, with plenty of food. Somewhere you and your gang can be free."

His eyes widen, for a second. "You can show me how to fly it?"

"I can give you a few lessons. But mainly, I can programme it to make trips."

Tyler looks away, suddenly dazed.

"Think about it, Ty. Pick a place, somewhere you've always dreamed of. Somewhere away from all of this."

"I'd kill someone, you know that," whispers Tyler, "for a proper chance to escape." He stares directly into my eyes and I feel a twist in my guts. "Better not be lyin' to me, bro. Or that someone could be you."

Chapter 25

We make a deal: I'll take Tyler to the Muwan and teach him to use it in exchange for the return of the Bracelet of Itzamna and Tyler's help to get into the EG's headquarters.

The fact that I'm in an alternate future is a relief, in a way. But how close is this timeline to my own? Tyler knows me but maybe we weren't good friends. I experienced a similar reality once. It was created when Martineau destroyed most of the Ix Codex.

Have I somehow jumped back into that timeline?

I need to talk to Tyler about what happened in this world's history. But it's going to have to wait – for now I can see he's completely focused on getting the Muwan. It's a good thing that Harry saw it, I realize, or else I'm really not sure that Tyler would have believed me.

"We'll go as soon as it's dark," Tyler says. "Sundown is in about an hour. It's just gonna be me, you and Harry."

"She's an amazing shot," I comment.

"Yeah, she was in archery lessons at her school. Now she's huntin' rabbits."

"She got two of their people today," I warn. "Maybe it's not safe to take her with us. If we're caught. . ."

Tyler interrupts. "Harry's the only chance we've got to find anything in them woods, especially in the dark." In a hollow voice he adds, "If we're caught, Josh, there will be blood. Not just ours."

When the sun has almost set we make our way through the streets. Tyler has a dark green, knitted beanie hat pulled over his bleached hair. He and Harry both carry arms; he a rifle, Harry her bow and a backpack of full home-made arrows. They don't offer me a weapon.

The roads are eerily dark; no street or house lights. Within minutes my eyes adjust to the ambient light. We arrive at the perimeter of Tyler's territory – or at least that's what I guess. The path is bordered by the stinking piles of rubbish just like the ones we passed before.

Harry leads us north along the railway tracks, now rusted and thick with weeds and shrubs. In perfect silence we walk as far as the bypass, across into a nearby field, until we reach the river.

A boat comes into view – a punt. I can just make out the figure of a tall black guy standing at the back. Another of Tyler's gang, waiting for us. He drops a long metal pole into the water. Tyler grabs one end of the punt and drags it closer. We jump on board, and then we're gliding down the river again, moving through dark water that occasionally ripples with silver light.

Through the stillness there's the creak of insects, a rustle that might be a fox chasing invisible prey. To our left, the woods loom on the crest of the hill, across a field.

Pointing, Harry says in a low voice, "Over there. That's where I saw the UFO land."

We're probably less than five hundred metres from where I hid the Muwan. At the place where the river meets the edge of the wood, we disembark. When we're about thirty metres inside the woods, we find a path. Tyler calls an abrupt halt. He holds up a hand for absolute, unmoving silence. Then I see and hear what has stalled him.

Ahead there's hot orange light flickering between the trees. Tyler hears me gasp; he clamps a hand over my mouth. Then I listen.

There's a rhythmic sound: unmistakable, chilling. Someone's being beaten – viciously, from the sound of it. The victim, a man, begins to cry out with every blow. We listen, appalled, immobile.

Tyler takes his hand from my mouth. "Is this some kind of trap?"

"No. . .!" I begin, indignant.

"Shh. Zip it."

The beating stops. The victim's cries reduce to faint moaning. A lone female voice speaks, announcing something; I can't quite catch her words. That's followed up with a group response. A low, measured chant.

"It's one of their ceremony things," murmurs Harry.

"Of course," Tyler says. "We should have checked the calendar. It's close to the solstice."

"Solstice?"

"Midsummer. It's a big deal in the new religion."

"New religion?"

"Yeah. All the other ones are banned: Christianity, Islam, Judaism, Hindu, everything. The EG don't like all that, they say them religions divide us. 'One Truth for One People', that's what they want. So now they invented a religion, made up of ancient stuff. Worshipping Ceres, and Minerva, and I don't know who else. Like in the days of ancient Rome. Basically, worshipping trees and plants and the moon."

"That's why Wytham Woods are sacred. . ."

Tyler puts up a hand again, for silence. "Harry's right – this is a ceremony. I bet it was a laugh back in ancient times. Horse racing, games and that. We learned about it during blue-blood 'education'. This new mad version of the religion, though, it's nothing to laugh about. They always start with the punishments. That poor bastard probably had an unauthorized shower."

"Showers are rationed. . .?" I murmur.

"Everything is rationed. Water, food, electricity."

We follow Harry deeper into the trees. She slinks along with practised ease. Tyler's right; it's incredible how well she knows her way around here. We begin to move parallel to the path, roughly ten metres away. The drone of their ceremony gets louder. A dull sensation seeps into my chest, cold horror at what's happened to the world in only two years. At the edge of my thoughts are the terrors I recall when Ixchel and I were trapped in the ancient Mayan city. Midnight ceremonies with chanting and ritual violence. Doesn't seem far from human sacrifice.

Harry leads us in silence to a clearing and whispers, "It's here."

You almost have to walk into the Muwan to find it in the dark. It takes me a few moments to find the tree where I hid the Muwan remote and my two mobile phones. But once I've retrieved them, I use the remote to open the cockpit and then climb up the ladder to clear away the tree debris I'd arranged as camouflage. Down on the ground, Tyler and Harry wait, motionless silhouettes.

Finally, it's ready. I'm about to invite them aboard when three beams of light appear in the woods. They stretch out across the clearing, pick up Tyler and Harry. A beam catches me right in the eye, holds steady for a second and then flashes down on to the Muwan.

There's shouting, panic, the sound of gunfire. I squash myself flat against the rear of the Muwan, absolutely rigid. The torches go out. The sound of heavy footfall surrounds us. The torches scatter. I lose sight of Tyler and Harry and guess they're under the plane.

Two more shots. Footsteps rushing at the Muwan. I slither across the skin of the craft, fall head first into the cockpit, turn on the running lights. The clearing floods with hard blue light. My fingers tremble as I start the engine, tap instructions on the control panel. Someone scrambles up the ladder – it's Harry.

"Get in the back," I hiss, and give the girl a helpful shove. "Where's Ty?"

One of the torch crew reaches the Muwan. He starts up the ladder, staring at me, his face half-lit by the running lights. He gives a sudden gasp, seemingly yanked away by someone else underneath. He cries out, once. Then silence. More shots are fired; one cracks against the cockpit window. I turn off the running lights. There's another tug at the ladder.

Seconds later Tyler's voice rasps into my ear. "See, didn't I say there'd be blood?" He shoves me hard, exasperated. He slumps into the co-pilot seat. I retract the ladder, and the cockpit slides into the closed position. In another second the Muwan is surrounded by an enraged huddle, banging the outside of the craft with tree branches. Bullets ring out, ricocheting against the bulletproof glass of the cockpit windows.

I touch a finger to the navigation controls and raise the craft to a height of ten metres. The weight limit warning light goes on. At least two people are hanging on to the metal stands, which I can't retract into the belly of the craft.

Tyler shifts in his seat. "What's going on? Why don't you just go. . .?"

"Can't. Two of them are hanging on. We can't take off properly."

"Lose them."

"If they fall, they'll die."

"Then fly nice and low!" Very slowly and deliberately he says, "Now, shift this flyin' saucer."

I take off gently, giving the hangers-on a chance to let go. At around five metres, one of them does. The second one seems to have decided to tough it out. Brave guy. He hasn't a clue where we're going.

We're back in Jericho three minutes later – our first chance to drop off our unwanted passenger and warn Tyler's gang. I put the Muwan down in the playground of the nearby primary school. Before we land, the weight sensors register that the second guy has dropped off. By the time I've opened the cockpit he's bolted at least fifty metres across the playground, into the night. Tyler watches him go, cursing.

"Pity he didn't fall off during the flight. He'll bring the rest of 'em over."

Chapter 26

Tyler rolls up his left sleeve and removes the Bracelet of Itzamna. "OK, bro, your end of the arrangement seems to be holding up. So here's your time machine."

I accept it without a word, remove my jacket and place the Bracelet of Itzamna into position on my own left upper arm.

"We gonna have to get everyone into the evac bunker." He pauses. "I think I might have killed one of the chippenpins out there tonight. You know what happens next; they'll be here soon. Don't expect mercy. Harry, you're gonna get everyone underground, OK?"

"Not a problem, Ty. What about you?"

Tyler nods towards the Muwan. "Me and Josh gotta get this thing out of Jericho until they've looked the place over. We'll be back in a day or so."

"No – wait. I need to get inside the EG Centre," I say, anxiously. "I have to get access to the Sect's computer records. . ."

"If you want to get in there, you need me. In a bit, there's gonna be angry chippenpins all over this place. We have to leave." He claps Harry on the back. "Don't let no one refuse to go into the bunker. OK?"

Then Tyler turns to me with a heavy sigh. "All right, Mariposa."

A grin breaks out on my face. "You called me Mariposa!"

"You could have been one of us, you know. All my main guys were from the capoeira group."

"That's why you're called 'Caps'?"

"Ha – no. It's cos of where we hid – with the captain. Harry's family had a nuclear bomb shelter. Her dad was ex-Army." Reflectively he muses, "Captain Donnelly. Completely mad, but brilliant. He was our leader at first. They killed him, of course; captured him. Tortured him to find out where we was hiding. Left his corpse out for us to find." His eyes meet mine and he smiles grimly. "It was meant to be a lesson."

"God, that's horrible. Poor Harry. . ."

"Yeah. Harry's only twelve, but she's in this to the death." He hesitates for a second and then says, regretfully, "You could have been my right-hand man, Mariposa. But you knew best. Had to stay with your girlfriend. Girls! Always was your problem, man."

"Wait, wait. Ty, I'm not the Josh Garcia you knew."

"Ain't that the truth. . .?"

"No, no. I mean, I'm from, like, a parallel universe."

Tyler looks mystified.

"Look – you didn't recognize the Bracelet of Itzamna. You'd never heard of Muwans. But the Tyler I know, he knows all about that. He knows all about the ancient plan to stop the 2012 superwave."

"You're doing my head in a bit, man."

"This time-jumping thing doesn't seem to be straight time travel, past and future and such. There are many universes. And the Bracelet of Itzamna seems to move you between them."

He shrugs. "Whatever. But I'm still getting this spaceship, yeah?"

"Of course, we had a deal. I can't take the Muwan back in time with me."

Tyler nods. "In that case, I'm fine with whatever you want to do."

"So you'll help me?"

"Said I would, didn't I? But not yet. Got to get your UFO out of here before the zombiefied Moon worshippers get here. Right now, us Caps, we're just an irritation. They're happy to wait until we starve to death. But if they find your aeroplane, they'll call for backup."

"Where do you want to go? Would you like to scout for somewhere safe to take your gang?"

"I was thinking exactly that. Your family had a place, didn't they? A holiday house in the Lake District somewhere. Glencoe, Glenride, something with Glen. It'll come back to me in a bit. Smart guy; we should all have listened to your dad."

I'm speechless.

Tyler looks into the blackness of the field that divides Jericho from the Controlled Zone. Pinpoints of moving light appear just at the edge. Now and again the beams lengthen. Torches; the invasion is coming. Tyler turns towards the Muwan. "Come on, then. Chop chop."

He tugs at me and I find myself following.

You family had a place.

What's Tyler talking about – a holiday home? Not in the world I remember. . .

When I'm seated in the Muwan, I start the system checks. Tyler's more alert this time, intently examining the control panel.

"I'll start flying north. When you remember the name of the place, I'll programme it into the system."

"Programme it into the system," Tyler says, admiringly. "This is incredible, you know that? How did a guy like you get a machine like this?"

But I ignore his question. "What did you mean, we should all have listened to your dad'?"

"About 2012. He was saying something was going to happen ages before it did. Well, to be fair, he wasn't the only one. But your dad, he said he had proof. Some ancient letter he'd found from a Mayan king."

The Calakmul Letter – my father's first clue to the existence of the Ix Codex.

162

"So . . . what happened after my dad died?"

"Died? What you talkin' about? Your dad didn't die, man. He left town. Tried to warn everyone, then he left. Went off to that place your family had, like I said, in the Lake District. The holiday cottage. The one you'd all go off to in the summer holidays."

My father is still alive. My father is still alive.

The shiver of anticipation I'm getting feels familiar. If I keep time travelling, this is going to happen again and again. I'm going to run into my father, as I have before.

Tyler's memories seem to be cheering him up. "Your dad, he was some sort of archaeologist, weren't he? He became obsessed with 2012, actually. And some ancient civilization. Not the Mayans, some other group."

The Erinsi. . .

"Yes," I say. "The Erinsi. They made the time-jump bracelet."

"Yeah, well, I'm starting to believe you. But your dad, back then. . ."

"People would have thought he was a nutter. . ."

"Who's laughing now?"

"Well . . . where I come from, my dad died saving my life. Just before he gave me the time-travel bracelet."

Tyler whistles. "Man, that is so, like, destiny!"

"That would be amazing," I say. "My dad, alive!"

Tyler becomes thoughtful. "Do you think, then, that your dad giving you that bracelet is meant to help you change things in your own time?"

"I dunno," I groan. "I think the time-travel bracelet might have caused enough trouble. It's more a case of fixing the damage that someone else did."

"There are other time travellers? That's mad!"

"I'm getting a bit fed up of them, to be honest. One of them – a joker called Arcadio – leaves me messages in code."

"Why's he do that?"

"Trying to make me do things, I guess."

"How do you know he's not messin' with you?"

Tersely I reply, "I don't."

My dad, still alive. In this world, he didn't disappear whilst flying over the jungles of southern Mexico. He may have found the Calakmul Letter, maybe even the fragments of the Ix Codex at J. Eric Thompson's house. But if he never tried to find Ek Naab, then Andres Garcia's search ended with some scraps of ancient parchment.

Which could mean that the Ix Codex was never returned to Ek Naab. The 2012 plan could never be completed.

My heart sinks. If this world doesn't even know about the 2012 plan, then how can I find out the missing piece of information – the location of the moon machine?

My trip here could turn out to have been waste of effort for me – and a dangerous bit of tampering with Tyler's reality.

I activate the holographic route map to show the terrain below. Tyler watches with interest for a few moments. Then he seems to slump. It's as though I'm watching the energy bleeding from him.

"I killed a man tonight," he says in a soft voice. Almost embarrassed, he turns to me. "He wasn't my first."

"Ty. I don't . . . know what to say."

"You ever kill anyone, Josh?"

"No. "

"Didn't think so."

My cheek muscles tighten, and so does my throat.

"You know what 'apocalypse' means?" Tyler's gaze is unflinching. "It means revelation."

"I didn't know that," I mumble. The emptiness of his tone sets my nerves on edge.

"There's a badness inside us all, Josh. When it all went down, some people weren't afraid of that bad; they made a friend of it. It gave them strength. They learned to kill without feeling, without judgement. Ordinary people like you and me. That's what happened at the end of the world. It weren't very pretty."

For a few minutes I'm still, trying not to imagine the things he's seen, things I hope I never see. I think of the Tyler back in my own timeline, of Ixchel, and everyone I care about. Maybe I can save them, if there's a way back for me.

More than anything, at this moment, I want to find a way to save the Tyler who's beside me, too. Listening to Tyler's unsteady breathing, I realize that I was wrong. Whatever else happens before I jump back to my own time, if I can help Tyler and his friends escape, it's been worthwhile.

Chapter 27

The horizon lights up with the edge of a rising moon. It casts an ashen glow over the rest of the night sky. Normally I'd play some music, but Tyler's melancholy is so dense that I doubt anything could penetrate it.

In brooding silence, he leans deep into his seat. I think about the blood that's on Tyler's hands, just from today. I get to wondering how much death he must have seen by now. How every act of violence I've seen seems slightly less horrifying that the last. At least for me, it still jars to see blood spilled and bones broken.

"Glenridin," says Tyler eventually. "Now I remember. That's the name of the place."

Tapping a few buttons, I find a town in the Lake District called Glenridding.

The England beneath us is wreathed in darkness. Major urban centres like Birmingham and Manchester are terrifyingly blank, like a black hole ate them up. But I notice pinpricks of lights clustered around some small cities, like Warwick, Lichfield, Derby.

"I rode on my motorbike through Mexico for hours, you know. And didn't see one person alive."

"They were there, no doubt. Hiding from you. Anyone with fuel is dangerous. That stuff is rarer than blood."

"You know, my first night in this time . . . I was even scared there might have been a zombie apocalypse."

This finally draws a low chuckle. "Living dead? Not so much of that, just lots of your everyday dead."

"What happened?"

"Plague. Some genetically engineered superbug, that's what people said. Got released from a lab by mistake when the computers went down. The security systems failed. There was a lot of bad things, Josh."

"How many people died?"

"Millions. There wasn't even anywhere to bury them. We took them to the stadium. Were going to burn them. Then people got worried that the ashes would spread the plague even further. So we just left them there. Can you imagine that, Josh? Tens of thousands of bodies, all wrapped in bin liners."

I couldn't imagine it, didn't want to.

"You know what the worst thing is? It's what you get used to. How it all seems to become normal. It's like in that book The Outsider, where he says that even if he'd been made to live his life inside a dead tree, he'd probably get used to it."

"Haven't read that. Who wrote it?"

"Albert Camus. I was reading it for A-level French."

I think of all my old school friends just like Tyler, working hard, looking forward to their future, only to have it blasted away in front of their eyes.

"Yeah . . . death became normal, all right. But killing, I can't get used to."

"That's good, though, yeah?"

"If you're going to protect your people, you got to be able to do what it takes. So I do what it takes, Josh. But it's eating me away. Little by little. I can feel myself being swallowed up by this other Tyler, one who doesn't mind so much."

"You're going to get out of that place, Ty. I promise."

"Sometimes it feels like it's true, what Camus wrote. The universe is indifferent. Nothing and no one gives a damn."

Tyler's morose mood is beginning to infect me. I know instinctively that I can't risk letting myself think that way. The only way I can let myself use the Bracelet of Itzamna is if I keep believing that we can improve things: me, Bosch and Arcadio; three travellers in time, linked by some unseen force.

But when time stops being linear, history becomes like a jigsaw puzzle. I keep picking up pieces and trying to find their place. And still I'm seeing only a bit of the whole picture.

The contours of the holographic map become more pronounced. Bodies of water appear between the countryside, blue in green. The Muwan begins to descend. My visor alerts me that our destination is ahead. In the eyepiece, landing controls light up. I show Tyler how to select a landing programme. The Muwan offers three landing sites. We pick one in the car park of the ferry port. The aircraft comes down in near total dark, on the shores of a huge expanse of black water, lit only by the occasional ripple of moonlight.

According to the dashboard, it's two o'clock in the morning. Not a good time to go knocking on the door of a family who haven't seen you for two years. I know we'd be more comfortable in the tent and sleeping bags, but until I know how safe this place is, we can't risk that. So I keep the air filters and the motion alarm going, but otherwise power down. Tyler asks if there's anything to eat. I take a couple of chocolate banana energy bars from the panel under my seat. We chew them slowly, watching stars sparkle above the shadows of lakeside peaks.

After a little while, Tyler speaks again. "There's something else I need to tell you. The Josh who was my mate, who was made a blue-blood same time as me . . . he and his old man didn't always see eye to eye."

"Is that why Josh became a blue-blood?"

"You don't ask to become a blue-blood. They test you and if you're compatible – most people aren't – then they make you one."

"What makes you compatible?"

Tyler shrugs. "There's this rare gene. They called it 'jelf'." Don't ask me what it means, cos I got no idea. You're either a carrier of the 'jelf' gene, or you ain't."

"A gene?" I wonder then, if it's the same gene that makes it possible for me to use the bracelet. "Do you know what it does? Where the 'jelf' gene comes from?"

Tyler scowls. "They didn't explain. Just grabbed us, tested our DNA, then made some of us into blue-bloods. Look - it weren't like a nice, helpful vaccination program at school, mate. It was like when they used to nab kids to serve in the navy."

"Maybe 'jelf' makes it possible for you to use hypnoticin - hip33, I mean."

He nods, curtly. "We reckoned it might be something like that, yeh."

"But it doesn't mess with your mind, does it?"

"What're you suggesting?"

"It doesn't, like – make you want to do bad stuff?"

Tyler snorts. "No. You're the same person after as you were before. No better, no worse. Just that you can use hip33 more than if you weren't made a blue-blood. And your eyes are blue. What makes some blue-bloods into bastards, Josh, is having that kind of power. Being told and believing that you're better than the rest."

"So you didn't want it – you were press-ganged?"

"Press-ganged – yeh, that's it. And if my mate Josh had gone with his folks like they wanted, he wouldn't have been made."

"What was his problem? Why wouldn't he go?"

"Josh didn't want to run for the hills like your dad. To be fair, a lot of people thought like Josh. Me included. We didn't have any idea how bad things would get. We wanted to get back to our lives. These people who said they were from the Emergency Government told us that everything would get straightened out. We wanted to believe them."

"Josh wanted to believe?"

"He had a nice life, was with a great girl."

"A girl? What was her name?"

"Emmy."

I stare. "Emmy! You're kidding. Emmy? Wow. I never thought she fancied me."

"Stop day-dreaming, muppet. Listen, things didn't fall apart overnight. At first it seemed like something that could be fixed in a week. Then they said a month. Food and petrol started running out; no one could get their money out of the bank. Hospital supplies started to disappear. Josh's dad wanted to go, even before the beginning. Well, Josh refused. He wanted to stay with his girl. His dad got crazy, tried to order him to leave. They had a massive row. Josh left home. He stayed at my house for a bit."

Tyler breaks off. There's a long silence.

"And then?"

He answers quietly, "No one knew it, but it was already too late. See, pretty early on a germ had escaped from a lab. When the computer security went down. Then the plague came. And things got really bad. The Emergency Government started to get really powerful. They decided who got medicine and who didn't. Josh and me, we were rounded up, tested. They tested Emmy too, but she didn't have the 'jelf' gene. They threw her out of the city. They threw anyone out, who didn't have at least one person in the family with the gene. A better tomorrow for the best, see?"

"You were a blue-blood, then. How did you get away?"

"They turned me against my own neighbourhood, Jericho. But instead of capturing people, I helped them to hide." He gave a bitter laugh. "The EG didn't like that. Not a bit."

"So . . . Josh's dad . . . he was right."

"Hindsight is perfect. But, yeah."

We're both quiet for a long time, staring through the glass at the sky. The moon is less than half full but it's bright enough to drown out most of the stars. Except for the Orion constellation, directly overhead.

With a teasing tone, Tyler says, "Emmy didn't fancy you in your timeline, hey?"

"Nope. She was a good mate though. Maybe if I'd never met Ollie. . ."

"Ollie?"

"Just some lying cow who broke my heart. . ."

Tyler chuckles. "So mate – did you ever get with a girl?"

"Yeah."

"You in love?"

I pause, wondering how much to admit. "Yeaaah. Wish I knew how she was doing. I kind of stranded her back there, when I time-jumped."

"Better get back to her then, bro. Stay in hell much longer, the sin's gonna end up sticking to you."

"Sometimes I wonder," I say, very slowly, "if she might be better off without me."

"True, that. Nice boys don't get caught up in gun battles."

Maybe it isn't meant as a hard statement. But his words take their effect - it's like the ground being pulled away from underneath. I can already feel myself dropping out of the sky, blue and green contours of the land rushing up to meet me.

Chapter 28

We don't sleep long – three hours at most. With the Muwan parked on the banks of a long, black lake, the dawn light wakes us, stripes of clouds turning pink. I open the cockpit window, stand up, crack my neck, have a stretch. A skinny mist hangs over the metallic waters of the lake, which is about ten metres away. The rising sun begins to light the distant hills to the west. A flock of Canada geese fly past, land with loud slaps in the water a hundred metres away.

Beside me, Tyler stirs, opens his eyes and stares at me. He looks at his surroundings, blinking. The line of his jaw is tight. He gazes at his hands.

I take out my binoculars and scope the place. The signs of neglect and dilapidation are all around. A moored ferry, falling to pieces on the wharf. Two abandoned cars in the car park, one with all four doors ripped away. Both petrol caps are open, I'm guessing from where the fuel has been siphoned away.

On a patch of pebble-dashed sandy beach, we stare into the water lapping at the edges of the lake. I reach down for a scoop and use it to wash my face, neck and hands. Tyler climbs out of the Muwan and wanders towards the water.

"Don't drink it. Who knows where they dumped the dead people in a place like this?"

We share two strips of beef jerky, a dried mango bar and a strawberry-cream-filled Submarino cake. As we eat, I notice Tyler giving me an appraising stare.

"You been working out."

"Yep."

"Still play capoeira?"

"I practise the moves, yeah. But it's no fun on your own."

"So? Teach people."

"Oh . . . I dunno." I think of the ways in which I've recently used capoeira, in self-defence, but also to attack. It's not a game for me, not any more. "I'm not good enough for that."

Tyler puts down his tea. He stands. "Show me." Then he's in a ginga stance. I watch him for a second, then climb into the Muwan, turn on the docked iPod, select an up-tempo version of the capoeira classic "Paranaue". A grin breaks across Tyler's features as he slides from side to side. "Come on, Mariposa. *Muito axé*!"

And we go to it. Real capoeira. Tyler flips and rolls around, throws in head spins, handsprings, sweeping kicks, slow at first until we get the measure of each other, growing faster as we become confident. The recorded music doesn't synchronize with your pulse quite the way it does when you've got the twang of the *berimbau* right next to you, but even so my heart thuds with effort and thrill.

By the time the song ends we're both smiling and sweating and it's back to the lake to cool down. Tyler's the real deal – a *capoeirista*. That should have been his life. Not becoming this isolated gang leader, holding on by his fingernails to survive. When it ends we embrace and Tyler whispers, "Thank you, my brother. I needed that."

I lock the Muwan, and we start looking towards the nearby road. Beyond that lies the town. From here there's no sign of any life. My guts coil like snakes when I think that I might be about to meet my parents; my parents-who-might-have-been. At least I can be certain that other-Josh won't be there; from what Tyler says, he'd never have been able to escape from the Controlled Zone.

173

Tyler insists on bringing the rifle, says I've got no idea how unpredictable life has become. We cross the road, head for the dark stone cottages of the village.

"What are we looking for?"

"Josh didn't tell me much about their holiday place. Only that it was in the middle of nowhere. He weren't too happy about that."

"But this is a village." There are rows of houses, several streets' worth. Nothing that matches Tyler's description.

"Let's start by seeing if anyone's home."

I stare, astonished. "You're joking, right? The place looks pretty abandoned to me."

Tyler shakes his head, grimly. "Stop going by appearances. In the badlands, people stay behind closed doors."

I spot a door partly cracked open. "How about there?" Then I get my first shock: the sight of two finger bones clutching the edge of the door. Tyler pushes the door with his foot, his finger on the trigger. The rest of the body comes into view – a skeleton in grey trousers and a ragged checked shirt.

Tyler shoves the body to one side with the side of his trainer. He steps into the cottage. I follow him into a kitchen. Tyler goes straight for the cupboards, opens them up. They've been cleaned out. He turns on a tap and waits. Nothing. Without a word, Tyler makes for a downstairs bathroom that we passed on the way in. I watch him lift the seat with a foot and shake his head, very grim.

"What?"

"You don't want to see."

Ignoring the advice, I poke my head into the tiny room. The toilet is full almost to the brim, dark solid matter at the base, clearer liquid above. There's very little smell. I guess bacteria have processed most of what was once there.

"Plumbing stopped working when the electricity plants failed. You had to go down to the river to fetch water. There was a time when people would charge payment in food to let you use an unblocked toilet. Those kinds of manners didn't last long. After a bit there were people who'd kill anyone who had anything they wanted." He looks thoughtfully towards the dead body. "Reckon he didn't want to let someone use his toilet or eat his food. Looks like they did it anyhow."

From there we go into the next house, and the next house, repeating what seems to be a practiced routine for Tyler. In the next five houses the dead bodies are in the bedrooms, tangled up in bedcovers dark with stains of blood and other gross stuff. Tyler takes his time checking drawers and cupboards.

"Someone's done these places over already. Someone around here survived. They've probably taken anything useful from every house."

It seems too much to hope that it's Andres Garcia. Why would he survive such a terrible pandemic of whatever this illness was?

Back in the ghost-town street, Tyler suggests we move the search away from the main village. Anyone who survived the plague couldn't have lived anywhere close to the rest of the population. They must have had access to a different source of water. They'd have had the means to protect themselves when people began to panic, to turn to theft and violence in search of food and medicines for themselves or their loved ones.

His gaze lifts to the rise of the hills. "Up there. They'd be high up, where they could see people coming. They'd have weapons, long range. To pick people off when they got close."

"So we look for a house on a hill with a trail of dead bodies leading to the front door?"

"There'll be no trail. Whoever survived this would know enough to move the bodies. And then . . . to incinerate them. They don't call it the 'badlands' for nothing."

175

I hand Tyler my binoculars, watch him sweep the landscape. Until he stops, his focus rock-steady on a white house, the last and highest building visible in the vicinity. He passes me back the binoculars. "That's the one. Just like Josh said – middle of nowhere. Bet you two cans of Coke."

The house is about a kilometre south-east of the ferry landing post. A narrow lane leads off the main road, past trees that shield most of the cottage from the lakeside village. We make our way up the lane, which is shaded by overhanging trees, a fast stream gushing to our right. The lane ends at a cottage of stone, painted white.

Behind some privet bushes there's a crackle, the sound of static discharge, pungent fumes in the air. Tyler lifts his gun and whispers, "Electricity generator. The petrol kind."

Another sound floats across the morning air. Piano chords and a saxophone. A slow, melancholy tune. Familiar as the scent of fig trees on a warm summer's day and the overripe garden vines I'd pass on my way home.

Blue in Green.

Breath catches in my throat. The music seems to knife through me, to occupy space between nerves and blood cells. I close my eyes to an overpowering sense that I'm living someone else's life. All I want, right now, is to escape.

From behind us, the click of a rifle being cocked. A woman's voice says, "Don't move." We stall. "Drop the gun. Do it." Tyler bends slowly and places his rifle on the ground. "Hands in the air. Turn around. Slow."

By the time I've turned, I recognize the voice. It's so different. Harsh. Cold. When I turn, the hard, pale eyes that glare at me over the rifle scope widen in shock. The rifle wavers.

"Mary and all the saints! Son, is that you?"

What do I tell her? She is Eleanor Garcia. But I'm not her son.

Chapter 29

Blue-grey eyes hold mine in a paralysing stare. They're only a grim reminder of my mother's. Lined, gaunt cheeks where her rosy complexion should be. A tired gaze, fearful, deep with pain. Her hair is thinner too, lank, unkempt. The woman who is not my mother wears faded blue jeans, a loose cotton shirt, and green Wellington boots.

Something about having a gun pointed at you makes you want to raise your hands. A couple of seconds later I realize I'm holding my breath. Then that my eyes are stinging, hot and salty. I don't even understand why.

"Josh. . ." breathes Eleanor. Her voice becomes huskier. "Josh. . ."

Tyler breaks in, "It looks like him, don't it?"

She raises the gun again. "There's something wrong with his eyes."

"They turned him into a blue-blood, like me."

There's a sound from the side door of the stone cottage. A Border collie bustles through the door, barking ferociously at Tyler and me. The dog is followed by a little kid in dungarees, a girl with long, dark curls and two button-cute brown eyes in the middle of dimply cheeks.

She stands there with a finger in her mouth, gazing solemnly at Eleanor with the gun and the barking dog. A man steps through the side door. I'm not surprised at all to recognize him. All anger in his voice melts away when he sees me.

The air is warming rapidly now that the sun has broken free of the lakeside peaks. Faintly, in the distance, I hear the sound of bleating sheep, responding to the raucous echo of the dog. For a moment we all just look at each other. Only the little girl doesn't seem traumatized. She walks up to the dog, less than a metre away from me. Pointing at me, she turns to Eleanor and Andres. "It's Josh!"

"Eleanor. . ." Andres says quietly, "lower the gun."

She does it, trembling as he moves in to take the rifle. Andres grabs hold of the dog's collar, orders it to stop barking.

He glances at Tyler. "You're Tyler Marks, aren't you?"

Before Tyler can reply, Eleanor takes a step towards me. Her eyes have started to well up. I'm still held in some kind of powerful grip. And I can't move.

"He's not Josh. . ." She turns to Andres. His beard is much shorter than I remember my own father's being. Little more than stubble. Hair's longer, though; greyer too. Strands of it touch his collar. I try to swallow as she repeats in a conspiratorial whisper, "He's not Josh."

Andres Garcia peers at me. "Who are you?"

I breathe out slowly. "It's hard to explain."

"Try."

"But it is Josh!" says the little girl. She's obviously noticed the friction in the air, won't come any closer. I guess she's been trained not to go close enough to catch a stranger's germs. It strikes me that if I didn't have the same face as their son, right now there's a chance I'd be on the ground, shot dead, right next to Tyler.

"What's your name?" I say to the little girl.

Eleanor and Andres gasp. But they don't move. The little girl stuffs almost a whole fist in her mouth and runs behind Eleanor, peeking out at me from behind her legs.

Tyler says, "He's Josh . . . but from a different reality." When he puts it like that even I can hardly believe it. "He's got some kind of bracelet on his arm lets him time travel into different realities."

"What nonsense. . ." Eleanor begins.

Andres interrupts her. "You really don't know your baby sister, Sofia?"

"My sister. . .?" I have to stop then. I'm closer to tears by the second.

"He's not Josh," Tyler insists. "Your son Josh works for them now, for the government. He's a blue-blood. They changed him."

Eleanor grows rigid beside Andres. But he says nothing. "Andres. What is he talking about?"

"I think maybe they'd better come inside."

Tyler's first movements into the house are cautious, suspicious. Andres takes Tyler's rifle, promising to return it when he leaves. Inside the cottage there's a warm, yeasty smell of baking bread. Kind of Blue on the stereo. Apart from an enormous freestanding pine table and some chairs, the only object in the kitchen is an upright piano. As I pass, I notice sheet music open at The Peacocks.

You could easily forget that this is an island of life in the midst of Armageddon.

Tyler asks, "How did you survive the plague?"

Andres answers carefully, "We stayed home. We'd spent most of the year stocking up so that we wouldn't have to leave the house."

"Yeah, but . . . people must have come, trying to get your food. How did you keep them away?"

Eleanor and Andres exchange a look and then glance back at Tyler. Immediately, he lowers his eyes. "OK." Something's understood between them, but I can't be sure what. I think back to Tyler's ominous words about the trail of bodies that might once have led up to their cottage.

From the moment that Tyler sees the food that Eleanor lays out on the table, he goes into a kind of joyful ecstasy. "Oh man," he groans. "You've got actual cheese. Actual bread. . ." He stuffs a chunk of crusty loaf into his mouth and pops a cube of crumbly white cheese in afterwards. His eyes close. "So good. We're down to tinned food."

"We have two cows," Eleanor says, speaking to Tyler while her eyes steal over to watch me looking at Sofia. "A few sheep. And a dog trained to attack anyone who tries to get near them. They give us milk. I learned how to make cheese, butter, yoghurt."

Sofia passes me her plate of bread. "I want some butter." Hey eyes are round and curious, watching me as I spread the creamy yellow butter. "Are you my brother?"

The whole room falls silent, waiting for my answer. "No." Sofia seems confused, disappointed. "I look like him," I tell her, gently. "And I am called Josh. But I'm from somewhere else. Another place. I have a mummy called Eleanor and a daddy called Andres, too. Just like your brother Josh."

"And a sister called Sofia?"

"No." She looks downcast.

I can't take my eyes off the little girl. Sofia. She's got to be around three, four years old. That means she was born around the time that in my own reality, my father disappeared. And suddenly it becomes very clear to me. I look at them and try not to notice the ache in their expressions.

"You didn't go looking for the Ix Codex," I say to Andres. "Did you? Because of . . . the baby."

"He . . . he's right. I was going to an excavation in Cancuen, in Guatemala. I had a lead, some information about the Ix Codex. But then Sofia came along, earlier than we expected. And I didn't go."

For a moment, no one speaks. Andres continues to regard me with a mixture of bemusement and disbelief. "But how is it possible that you know about this? I don't remember telling you, Josh."

"You didn't. Where I come from, I found out when you went missing. They told us you'd been murdered, your body put on a plane that crashed, to make it look like an accident."

"Murdered?!" Andres tries to laugh.

"Sofia's a nice name for a sister," I say wistfully, watching the dark-haired little girl wrap her arms tightly around her mother's thighs, huge brown eyes gazing into mine. This little Sofia saved her father from making the fateful trip to Ek Naab. So he gets to live, in this timeline. But the Ix Codex was never found, and now the whole world is paying.

Eleanor picks up Sofia in her arms, kisses her cheeks and takes her to the living room to watch a DVD. Soon I'm hearing the faint strains of the Dora the Explorer theme music from the television. She comes back into the room, leaving the door to the living room ajar.

One factor changed – the creation of Sofia – and the destiny of the universe is altered.

Every time I think I've found the zero moment – the starting point for all the changes in my own history – I find that it goes further back.

Arcadio and his cryptic messages; he quoted a writer named Calvino, warning me against searching for the zero moment. As if to say – don't try to go backwards to change your own history, because it's sure to fail.

Well, he was right. I tried to go back in time and change the past so that my father didn't die. But all I did was to cause an event that led up to his death.

Arcadio wrote the zero moment quote in lots of copies of John Lloyd Stephens' Incidents of Travel in Central America, Chiapas and Yucatan. He tattooed himself with a page reference to that book – his way of leaving himself a message in case using the Bracelet of Itzamna caused him to lose his memory. I'd always assumed Arcadio wrote them to remind himself who he was, to warn himself about the dangers of travelling in time.

But what if he was also warning someone else – me?

Chapter 30

Was Arcadio trying to tell me that some things are set in stone? Or was he telling me that time travel is dangerous; don't meddle with the past because you can't predict the consequences?

I haven't travelled into the past this time, but into the future. Yet it hits me now that if something goes wrong here and I get stuck – then I will change my own timeline too.

At the very least – I will cease to exist in that history.

And Ixchel. Instead of finding me again, seconds after she's seen me disappear with Madison, she'll wait and wonder and live a life of what-could-have-been. Thinking about it, my insides feel cold and loose. Ixchel wouldn't be the first person to lose someone they cared about to time travel.

Susannah St John lost Arcadio.

Simon Madison lost his father, Martineau.

And if anyone cared about Madison – perhaps Ollie – then she's lost him too. Poor Madison, I almost feel sorry for him now; wandering about in a vacant region of post-apocalyptic Mexico, without food, clean water or fuel. Will he even survive?

Andres is clearly at a loss for words. When he looks up again, I sense that he's come to a conclusion about me.

"You really are from an alternate reality?"

"I travelled through time, from June 2012," I say.

"Do you have a spaceship or something?"

"Actually," I smile, "I kind of do. But it doesn't travel in time. I have to leave it here."

"If it doesn't travel in time," Andres says, "then where did you get it?"

"Someone must have left it for me. . ." Such traces of my invisible co-conspirator make me uneasy. It's like looking into a mirror and seeing someone other than you staring back. "I'm not the only time traveller," I admit, with reluctance. "We kind of work together."

Arcadio. It has to be.

Eleanor says, "What are you doing here?" She still hasn't smiled, hasn't softened her expression one tiny bit. She can't even look at me when I'm looking at her.

"I came to find out what went wrong with a plan to save the world from the 2012 superwave. But I don't think that plan was ever used in this reality. So now I need to find out how the Sect . . . the Emergency Government . . . took over the world. Then when I go back to my time, maybe I can stop them."

"You won't change anything for us, then?"

I can't read Eleanor, can't tell whether she thinks that's a good thing or not.

"Truth is," Tyler says blandly, "even with all his 'time travel' and his spaceship, there's nothing he can do to help us. We're stuck with the Emergency Government. So it's back to prehistoric times for everyone except the chosen few."

Andres asks, "You mentioned 'the Sect' . . . what's that?"

I tell them all about the Sect of Huracan and their carefully constructed plans to prepare a "new world order" after the collapse of civilization. Over the next hour I end up telling Tyler, Andres and Eleanor all about the Ix Codex and Ek Naab, the ancient Erinsi plan to protect the world from the 2012 superwave. Then we come to the subject of Zsolt Bosch, the twenty-second-century scientist who discovered the Erinsi ruins.

"But if Bosch hadn't time travelled, that 2012 plan would have worked," Tyler observes. "So it's like he caused all the trouble."

Warily, I agree. I'm beginning to wonder if Bosch wasn't born into this very timeline. In his world, the Sect of Huracan secretly controlled every major government. I'd say, from what I've seen, that they could be on the way to that.

Andres says, "I don't understand why you started to time travel."

"Because this other time traveller left me messages, a series of postcards sent to me during December 2010. By a guy called Arcadio." There's a pile of Sofia's drawings and scrap paper at one end of the kitchen table. I take a piece and write out the entire text of Arcadio's postcard messages to me. "Like this."

WHAT.KEY.HOLDS.BLOOD.
DEATH.UNDID.HARMONY.
ZOMBIE.DOWNED.WHEN.FLYING.
KINGDOM'S.LOSS.QUESTIONABLE.JUDGEMENT.
FINESSE.REQUIRES.PROPER.HEED.

"He hid the name of the location of where I had to go with an acrostic, you know, where the first letter of each word is a letter in the secret message. Each postcard showed a different Mayan ruin. The secret location was Tlacotalpan."

Andres smiles. "Ingenious."

"What are the dots for?" Tyler asks, poring over the words.

"It's in code. A Caesar cipher."

Tyler asks, "So who is Arcadio?"

"Great question. But I don't know the answer."

Andres says, "It seems certain that your friend Arcadio is a person who enjoys codes."

"Codes and quotations. He's cryptic! I've found messages from him with bits from a writer called Borges and another called Calvino. And he particularly likes to leave messages in a book by that explorer, John Lloyd Stephens."

Andres pushes back his chair, dazed. He leaves the room, returns a moment later. In silence, Andres lays four books down on the table. The first two I recognize – both volumes of Incidents of Travel in Central America, Chiapas and Yucatan by John Lloyd Stephens. The other two are Labyrinths by Jorge Luis Borges and If On A Winter's Night A Traveller by Italo Calvino.

Transfixed by the sight of all those books together, I glance across at the page where I've written the postcard messages from Arcadio.

I steady my nerves with a sip of hot pine needle tea. "Yes – those exact books. In fact – everything you'd need to know to be Arcadio . . . is in this room, right now."

"That's well spooky," comments Tyler.

Andres says, urgently, "Do you know what these are, Josh? They are the only books I managed to bring from home."

Through lips that feel fuzzy, I murmur, "These books were all in our house. . .?" I guess I'd never paid much attention to my parents' book collection.

"Yes."

"Maybe you're Arcadio," Tyler says to me. His tone is playful but each word swipes me like a cane. "Maybe you do stay here. You read those books. And then you go into the past and write all those messages."

Silence falls over the four of us. I'm totally unable to speak, hyper-aware of the breath in my throat and mouth. I want to argue, to protest, the way I always have when Ixchel accused me of being Arcadio, predicting that I would desert her.

Tyler's suggestion has an unmistakable sting of truth.

Yet I can't be Arcadio. Don't want to be. The idea of being trapped here in this nether-future, without Ixchel, growing up amongst the ruins of modern civilization?

It's everything I've been fighting to avoid.

"You could be happy here, with us," says Andres, gently. "It would make Eleanor and Sofia happy too."

"I can't stay here," I blurt. "I won't."

Tyler says, "What if that's the only way to help people in your own timeline? That girlfriend you talked about, the one you said you were mad for. Or your own mum, and everyone else?"

"No," I say, desperate. "It can't be! That's why I have to go back with something, anything that can help prevent this future from happening." I stand up. "Tyler, you promised to help. I want to go now. Take me to the EG Centre. Or to the Futurology Institute. I'm pretty sure that's where the Sect was building its new headquarters."

"The Futurology Institute is the EG Centre," says Andres. "They never finished that building; it was commandeered by the Emergency Government."

The Sect's fingerprints are all over that.

"And no one thought that was strange? That the Emergency Government would set up in Oxford of all places?"

"Less strange than you might think. Hitler planned to use Oxford as his capital if he conquered England. It's one of the reasons why Oxford wasn't bombed."

I move towards the door, but Eleanor stands in my way.

"No. For God's sake, child, you may not be my son but there's no way I'll stand by and watch you get yourself killed."

Andres stands up too. He lays a protective hand on my shoulder. "She's right. We're not letting you go like this."

For a moment I'm completely dumbfounded. Montoyo and my mother in my own reality, Andres and Eleanor in this; they all want to stop me doing what I know needs to be done.

"What you need is a plan," says Tyler. "Lucky for you, I was taught by one of the best – Captain Donnelly was a brilliant strategy man. Reckon you're a bit short of one here."

Frustrated, I say, "I need to get into the Sect's offices, make copies of their computer files. When I get back to my own time, we can analyse their data, work through it backwards and find out what they did to be able to take over. There'll be a weakness that can be exploited."

Tyler and Andres laugh. "How they took over?" says Tyler. "I already told you about hip33, didn't I? That's how. Without hip33 they couldn't have made enough people do what they wanted."

"It was more than that," says Andres. "A great deal of planning and organization, I suspect. But broadly, yes. Tyler is correct. Without hip33, the Emergency Government could simply not have achieved their aims."

"Then it's simple. I get in; I take some vials of hip33 and their data. When I get back to my time, my friends analyse hip33 and make an antidote. That way we're covered – if we can't stop the 2012 superwave, we'll stop the Sect."

"It's not 'you get in'; it's 'we'," Tyler says. "Three of us, Josh. That's the minimum team you'll need to pull off a heist like this."

He looks expectantly at Andres. "So – Dr. Garcia. Are you in?"

Chapter 31

By the time we're close to finishing the plan, night has fallen. Tyler has drawn maps of the EG Centre's treatment labs, from memories of the months he spent as a 'blue-blood' agent. He tucks them carefully into his pocket.

Before they light candles and gas lamps, Andres and Eleanor go through a ritual of pulling down the blackout blinds. It's protected their secrecy before; it will again. Sofia wants me to read her a bedtime story but Eleanor vetoes the idea. "We don't want the baby getting confused," she says firmly.

We decide to leave at dawn. Tyler and I get our heads down for a few hours in the third bedroom: other-Josh's room. I notice a stack of guitar tabs printed out from the Internet. Posters of Arctic Monkeys, Green Day and Muse on the walls, from when other-Josh used to come here for his holidays. So, we have that in common.

I can't sleep, so I go down to the kitchen and pick up one of the books – the one by Borges. I find the essay that Arcadio quoted from in his letter to me, the one he left with Susannah St John. The title is "A New Refutation of Time".

And then I hurl the book across the room. Is this me becoming Arcadio?

A little while later, Tyler shakes me awake. In the candlelight his eyes seem wild, filled with the call of battle. We change into jogging outfits and running shoes – the first part of the plan is to pass ourselves off as a bunch of guys going for a morning run.

As we stand on the threshold of the cottage, Andres kisses Eleanor goodbye, stroking her hair. It seems a bit odd, after months of seeing my own mother with Carlos Montoyo. Maybe I actually miss him.

With some reluctance, Eleanor puts her arms out to me for a hug. Feeding me in her own kitchen may have softened her attitude to me a bit, but she's still wary. When I'm close she whispers, "Don't worry now, I'm not confusing you with my boy. But you be good to your own mum, you hear?"

In pale blue light, we stroll down through the deserted ghost village, back to the Muwan. Andres stands for a few minutes in silence, simply marvelling at the machine. I climb in and prepare for flight, taking time to show Tyler what to do. "It's a shame you didn't leave a manual in the glove box," he says.

Then we're inside, strapped to the seats and taking off. I show Tyler how to measure the power left before a recharge, and calculate what he needs to reserve for a final trip to Ek Naab.

Once this mission is over, I'll hand the Muwan over and Tyler will use it to fly his gang out of Oxford. We agree that it's safest to bring them back to Glenridding – for now. It'll take several trips and once the power in the Muwan runs out, a return to Ek Naab is Tyler's only hope of refuelling. If he can't persuade the people of Ek Naab to let him in, then the Muwan is no further use to him. And he'll be stuck in Mexico!

"You let me worry about that," he says, confidently. "I can be pretty persuasive."

Tyler reckons that there is only one place in the Controlled Zone where we can hope to hide the Muwan, close for a quick getaway from the EG Centre.

"The university parks. There are trees round the back, fairly tall, good cover. Maybe you can squeeze in between some of them."

But when we arrive I can see he's asking the impossible. There's no way to get between those trees. So I bring the Muwan down in front of a huge rhododendron and then hover along the ground, pushing a path through. When we get out we take a look. It's not very well hidden. I can just see us returning to a small crowd of fascinated children and dog-walkers. When I mention this, Tyler says, "Dogs, in the city? No. They were all eaten a long time ago."

Five in the morning. The air is damp, cool, smells faintly of wood smoke. Somewhere in the vicinity, there's been a fire. The chorus of birds is almost deafening. A crowd of starlings swoops over the middle of the parks, over what used to be a rugby pitch.

I take two dart guns from where they're stored under the seats. They only fire tranquillizer darts but still, they pack a punch. Tyler hangs on to his own rifle. I hear Andres ask him quietly if he's killed people before; does he want Andres to handle the gun? They exchange an intent glance. Tyler says it's OK, man, he's cool with whatever needs to be done.

We're three joggers out for some early morning exercise. Shorts, running shoes and T-shirts are all we need. The Bracelet of Itzamna is just visible under the sleeve of my T-shirt so I've borrowed a sweatshirt from Andres.

We set off, jogging within twenty metres of one another. The park is still deserted. We cross to the road without seeing anyone else. Then we head down the empty road. Nothing in sight is moving. The street is clean, empty, no parked cars. No heaps of burned or rotting rubbish.

To the right of the Natural History Museum, where I remember there being a car park, is a brand new building, all glass and butterscotch-coloured concrete.

The Futurology Institute.

"How're we going to get in?"

"They know you," Tyler says. "The other-Josh has to check in for his hip33 injections, so they'll recognize your face. And I've got the chippenpin chip."

Tyler leads us to the entrance. He pushes me ahead, through the revolving door. Inside, a security guard glances over the book he's reading. There's instant recognition in his eyes, but also a hint of confusion. I guess I must look enough like other-Josh to pass for him, but he can sense that there's something not quite right.

"Mister Garcia. Sorry, I didn't see you go outside again. . ."

Tyler and I glance at each other for a fraction of a second. The plan to pass myself off as other-Josh seems to be working, but I'll have to be extra careful not to step out of "character".

I say the words that Tyler's instructed me to say: "I've rounded these two up. Tyler Marks and one of his gang. They were trying to infiltrate." Then I turn around, pointing a dart gun at them. Andres and Tyler step forward, hands in the air.

The security guard looks even more confused. He flashes me an imploring look. His hesitation is crucial. In another second Tyler grabs his head and slams it down on the desk. I hear the guard's nose break. He groans, loudly. Tyler whacks him one more time. The man passes out, bleeding all over the desk. We drag him to a nearby room.

The secret facilities are underground, in bomb-proof bunkers. I guess the Sect saw Armageddon everywhere.

At the threshold door, Tyler lifts his right arm, letting the scanner read his chippenpin chip. Tyler leans over the control panel and taps the "Admit EGRI" button that's flashed on to the screen.

"Why's there so little security?"

"Classic reliance on technology. They honestly believe a chippenpin won't threaten them. A better tomorrow for the best – it's supposed to be such an honour to be included. But this won't get us far, you wait. To get any deeper inside, we're going to need blue-blood DNA. If you have a chip you can fake it – got mine hacked so that I show up as one of the nice, loyal drones. But DNA? There's no faking that."

"But this other Josh – he's a blue-blood. He should be on the system."

Tyler grins. "Standard! Get your thumb ready, blood-brother."

Tyler leads us through a maze of corridors. A minute or so later we arrive at a glass door that blocks any further progress. There's a small printed sign pasted to the glass above a panel that opens at Tyler's touch. Underneath there's a depression with a hole in the middle, and a pad about the size of a thumb, coated in a metallic substance.

Tyler takes my left hand and places the left thumb against the depression and there's the sound of a spring. I feel a tight biting sensation; pull my thumb away to show a bead of bright red blood. Tyler guides my hand to the metallic pad. I place a drop of my blood on the biosensor. A couple of seconds later, a mechanism inside the lock clicks. The door slides open. Tyler jams his foot against the door.

I mutter, "What key holds blood."

Tyler throws me a sidelong glance. "I always knew you'd open doors for me."

Chapter 32

Once we're inside the secure area there's a noticeable change in atmosphere. The air is climate-controlled; it hums with the sound of machines. Louder than I ever remembered; the background buzz of energy being consumed.

Andres and Tyler hide their weapons under their shirts. I slide behind them with the dart gun. Tyler leads with his hands on his head.

A white-coated technician steps out of a side office. He's immediately on his guard.

"Josh Garcia . . . what's going on; why have you come back? Didn't you already get your medication?"

Tyler says, "Shoot him. Now."

My tranquillizer dart sinks into the technician's thigh. Tyler catches him as he falls. He clamps one hand to the guy's mouth.

But as the technician collapses, one hand clutches at his hip. There must be some kind of panic button in his trouser pocket because a second later a klaxon starts sounding. It's the exact same noise I remember hearing when I was escaping from the Sect's institute in Switzerland.

We freeze, waiting, wondering what's going to be unleashed. It could be anything. Then trails of blue LED lights appear on the carpet, tiny arrows pointing towards the doors.

That technician set off the fire alarm. Any second now the place will burst with activity. Our time is running out.

Tyler grabs Andres and points to a corridor about three metres away, to our left. "The techie bloke reckons he just gave your Josh his medication, yeah? I'm pretty sure the treatment rooms are down there. He's got to be in one of them."

"My Josh. . .!" Andres looks torn. "But who's going to cover the two of you?"

"We'll manage. You can cover the exit when we leave. Give us some firepower, just in case."

"OK – I get my boy out, then what?"

Tyler says, "Meet us back at the UFO."

"What if he doesn't want to leave?"

"He knows he made a mistake, years ago. You're his dad. But inside the CZ, there's no way he could ever contact you. You don't know how many times I've wished that Josh was with me the day I escaped. But he wasn't, yeah, and I can't change that. You have to trust me, when Josh sees you, he's gonna want to go with you."

The klaxon pounds, seems to get louder. Andres stares at me one last time. "Good luck," he manages to say. I nod in reply. This isn't how I envisaged saying goodbye to him. Then he's gone, rushing down a darkened corridor.

Tyler pulls out his gun. Somewhere down a corridor to our right, doors start opening. People on the early shift, coming out of their offices, coffee cups in their hands. The faces I catch sight of are perplexed, bemused. I hear someone loudly complain about "blasted fire drills. . ."

Tyler ignores them, marches me right past.

A group of three technicians in lab coats step out from behind another door. They stare at Tyler, glance down at his gun. A woman asks, "Is this a drill?" Tyler raises the gun, points it directly at the woman's head. "Not today, sister. Give us some hip33."

The woman turns to me and stares, blankly. "Josh Garcia . . . what's going on?"

194

From behind us there's another voice. The sound of it tears down walls in my head. I should have been prepared but I'm not.

Marius Martineau.

I watched him die in the rainforest of the ancient Maya. I took his time-travel bracelet. I thought that was the last I'd ever see or hear of the twisted, power-crazed psycho. But no.

In this future he's alive and well.

He speaks lightly, says my name. As I turn, he shoots two bullets at Tyler. One smacks into the door frame right next to his head. The second takes Ty in the shoulder. He falls, firing his gun blindly down the corridor. But Martineau's taken cover.

At Martineau's command two technicians fall on Tyler. They wrestle the rifle out of his grip. I fire tranquillizer darts into all three. It takes a few seconds for the poison to take effect. In those seconds one of the technicians grabs Tyler's rifle, tries to aims it at me.

The bullet whizzes past my ear and smashes the lighting tube. It explodes with a burst of electric fire. There's hot, sharp pain as my hands and face are sliced by flying shards of glass. I flinch, feel blood streaming out of the wounds. I drop the dart gun. We're plunged into semi-darkness. The only light comes from behind the open door to the lab.

Martineau's voice cuts through the shadows. "Garcia. It's over. Give yourself up."

I'm close to panicking. Tyler went down hard; he's going to lose blood, fast. I have to get his rifle. I drop low to the ground and begin to crawl. Two more bullets ring out, firing just above my head. There's movement further down the corridor. Lights begin to go on.

I make a dash for it, leap into the lab that Tyler and I were trying to reach. Martineau's bullets crack the air behind me. There's no time to reach Tyler – I have to get out of the path of Martineau's gun.

195

"I don't want to kill you, Garcia, you're an asset. But if I have to, I will."

I jam a chair under the door. The room is obviously some kind of treatment room, with three patient couches and an examination screen. Martineau starts kicking at the door. Any second now, it's going to buckle.

I open first one fridge and then another. The second is full of tiny plastic vials with screw caps labelled hip33. I grab a handful, stuff them into the pocket of my hoody.

The door frame splinters. I take another chair and hurl it at the light fitting. The filament crackles for a second, fizzes brightly. Then I'm plunged into darkness. The door bursts open. I dive on to the floor and slide under one of the patient couches. I hear Martineau step inside, his footsteps crunching loud on broken glass. Outside the door, Tyler's breathing is fast and ragged, broken with gasps of pain.

My hand goes to my Bracelet, ready to zap myself back to the past.

Then I think of Tyler. He's going to die if I leave him here. There can't be much time. How quickly can you bleed to death? Without Tyler, how much longer will his gang survive?

And what about Andres? How will he get his son out of here? Without the Muwan, I doubt they'd even get as far as Jericho. Voices from the other side of the door confirm my worst fears – reinforcements are on their way.

But this world, this reality isn't mine. I didn't create this future. My own timeline is waiting – and I might just have the antidote to the Sect.

One finger rests on the Crystal, ready to press.

Martineau fumbles in the dark, hunting me.

And I can't do it – I can't leave.

Maybe I didn't create this future – up to this point. But now I've interfered. Tyler and Andres are in terrible danger – because of me. It's down to me to help them.

I hold my breath, waiting, perfectly still. Martineau is less than a metre away; I can smell the coffee on his breath. In the darkness, I sense him turn to face me.

"Should have taken a shower, boy; your stink betrays you," he sneers.

I roll hard to the right, under the second patient couch, then leap up and on to the nearest bed. Martineau fires, first at where I was, then randomly into the room. I vault over the beds and manage to land within two metres of the door. Another bullet tears into the wall above my head as I hit the ground, land on my palms and then spring up, twisting my body around in a hand flip.

I miscalculate – slam into the broken door. For a second I lie there, bruised, cut, defeated.

A foot shoves against the door. Light spills into the treatment room. I see Martineau crouched behind me, pointing his gun. I watch as he slowly stands up. The corridor outside is packed. Someone asks Martineau if they should tie me up. From outside, I hear Andres call, his voice torn with despair.

"Give it up, boys. Josh isn't here. He's gone!"

Martineau towers above me, framed in a network of torch beams, his dressing gown flowing like some demonic cape. All the malevolence of his new world order seems to be concentrated in his shadow. And I can't see how I can fight this any longer, I simply can't.

I hear Andres struggle against his captors. I see a silhouetted guard glance upwards as he looms over Tyler. "This other one is bleeding pretty hard."

Trembling, I drop my head. "Let me hug my friend before he dies."

Martineau and the gathered audience are baffled at my request. But they don't stop me. I lay across Tyler's chest. I put my arms around his shoulders. He's shuddering, going into shock. I make sure to get a firm grip.

"All right, that's long enough. . ." Someone plants their foot against the back of my calf. I slide a hand around Tyler's neck and grip on to the Bracelet of Itzamna that's around my other arm. Tyler stops shaking the instant I grab him. I grip tighter; push my index finger hard on the Crystal Key. There's a sort of strangled sound of confusion from Tyler. The guard starts kicking me, trying to dislodge me. But it's too late.

There's the sound of gasps from everyone around me.

Martineau's roar of fury.

Very softly from Tyler, "Oh no. . ."

And Andres Garcia crying out, a sound I'll remember for many years, "Josh!"

Chapter 33

The scent of sun-warmed pine needles begins to fill my head. The peace of the woods is disorienting after the blood and the bullets, the darkness and the panic.

My first thought is of Ixchel. Is she here? The possibility that there's a problem with the Bracelet and we've travelled to the wrong reality is so nightmarish that it sucks all the air from my lungs. My hands are shaking when I lower Tyler to the ground. For a second I hold my breath, checking for a pulse in his neck. He's alive. I breathe quietly for a minute, trying to get my head together. Ixchel shouldn't be too far away. It's hard to remember exactly how long we were in the woods, fighting Simon Madison, before I zapped us to the future. Less than ten minutes though, for sure.

That would explain why it's still so quiet around here. They should arrive any minute.

I'm about to go and investigate, but the second I turn away I hear Tyler groan once, very loudly. He rolls on to his side just in time to vomit. I barely manage to slide out of the way.

When he's finished, Tyler shifts around for a second or two, as if he were drunk. Abruptly, he sits up. The right side of his face and hair is smeared in his own blood. He stares blankly at me for a moment, trying to focus.

"Your shoulder..." I say. A dark patch of blood stains his right shoulder. Tyler glances at it and flexes his right arm, grimacing with pain. "Scumbags put a bullet in me. Again."

I gaze at him, stunned. "But you're OK? I thought. . ."

Tyler stares back in silence. He wipes his mouth with the back of his left hand. "You thought I'd had it? That's the point. Get yourself shot in a closed environment, you'd best lay low. Play dead."

"It doesn't hurt?" I wince in sympathy, thinking of the time that Madison shot me in the thigh. Pure hot metal torture, that's what I remember.

"Course it hurts. But after a few minutes the endorphins kick in." Tyler heaves a sigh. "I've had worse than this. Be glad when we get the bullet out, though."

"What if they'd actually finished you off?"

"They took my gun; I wasn't a threat." Tyler doesn't seem very interested in discussing it any further. "Where are we?"

"Somewhere outside San Cristobal de las Casas. That's a town in Mexico. It's June 2012. And in about eight minutes my girlfriend and I are going to ride into the woods on a motorbike, chased by a raging psycho from the Sect."

"Mexico," Tyler responds, levelly. "2012?"

"And Marius Martineau's massive fool of a son is about to ride in."

"Shouldn't we hide?"

"The Bracelet should have put us down at least twenty metres away from them. Best to stay put, right here, until it's all over." I glance at my watch.

"Until it's all over? What does that mean?"

"We've gone back to my last point of origin, but exactly ten minutes before I set out, and displaced by around twenty metres. That's how I know what is about to happen: I've been here before. I've seen it, but from a different viewpoint. Simon Madison – Martineau's son – Ixchel and me, are about to come crashing into the woods on motorbikes. Then he wallops Ixchel. I drag him into the future with me."

"The future."

"Yep – 2014. Where I met you."

"So right now there are two yous running around?"

"No. There were two of me where we've just been – me and other-Josh. But the Josh that is about to come into the woods chased by Madison, he is me. He's me from a couple of days ago, before my trip to 2014."

"Pure madness."

"Yeah, it is a bit. It's like looking in a mirror – with a time delay. I see him, I know about him, because he's in my own memory. He is me, but he doesn't know about me. He's about to time-jump into the future – to 2014 where he'll meet you. I have to keep it that way. Or else . . . or else I'll create a time paradox. Or something."

"What if you did something to help him?"

"I could. Once, I actually did – I did something to help myself, ten minutes in the past. But this time, I know that I didn't do anything, see? So I won't."

Tyler gives me an incredulous stare. "Huh?"

I try to think of another way to explain it. "If I were sitting here now, remembering that I left myself something handy, a weapon or something, then I'd go, aha, I need to go and leave that in place right now, so past-me can find it."

"But you're not going to?"

I sigh. "No, see, because I didn't."

We're silent for a minute. I look at Tyler's shoulder. He's trying to find a comfortable position for his arm and failing.

"You're losing blood."

He grits his teeth. "I know, muppet, we need to tie it up."

I stand up and take off my hoody and T-shirt. I pull the hoody back on and tear the cotton shirt into strips. Tying the cloth hard and tight, I bandage Tyler's shoulder, then use the rest of the torn shirt to wipe Tyler's face. He grimaces. "Wipe your own face."

"No need to thank me."

"Thank you for what, Josh, for dragging me back to hell?"

"Funny, I thought we just came from there."

"Didn't I make it blatantly clear, moron, I don't want to go through the end of 2012 again?"

"We're going to prevent it. It won't be like what happened in your timeline."

"Prevent it – how?"

"I've got the sample of hip33. Someone will be able to synthesize an antidote. The Sect won't be able to use their mind control."

"And the superwave, you've got some way of stopping that too?"

I don't answer. Tyler's got a point – my mission has only been partly successful.

I'm no clearer on what can be done to stop the superwave. Bosch came from a future where the superwave isn't stopped. I've just been to a future where the superwave isn't stopped. In fact, the only future realities that seem to be linked to any time travelling – they all seem to be doomed by the superwave.

Maybe it can't be stopped?

Maybe it is fate.

Tyler breathes hard through his mouth, struggling to contain the pain. This waiting is tough on him, I can see. "Why you?"

The question throws me. I peer into the woods and once again glance at my watch. Surely it must be almost time for the motorbikes to arrive. When I look back, Tyler is still facing me with a hard, expectant gaze. "Why me?" I say. "Because some scientist from the twenty-second century time travelled, changed the past. He genetically engineered four boys to be able to resist some poisons, and used those poisons to protect all his secrets. I'm descended from one of those kids – from his own son, actually. I was born with a gene that protects me. So – that's why me."

"But why are you the one who's time travelling? Your magic bracelet – is that poisoned too?"

"No . . . no, it isn't. But you need some kind of gene to use it."

202

"The 'jelf' gene? The one they test for before they make you a blue-blood?"

"Yeah, when you told me about 'jelf' I did wonder the same thing," I admit. "That's why I asked if you know what it does."

"If it's 'jelf', then you were born with it."

"I don't know if I was born with the ability to use the Bracelet, or if it's one of the things the Sect changed about me. The first time I used it, was after they changed me."

"The Sect . . . you mean the Emergency Government?"

"Yes. They started their genetic engineering programme a while ago. What you called making blue-bloods – they tested it on me a while back."

"Reckon any blue-blood can use the Bracelet?"

"No idea, Ty. Want to give it a go?"

Tyler stares at me with curious detachment. "You're playing with people's lives."

"It's not a game."

I lean back, follow a brightly coloured bird as it flies from a low branch and up into the tree canopy. The needle-clad branches are pine-dark silhouettes against a featureless, whited-out sky. I turn around slowly so that the world seems to rotate, stretch out my arms and feel the warm air, heavy with moisture as it clings to my fingertips.

Without looking down at Tyler I say, "It's going to rain."

Chapter 34

A light drizzle begins. Seconds later the tension snaps. The high-pitched roars of two motorcycle engines shatter the stillness. The dull, metallic throb of helicopter blades whirring follows close behind. Moist wood cracks and breaks as the motorbikes enter the woods. We hear wheels spinning, loose soil and pine needles sent flying into the air.

For a second or two Tyler looks at a loss. I indicate that we should both lay low. We scramble for cover behind two thick-trunked pines and try to catch a glimpse of the action.

Ixchel's and my encounter with Madison takes place noisily, a little distance away. We're close enough to hear everything but our view is obscured. It's difficult not to intervene, especially when I recall the swingeing blow that Madison delivered to Ixchel.

But Tyler is injured, and what's happening barely twenty metres away – that is my past. Already written, already part of me. I can no more disturb that than I can rip out my own memory.

So I close my eyes and try to block what I'm hearing. Until I hear Ixchel yell, until there's no sound but the incessant pounding of the helicopter blades above. Slowly, I rise to my feet and prepare to scare the wits out of Ixchel.

When she sees me, she flinches. "You came back for me."

I reach for her, trying to find words, but I can't. She lets herself be pulled close, lets me hug her tight, but after a few seconds she pushes me away. Her eyes are filled with eagerness. It takes another few seconds of gazing into my eyes before Ixchel understands. When she does she pulls away, confused and hurt.

"You've already been? How long have you been gone?"

"Hardly at all. A couple of days."

Her voice becomes colder. "Why didn't you come back for me?"

"Madison was there. I had to run."

"Josh . . . what happened?"

Tyler emerges from the trees, one hand propping up his injured arm. Unsteadily, he makes his way over. "This your girl, Josh?" He wavers. I grab hold of his good arm and take some of Tyler's weight. "The name's Tyler. Josh speaks very highly of you."

Ixchel's eyes run over both of us, struggling to comprehend. "Tyler. . ." she says after a while. "Interesting move, with the hair. And they did something to you, didn't they? Like with Josh. They changed your eyes, too."

Tyler tries to smile, but wobbles, falling against me.

"How bad is he hurt?"

"He's losing blood," I say. "Will you phone Montoyo? I struggle to keep Tyler upright. "Mate, I'm so sorry. People are always getting shot at because of me."

Ixchel makes the call. She has to cover one ear to be able to hear about the drone of the helicopter blades. Her face seems very controlled throughout. My guess is that there was some yelling on the other end of the phone.

"Montoyo is sending someone. But they're going to take at least twenty-five minutes to arrive. We need to get away from here. The police bike is still here . . . and that helicopter is going to be tracking us."

"The Muwan can take out the helicopter with an ion burst," I say. "But the Mexican motorcycle cops are going to be here soon, and that's definitely a problem."

Ixchel retrieves our Honda and the helmets we didn't have time to put on when Madison gave chase. Meanwhile, I prop up a fading Tyler and give him my helmet. We just manage to squeeze the three of us on the bike, with Tyler in the middle. He flinches when the bike starts moving; each bump we ride over seems to cause him agony.

But even the Tyler I knew was a tough, resilient guy. And this Tyler is battle-hardened, a leader, a survivor of the apocalypse. I know I can count on him.

We ride through the woods, weaving through the pines for around thirty minutes. The fresh hillside air of the woods is replaced suddenly by the acrid smell of hot asphalt. A light drizzle begins to mist the air; I have to squint to keep the moisture out of my eyes.

Ixchel keeps her phone dialled in to Ek Naab so they can track us. The Sect helicopter is a persistent irritant in the sky above us. It can't land, but on the other hand we can't risk coming into the clear. Eventually, the Muwan arrives from Ek Naab. We're deep in the forest by now; according to the satnav, several kilometres from the nearest road.

We watch through the pine canopy as two electrical bursts erupt from the Muwan Mark I: the ion volley in action, at last.

The helicopter doesn't wait for a third. It visibly falters, then stalls once and loses altitude. It turns and heads back towards San Cristobal. Those electrical bursts will have taken out most of their systems – I guess they're lucky to be alive.

Once the helicopter's out of the way, the Muwan finds a clearing in which to land. The pilot is none other than Rafa himself, who prepped the craft for my Crazy Benicio lesson. Rafa says nothing at all as we get Tyler into one of the passenger seats: a combination of sheer brute force, dragging him up the ladder and the odd moment of cajoling.

Then Rafa sends me back outside so that I can stow the motorcycle. Once I'm back inside the Muwan, he closes the cockpit and pulls away from the ground on a heading for Becan.

"You're in deep trouble, my friend."

"What's up . . . is it Benicio?"

"I'll get him later. He's OK, apart from a slight run-in with the police. Your motorbike clocked up quite a few suspicions; they traced it back to Benicio. He reported it as stolen, said the thieves shot him in the leg, so the cops are leaving him alone, for now."

"That was quick thinking."

"Sure was. But you, on the other hand, you managed to let the NRO capture a Muwan Mark II."

There's nothing I can say to that, so I turn to watch Ixchel looking at Tyler. He's pale now, looks barely conscious. From under my seat I take a bottle of water. Rafa points me to a packet of emergency supplies that he's tossed on to the floor of the Muwan. Passing two painkilling tablets to Ixchel, I tell her to help Tyler. He swallows them with difficulty.

As I stare at Tyler, his throwaway comment a little while ago returns to me:

Reckon any blue-blood can use the Bracelet?

I thought he was just being flippant. The possibility hadn't even occurred to me. But when I really think about it – the idea might actually stand up.

The truth is that I don't know how or why I can use the Bracelet. I always assumed it was because of being a Bakab Ix. Montoyo can't use the Bracelet of Itzamna, but I can. So can Blanco Vigores – another Bakab. So could Marius Martineau, who, like his son Simon Madison, carries the Ix gene.

But what about Bosch? What about Arcadio?

Tyler's been altered genetically by the Sect, just like me. Could it be that Tyler also has the gene that lets him use the Bracelet of Itzamna?

Back in the Garcias' house in the Lake District, I mentioned that anyone in the room had the knowledge to become Arcadio; I'd just written down the text of Arcadio's coded postcard messages to me. The two books that Arcadio liked to quote from were in the house: the books by Italo Calvino and Jorge Luis Borges.

And Arcadio's all-time favourite, Incidents of Travel in Central America, Chiapas and Yucatan by John Lloyd Stephens; that was in the house too.

Is it Tyler who will read those books?

Tyler is a leader, a man of action. I can see him having the drive to become Arcadio. To spend half a lifetime obsessed with the secrets of time travel. He has the blue eyes; he knows about the whole story of Arcadio and me and Susannah St John.

There are no photos of Arcadio – no portraits. He wouldn't let his image be recorded. And everyone that I know who has met him is deliberately vague. Almost as though they're trying to throw me off the trail.

Did Arcadio tell them never to describe him? Was he trying to hide his identity – in case I tried to change his past?

Rafa pulls me back into the world of trouble that's waiting for me in Ek Naab. "The NRO found the Muwan you left in that cavern in Tacana." He shakes his head, gravely. "I've never seen Chief Sky Mountain this angry. I wouldn't be surprised if he threw you into the cenote all by himself, Josh."

I could try to defend myself, to explain why we went to Chile, why we had to outrun the NRO, why I didn't make it back to Ek Naab.

But I don't, I can't. I'm distracted by one insistent thought.

Is Arcadio sitting in the back of this Muwan?

Chapter 35

Well, it's back to face the music in Ek Naab.

There's no doubt that Benicio was right in his prediction: my future as a Sky Guardian is on the line. Taking a Muwan without permission, without an assignment – that was bad enough.

Montoyo won't be surprised at what I've done – he knows me too well.

But losing a Muwan to the NRO is in a different league.

Just one ace left to play. Hopefully the vials of hip33 in my pocket will swing it. Ek Naab's Chief Scientist, Lorena, has a team that will be able to crack the secret of the Sect's plans for mind control.

It's not the same as using the 2012 plan to protect the planet from the superwave. But it's a start – a kind of hope. A tiny consolation in the empty void of terror that lurks somewhere ahead.

Perhaps for the first time, I have a real sense of what we're up against. The cosmos and the world's reliance on computer networks are going to do almost all their dirty work for the Sect of Huracan. Like the hurricane they're named for, that cataclysm will crack open the door. And then the Sect will blow it open with a world of chaos. Total disorganization as financial and communication networks grind to a halt. Every government in the world will be brought to the brink of collapse.

All the Sect need to do is to be the first organization to get the world back on its feet. They'll control the destiny of the whole planet. From what I've seen, they've spend decades planning for the collapse.

I've only seen the after-effects, but that's enough to give me night terrors. In fact, I don't know how I'll sleep again until I know Lorena has the antidote.

There are already thousands of secret members of the Sect, smug with the knowledge of their specialness, the fact that they've been selected to survive the apocalypse. I reckon they don't even think what they're doing is wrong. For a chance to rebuild the future according to their own plans, they're prepared to let pandemonium rule, to let billions die – wiped out by what they see as a natural disaster.

A better tomorrow for the best.

Or is it really a "natural" disaster? From what I've seen of the leaders of the Sect, Marius Martineau and Melissa DiCanio, they might even be capable of helping along a natural disaster. DiCanio's company, Chaldexx Biopharmaceuticals, would probably have access to genetically engineered biological weapons.

What if it is no accident that a plague is unleashed after the turmoil of 2012?

The thought of what might be waiting for us all, just months from now, puts ice in my veins. I'm determined, Montoyo is determined, the whole darn city of Ek Naab is determined. But against that, I can't forget that in Bosch's future and the only future I've seen, the Sect win; the galactic superwave hits the planet and the Sect take over.

What if there is no way to prevent what is coming?

I glance at Tyler. The white-gold of his bleached hair is edged with his own blood. He's dozing now, relaxed. Trusting us to get him to safety. Trusting people in Ek Naab to put things straight in this world. I get a pang of guilt about what I'm doing to Tyler. The way I see it, either he goes back to his grim post-2012 future, or I do. One way or another, the destiny of his reality and mine are intertwined.

Either Tyler is Arcadio, or I am.

The homing signals of Ek Naab register in the navigational readings. Rafa selects an automatic docking programme and steadies one hand on the steering controls, just in case we need any adjustments to the final descent. The hangar bay opens like a yawn in the woods. Rafa guides the craft inside. Just before we land we send a signal calling for an emergency-response medical team.

When the cockpit opens there's already a stretcher waiting, with two medics. Beside them is the stocky, muscular figure of Chief Sky Mountain, the mayor of Ek Naab. His tanned skin and a thick white plait give him an air of stark gravity. He's dressed in a plain white linen tunic-shirt and loose trousers and wears a calm expression, but his mouth is a tense, thin line.

Slightly frazzled, I clamber out of the cockpit and help the medics to get Tyler out.

"You again!" one of them exclaims to Tyler. I pause for a second and then realize that this medic treated Tyler after he was kidnapped in Brazil. He recognizes Tyler, even with the bleached hair.

But not this Tyler. In this Tyler's reality, Josh never went to Ek Naab, neither did Tyler.

One of the medical team inspects the wound dressings and prepares to whisk Tyler away for surgery. She doesn't bother to ask me what we've been doing risking our lives – again.

Ixchel gives me a hurried kiss goodbye and then goes with Tyler, something that the chief suggests rather forcibly.

Chief Sky Mountain stands by the entire time, patient and unmovable. When Tyler and Ixchel have gone, I turn to him very reluctantly.

"Sir . . . Chief . . . I've got good reasons for what I did," I begin.

"Is that so? Then you'd better come and address the ruling Executive. They're waiting for you. Some people think it's time you were stripped of your Bakab status."

I try to avoid his eyes, but the mayor of Ek Naab won't let go, holding me in an appraising stare. Can this mean what I think it means? I can't even speak. After everything I've been through trying to do my duty, trying to serve the 2012 plan, they're just going to throw me aside?

"Who thinks that?" I say, my voice cracking.

"Lizard Paw and Rodolfo Jaguar, your fellow Bakabs. And possibly Lorena, too. She's had trouble with you in the past, I believe, stealing tranquilliser darts from her labs."

"And you, Chief, what about you and Montoyo?"

The chief takes a step forward and puts his hand on my shoulder.

"You're the Bakab Ix, Josh, son of Andres, grandson of Aureliano. Your sixteenth birthday is weeks away. You could be Bakab soon, my boy. But there's no denying it – you have been and continue to be reckless. Allowing the NRO to capture a Muwan Mark II is, without a doubt, a most serious breach of our security."

I nod, white in the face, fighting to stay calm. "Right. And Montoyo? What does Carlos say?"

"He supports you, of course. He always does. And who among us knows you better than Montoyo? Montoyo is a man to whom I'd entrust my life." There's a lengthy, considered pause. "Which is why, Josh Garcia, you will also have my support. As the mayor, I carry the vote of Blanco Vigores, in his absence."

"That's three against three."

The chief grins. It's a rare sight. "Ah. But as mayor, the casting vote is mine. . ."

Montoyo backed me up.

I stand motionless, feeling a tingle in my fingers and along my arms, hairs rising at the back of my neck.

Even without knowing what really happened, Montoyo put his reputation with the rest of the ruling Executive on the line. He supported me.

The chief begins to move away. When he sees that I haven't budged, he halts. "What are you waiting for, Josh? We need to get to the Hall of Bakabs right away!"

"I need a moment," I mumble, unsteady.

Again, he smiles, this time more gently. The chief sets a broad palm on my shoulders and gives me an affectionate pat.

"Don't be nervous," he says. "Montoyo tells us wonderful things about you."

"Montoyo says good things?" I echo, stunned.

"He's protected you where possible, Josh. Even more since he became close to your mother. You won't find a stronger advocate in the city. Montoyo urges the ruling Executive to include you now, to heed your counsel."

Then I say something that I can hardly believe I'd ever admit. "But I'm . . . I'm still just a kid."

"You've had more experience in your young life than most people will get in a lifetime."

"Seriously?"

"Josh, I've always suspected that your role in the destiny of Ek Naab goes far beyond your being the Bakab Ix. Montoyo has kept us informed of your exploits."

"He . . . he has?"

Chief Sky Mountain chuckles dryly. "I doubt he's been comprehensive. Carlos is most definitely one for keeping secrets. But he's told us enough. About your messages from the time traveller Arcadio. About your own forays into time travel."

"Ixchel and I . . . we copied out part of the Ix Codex, with Itzamna. . ."

"Exactly. And now you return with your old friend Tyler, from England. Who – unless I'm very much mistaken – has grown into a man since he was last here."

I can't remain silent any longer.

"He's from the future. I . . . I know I wasn't meant to time travel again, but I did. Something had to be done, you know? So I went to 2014. And Chief . . . I've seen how everything turns out."

Chapter 36

A flicker of anxiety crosses the chief's face. "Montoyo was right; you couldn't resist the lure of time travel. May I ask how you got hold of the Bracelet of Itzamna?"

"It's a time-travel device," I say softly. "There can be more than one at any point in time."

"It seems we've got you back to Ek Naab just in time." He lifts a single finger. "For now, say nothing of this to the ruling Executive. I can't guarantee that they'll accept the voting if you add a further misdemeanour to your record."

Without another word, the chief turns away. He doesn't even bother to check that I'm following, but leads me out of the aircraft hangar, past the jumpsuited engineers and the stench of hot metal and oil, through the starkly furnished offices of the Sky Guardians and out into the city, opposite the black cenote of Ek Naab. We cross over to the pyramid that houses the Hall of Bakabs and enter through mahogany wood doors.

It's only the second time I've been invited inside. The last time, I was installed as the Bakab of Ix and introduced to the ruling Executive, the guardians of all secrets in Ek Naab. It's the place where I first learned the awful truth about 2012. The mere memory of that sends a shudder of cold apprehension into my bones. But this is no time to show weakness. I make an effort to walk tall; I catch up to the chief. By the time we enter the dining hall, we're side by side.

Three other members of the ruling Executive are already there, sitting at one end of the huge table. Lorena, the Chief Scientist, and the two other Bakabs of Cuauc and Muluc, Lizard Paw and Rodolfo Jaguar. When they see us, they stand. The chief nods and they sit. We join them at the table, which is laid with glasses, carafes of juice, water and wine, bowls of soft fruits, guavas, prickly pears, loquats and strawberries.

Everyone is dressed in their work clothes: Lorena in her white lab coat, me in the fresh Muwan Sky Guardian uniform I changed into before getting into the aircraft, the chief and the two Bakabs in variations of the pale-coloured linen clothing that is every-day wear for most people in Ek Naab.

Montoyo, brooding and impassive, breaks off his quiet conversation with Lorena as we enter the hall. It's plain to see that the meeting has been called in a hurry. From the expressions of the other three members I can tell they're anxious as well as expectant. Only Montoyo seems impassive.

Five members of the ruling Executive. Blanco Vigores, the fourth of the Bakabs, is missing.

The chief pours himself a glass of water and sips. He stares at each of us in turn.

"The NRO have acknowledged their capture of the Muwan Mark II. They're well aware of our anxiety for its return. They've indicated willingness to hand the aircraft back within twenty-four hours. Their price," he adds, pursing his lips, "is full cooperation with us with respect to the 2012 plan. Full access to the Ix Codex, the Revival Chambers and to the moon machine."

The other three don't react, except to swivel their eyes in my direction.

"OK," I begin. "It's my fault they have the aeroplane, I know that. And I'm really sorry! But surely one Muwan Mark II isn't worth all that?"

Lizard Paw says, dismissively, "If the NRO build a fleet of Muwan Mark IIs, it is simply a matter of time before they could conquer the city."

"But not before we've sorted out the 2012 problem, right?"

There's a collective gasp. "Before or after," says Lizard Paw, "it's no trivial matter for the secrets of Ek Naab to fall into foreign hands." He flashes me a disdainful glance. "If this reckless child hadn't been allowed to risk so much so often, he might have had the humility to keep out of matters that are beyond him."

"Yeah – I risk so much so often – usually my own life," I counter.

Montoyo cuts me off, raising one hand. "Josh's actions have secured the Ix Codex for the city. He has, as he says, risked his own blood and that of his friends to protect the Ix Codex. And on more than one occasion. Aside from our own Chief Sky Mountain, no one at this table can claim to have more 'skin in the game'."

Rodolfo Jaguar says, "The boy's courage isn't in question, my friends. His judgement is."

Lorena gazes at me with kindness in her eyes. "Josh. We know how dedicated you are. How determined. But you are still so young. I fear that we've exploited you. Allowed you to assume too much responsibility. I don't blame you for exceeding boundaries that were not clearly set."

"Huh. Sounds like you've been talking to my mother," I mutter.

"These are personal opinions that are being expressed here," says the chief. "But to the collective decision about whether or not to remove Josh Garcia's status as the Bakab of Ix, his right to be heard now and his right to succeed Carlos Montoyo on his sixteen birthday; my dear friends, please, speak now."

Montoyo says, "Josh remains as Bakab Ix."

Lizard Paw folds his arms. "We remove the Bakab status."

Rodolfo nods. "Remove."

Lorena reaches across the table and squeezes my hand. "Remove. To protect you, Josh, before your mother loses a son."

Chief Sky Mountain clears his throat. "I myself vote for the boy to remain as Bakab. As proxy to the absent Bakab of Kan, Blanco Vigores, I add another vote. Not only the right decision, in my mind, but assuredly how Blanco himself would have voted. We all know of our colleague's close interest in Josh and his keen approval of the boy's adventures. Since the voting is tied at three-three, I use my mayoral casting vote in favour of Josh."

"That's outrageous," breathes Lizard Paw, quiet with rage. "The vote is very obviously three-two to us."

"The regulations that govern our voting have been obeyed," Montoyo says.

"Now that the young man has the Executive's ear once more," says the chief, "may I suggest that we turn our attention to the other matter at hand? Do we accept the NRO's offer?"

Montoyo glances at each member of the Executive in turn. "I believe that the correct decision is to continue with our mission, to protect our secrecy. Thanks to Itzamna, Ek Naab alone has sufficient knowledge to enact the Erinsi's 2012 plan. We don't need the NRO."

"You're wrong," says Rodolfo Jaguar, his dark eyes flashing with anger. "And you know it, Carlos. We don't have all the information we need – we don't know the location of the moon machine. Most important of all – we don't have a member of the Erinsi.""

"Not strictly true," says Montoyo. "That location of the moon machine is buried somewhere in the Books of Itzamna. We simply have not yet succeeded in decoding it. As for the Erinsi – there are other Revival Chambers. We can rescue other survivors."

"After years of trying?" sneers Rodolfo Jaguar.

Lizard Paw says loftily, "The NRO claim to have information vital to our cause. We should cooperate."

Lorena snaps, "You're deluded! Have you learned nothing? The NRO captured Andres Garcia; they stole the wreckage of Aureliano's Muwan when it crashed. Have you forgotten how they imprisoned Josh's father until shortly before his death? And now they use the lives of a mother and an innocent child as tokens in some ridiculous game! You don't make bargains with people who behave like common gangsters."

Lizard Paw sighs, then glances at me, a cautious look in his eye. "On the one hand, obviously the NRO are not to be trusted. On the other, do we have a choice? Shouldn't we hear the NRO out at least, learn what they might know before we decline their offer?"

The chief mutters, "You know as well as the rest of us that there isn't time to negotiate. Their offer is clear. And our time is about to run out."

I glance from Lizard Paw to the chief. "Huh? Why? December twenty-second is six months away. There's loads of time."

But from the grim expressions of the ruling Executive I can tell something is wrong.

After a taut silence, the chief responds. "No. The moon machine is solar-powered. It requires at least six months of charging before enough power can be generated. In fact . . . if it isn't activated very soon . . . it's likely that the superwave won't be fully counteracted."

The chief holds his breath for a second or two, then releases it. "The Erinsi themselves hold the secret to how to activate it. We have a date, an absolute date by which the device must be activated. That time is seventy-two hours from now."

Chapter 37

I'm the first to burst in to the silence. "But . . . but why? Why do all that planning stuff and then leave it in the hands of some people who might not even survive?"

Lorena says, "The Erinsi didn't have any idea what the society would be like."

"How could they trust a society they didn't know?" Lizard Paw says.

Lorena agrees. "A technology that can counteract the galactic superwave could be lethal in the wrong hands."

And then the chief refers again to the secret that Montoyo told me in absolute confidence: "The five Revival Chambers were designed to keep a total of one hundred and five members of that civilization alive, in suspended animation. Only three Erinsi are needed to activate the moon machine. There are simply no written instructions beyond the ones that say three living Erinsi are needed. Without them, we can do precisely nothing."

I say, "So we do what Carlos said – we find three Erinsi survivors."

The chief nods. "With the cooperation of the NRO. We've been trying to find more Revival Chambers, as you may know. . . Our own chamber, here in Becan, was empty of Erinsi survivors. Those Erinsi were lost to us thousands of years ago."

"I know – Bosch did that. But to be fair – he didn't know what it was. Bosch didn't know about the 2012 plan back then."

"Itzamna – the original meddling time traveller," Lizard Paw says bitterly.

Ignoring the time-travel jibe, I say, "But there are other chambers!"

The chief shakes his head grimly. "We thought we'd achieved a breakthrough with locating the Revival Chamber in India. Unfortunately it's completely inaccessible. The entire area is rife with military training camps."

"What about the others in Iraq, Australia, China?"

"We found the Chinese chamber some time ago. Like the chamber in Mexico, it's been empty for centuries. As for the chamber in Iraq – it was discovered by United Nations weapons inspectors before the Iraq War. It has been controlled by the NRO for years. The US troops left Iraq at the end of last year. Anything that could be gained from that base, the NRO would have taken long ago."

"OK, so how about Australia?"

"We can't find the chamber," the chief says, shortly. "Either the location in the Ix Codex is incorrect . . . or the entrance has been moved."

"By the NRO?"

"Possibly."

"What about the Sect?"

"We saw no evidence of any human presence at the presumed location of the Australian chamber. It's in the middle of a desert."

"So in fact . . . we're missing the location of the moon machine, the precise location of the fifth chamber . . . and we don't even have one Erinsi survivor?" I stare around the table. "We're completely stuffed."

There's an uncomfortable silence.

"I mean – am I missing something?" I continue. "Because it looks pretty simple from where I'm standing. The NRO is our last hope."

It's obvious from his bristling body language that Carlos Montoyo is furious at the idea that we would hand over the secret technology of the Erinsi to the world's most powerful military nation.

"Would it really be so bad?" I say. "Look – no one here has a bigger grudge against the NRO than me. I can't forget what they did to my dad." Ixchel's words return to me. There's a lump my throat as I say, "But maybe I can forgive. Because when it comes down to fighting the Sect, aren't the NRO at least on the same side as us?"

"Our role is to maintain the status quo," says the chief. "The superwave is going to destroy the vast array of computer networks – the nervous system of the planet. But that is not caused by anyone on Earth. It is a freak of nature. All we are here to do is to prevent that one terrible incident. We don't take sides!"

"The NRO had access to the chamber in Iraq. They might have revived some Erinsi survivors."

"Possible but unlikely," Lorena says. "It takes a particular combination of Erinsi technology to activate the Revival Chamber."

"Yeah, I saw the Sect trying to do it. Took them months; they kept failing."

She continues, "To activate the Revival Chamber you need the Adaptor, which I suppose the NRO might have found. But you also need the Key peptide."

"We've got the Key . . . the Sect, they have the Key. Why wouldn't the NRO have it too?"

There's an uncomfortable silence. "Josh, it took us a long time to decode the inscription on the Adaptor," she says, "to realize that it was an amino acid sequence."

"The NRO aren't stupid."

"No. . ."

"And for all we know they've got an inside man in the Sect."

"Again, unlikely. . ."

222

"But not impossible," I insist. "The NRO might have the Key. They could have revived Erinsi survivors. Which means they could help us."

Lorena hesitates. "Most of this is conjecture. But it's theoretically possible, yes."

"I think what Josh is saying," Lizard Paw says smoothly, "is that for now, we ought to decide to begin negotiations with the NRO. Let them put their case. If they really can help, we let them."

"It is evident," says Rodolfo Jaguar, "that there's no other choice."

"You're wrong," Montoyo says, firmly. "There has to be another way."

I say, "Carlos, Chief, look, I know you guys are duty-bound to hold the line against the outside world and all that . . . but you have to listen to them."

"Rather ironic," Montoto says, sourly, "that after we preserve your right to be heard in this arena, you choose to go against us."

"Maybe that should convince you that I'm right. Listen . . . there's something I haven't told you yet."

There's an expectant silence.

"I've been to the future," I begin, but my voice goes up at the end as the nerves grab hold of me. "I've seen the future – after 2012! The superwave on its own is not going to destroy civilization."

The five members of the ruling Executive simply stare at me, gaping.

Montoyo says, "You time travelled again? But we strictly forbade that!"

"I went to the future, OK? It wasn't even our future, it was a parallel future. Maybe even Bosch's future, where the Sect of Huracan ruled the world. I saw how that all began!"

The shock continues to work its way through the gathered ruling Executive, apart from the chief, who merely shakes his head, staring at the table.

"Yeah," I continue. "It's going to be bad. But what really finishes the world is a plague. A bacteria or some biological weapon escapes when all the computer security is down. And the Sect! They have this mind-control drug. You need a special gene to be able to use it, and the Sect is made up of people who have the gene. They start testing for anyone who can use it and force them to join the Sect. Then they do some genetic-engineering thing, which makes the mind-control drug work really powerfully. I bet you anything it's the same thing the Sect did to me when they captured me in Switzerland!"

I notice Lorena watching closely. No-one interrupts me – they're rapt with curiosity.

"They take over almost immediately. Everyone has to listen to the Sect, to do what they say. That's their whole plan. The superwave just makes it possible for the Sect to act."

"You think," Montoyo says with obvious difficulty, "that your trip to the future should be used as a basis for our decision-making here. . .?"

"Why not? Isn't that what Bosch did? He was from the future. The Sect were in charge; he tried to change the past. . ."

". . .and very likely, he ended up causing the Sect of Huracan to come into being! They recruit from the descendants of exiled Bakabs of Ix, after all!" says Montoyo. "From Bosch's own blood!"

"Which explains how come I've got the gene," I insist. "I always assumed it was the Bakab gene. But it wasn't – that was just something which Bosch introduced to protect Bakabs from the bio-toxin in the Books of Itzamna. The gene I've got, the gene that lets me use the time-travel bracelet, the gene that all the members of the Sect have – it was in Bosch!"

"He's right," Lorena admits. "Josh is a direct male descendant of the Bakab Ix – who was a son of Bosch. Forgive me – I should have realised that myself." She gazes at me, intently. "Josh – this is important – do you have any idea what the gene does?"

224

I shake my head. "All I know is that in the future, the Sect call it 'jelf'"

"Typical lack of clarity from a gene's given name," she mutters. "But thank you – I'll do some research."

"But there's more - I got hold of the Sect's mind-control drug," I say, thrusting a hand into my pocket and fishing out a few plastic vials. I drop them on the table in front of Lorena. "You can analyse it, find out what it does, make an antidote. Then the Sect won't be any threat. Give the antidote to the NRO instead! Trust me, the whole world is going to need it."

Lorena picks up a vial, lifts it to the table light and examines it. She lowers her glasses and turns to me. Her expression turns to one of hope. "Or – even better – we could use it."

Lizard Paw asks, "Meaning what?"

Lorena smiles. "Maybe there's another way to deal with the NRO after all. . ."

Chapter 38

The chief asks tersely, "Lorena – how fast can you analyse this hip33?"

"A few hours, maybe less."

"And the antidote?"

She shrugs. "More difficult to say. Months, at least."

"Before December?"

"It won't be much use to us any later than that."

"Please, Lorena, don't be evasive. Before December, or not?"

She's silent, then: "I'll do everything in my power to achieve that, Chief."

I ask, "What did you mean about another way to deal with the NRO?"

Lorena replies, "From what you've told us, the Sect of Huracan relies on certain individuals to use this mind-control drug, correct?"

"They call them blue-bloods, because after the genetic engineering their eyes turn blue. The way mine did."

Lorena smiles humourlessly. "As I suspected. Now we know the aim of the Sect's genetic alterations to you, Josh. We may have an advantage; a shortcut to an antidote. When you were altered, I had your genome sequenced. The secret to how hip33 works is there, somewhere. Locked inside your DNA."

"Lorena's on to something," I tell the others. "Because I've used hip33. When I was time travelling in the Mayan past. Marius Martineau injected me with it. Made me have some weird mental power over this warrior who was trying to kill me. The guy wanted to slit my throat but he just couldn't. It was something to do with my voice."

Lizard Paw interjects, "What you're saying, yes, is that Josh can use hip33?"

"I could have told you that," I say.

Lizard Paw smirks. "Well then, colleagues, I suggest we send Josh as our emissary to deal with the NRO. But with the advantage of hip33."

Lorena's cheeks turn deep red. "Josh? An emissary? No . . . I really think that . . ."

"I'll do it," I interrupt. "Come on, it's me or Tyler, right? And he's in now shape right now. Anyway – I wouldn't let him. This isn't even his reality. Why should Tyler risk his neck for us?"

"You think they'll just hand over the Muwan Mark II, no further questions?" Rodolfo says, incredulous.

I nod. "If I'm using hip33, they just might. All right, Lorena, I'm up for it."

She sighs and shakes her head. "Dios mio, Josh. How am I going to face your mother?"

Montoyo chuckles. "Don't worry, Lorena. We'll face Eleanor together."

"We have agreement then, yes?" says the chief. "Lorena will analyse the hip33. We'll hear the NRO's offer. If it should come to a face-to-face meeting, Josh will be dispatched, dosed with hip33. And if Eleanor Garcia objects . . . well, Carlos and Lorena will find a way to persuade her."

One by one, the five members of the ruling Executive agree.

The chief gazes at me with a benign smile. "Well done, Josh. It appears your recklessness may have paid off – again. You've given us a third way."

For a couple of minutes I don't know what to say. I'm suddenly hyper-aware of the person who's missing from this gathering – the fourth Bakab, Blanco Vigores. What would he say if he were here? The people of Ek Naab seem to have given up on the idea of ever finding him. You hardly ever hear him mentioned. It's as though somehow, people are relieved.

Despite the chief's confidence, I have no idea what the inscrutable old man would have thought about all this. And neither, I suspect, does anyone else. Blanco Vigores is totally unpredictable.

In all his long years living in the city, no one ever seems to have gotten close to Blanco. His origins are an enigma. Montoyo once told me that in his memory, Blanco had always been an aged, bald man. His disappearances from the city have become so frequent that he's easily forgotten.

The ruling Executive disperses, exiting through the front door of the Hall of Bakabs. A small crowd of curious onlookers has begun to gather. Rodolfo Jaguar and Lizard Paw stop to talk to them, clearly basking in the attention.

The chief, however, seems irritated by the fuss. He takes a call on his mobile phone. Out of the corner of my eye, I notice him grab Montoyo by the arm and lead him away from the crowd.

I'm wondering what the two men are discussing when Benicio pushes his way through a cluster of students. He's limping, walking with an aluminium crutch propped under his shoulder. When we spot each other we both grin. I'm so relieved to see Benicio safe and sound that for a moment I forget the tension of the last hour.

Benicio claps an arm around my shoulder. "Hey, cuz! I just came from your buddy Tyler's hospital bed. That dude has grown!"

"Tyler's awake?"

"He's still under the anaesthetic. But he's going to be OK in a few hours. They gave him a little blood, stitched him up. Ehhh . . . a bullet graze to the collarbone. Painful! But he's gonna be OK."

"How about you?"

Benicio grimaces. "I was lucky – the bullet just missed an artery."

"Wow. What now?"

He frowns, ironically. "Well, looks like the end of the world again. . . "

"Maybe not."

"Oh, you're confident?"

"There's a lot going on. . ." I glance over my shoulder at Montoyo and the chief. They're deep into what looks like earnest discussion. "I don't know how much I'm allowed to say."

"So – what was it like? The future – was it bad?"

"It was pretty bad. And what I saw was just the tip of the iceberg."

"Man, I envy you. Time travel! You have to take me sometime."

I laugh. "Not likely. I'm done with it."

"What about your destiny and everything? What about Arcadio?"

"I'm not Arcadio."

"How can you be so sure?"

"Because. . ." My thoughts go to Tyler. "Look, don't ask me how it all works, this time travel stuff. I'm only a beginner, right? But I'm one hundred-percent sure of this; I won't time travel again. So Arcadio can't be me. I can't be him."

"Unless you change your mind someday. . ."

"Which I won't," I say, emphatic.

A lopsided smile appears on Benicio's face. "Dude. Maybe you're Arcadio. And maybe not. But while you've got that time-travel bracelet on your arm, the way I see it, anything's possible."

Then we both stop talking, because at the edge of the crowd we see Ixchel. She's alone. Benicio taps me lightly on the arm and waves at her. Then he hobbles away as I set off towards her. After a nervous few seconds, we step forward and hug each other. The moment my arms are around my girlfriend, I feel her relax.

"They said they were going to stop you being a Bakab."

"Yeah. But it turned out OK. Montoyo stood up for me, can you believe it?"

"Actually, yes. I think he really cares about you. But sometimes you're like – the button he has to press to get something done."

"I'm a button-man for Montoyo," I laugh. Then I pause. "I hope you're not mad that I stayed in the future without you."

"I'm very, very mad," she says, "so you'd better make a nice apology." Ixchel raises an eyebrow in suggestion.

I take her hand and lead her to a quiet spot behind some shrubs. Once we're shielded from the crowd, which is now dispersing, I give her a proper kiss.

But a moment later we're interrupted. Montoyo's hand lands squarely on my shoulder.

"Josh – control yourself! There'll be time for such things later."

When I look up, I see the chief and Montoyo. It's obvious that their patience is stretched.

"This is why you can't take fifteen-year-olds seriously," the chief says, and I'm only half-convinced that he's joking.

"OK, OK! I'm listening!"

"We've just received a communication from the NRO. They want two of their own Muwans to be led directly into the city."

"They must think we're idiots!" I say.

Montoyo shrugs. "Their offer is substantial. More than the return of our Muwan Mark II."

"They'd have to offer the moon on a stick for us to let them inside the city, though, right?"

"The 'moon on a stick' isn't too far from their offer."

"Seriously. . .they must be desperate!"

Montoyo gives a rare smile. "I'd say, Josh, that 'desperate' is precisely what they are."

The chief nods. "Aboard one of those Muwan will be Ninbanda – a survivor of the Erinsi civilization. The NRO took Ninbanda from the Revival Chamber in Iraq. Ninbanda knows how to operate the moon machine."

I gasp. "Whoa . . . so it's true! The NRO has one of the Erinsi. . ."

Chapter 39

A couple of hours later Ixchel and I are in the café outside the Central Library drinking chocolate milkshakes when my Ek Naab phone buzzes.

It's Lorena. "Josh, I'm holding the results. The lab has analysed the contents of those hip33 vials!"

"You've cracked the formula?"

"Where are you? You need to see this."

I put my phone back in my pocket. "Lorena's lab have analysed hip33. The thing that Martineau called hypnoticin. She wants us to get up to her lab right now."

We don't even stop to finish the milkshakes. Minutes later we're in Lorena's lab. She pushes open the door to her office and leads us inside.

"I wanted you to be the first to see this." Lorena holds out a computer printout. "This is straight off the protein sequencer."

SEQUENCE: HIP33

AGYLIHRPPREIKGR

For a moment I'm frozen, staring at the printout and feeling stupid.

Lorena is showing us the fifteen-letter amino acid sequence that gives the formula of the Crystal Key – a vital part of the Bracelet of Itzamna's time circuit.

The fifteen-letter inscription that is carved on to the Adaptor, which activates the Revival Chambers.

The same fifteen-letter sequence that Arcadio left encoded in antique copies of books by John Lloyd Stephens, in case he ever forgot how to make the Key.

Lorena told me the secret to the working of hip33 was buried inside my DNA. This is part of that secret – part of some mysterious biological circuit that allows me to influence weaker minds when hip33 is injected into my blood.

Just like Arcadio told me in his cryptic postcard message:

WHAT.KEY.HOLDS.BLOOD.

Then an idea grabs me, a dumb idea, maybe, but so obvious to an Internet addict like me. . .

"Lorena . . . can I use your computer?"

Before she can object I'm already jumping on to a chair, sliding up to the nearest computer keyboard and typing the fifteen-letter sequence into the address box of a web browser.

www.AGYLIHRPPREIKGR.com

A website appears, flame-coloured graphics and strange flashing symbols. There's a growling, mysterious audio track. Everything about the site is a warning.

"It's not possible. . ." I exhale.

Lorena stares at me in complete bewilderment. Ixchel's beside me in an instant. "What does this mean?" She can't tear her eyes from the screen.

"It means that what the Erinsi called the 'Key' . . . is exactly that! It's the key to everything."

Ixchel murmurs, "Ninhursag."

I turn to Ixchel, confused. "What did you say?"

Ixchel taps the screen gently. "Ninhursag. That's what is written there . . . those flashing symbols. It's Ancient Sumerian. One of the languages I've been studying. Of all written languages in known history, it is the closest relative of Erinsi script."

Lorena gasps, then nods and smiles. "Clever girl! You're absolutely right."

"It is, though, isn't it?" I say, wonderingly. "The writing looks just like that inscription on the other side of the Adaptor. . ."

"Indeed," Lorena says. "One side of the Adaptor has an inscription in your friend Bosch's own secret code using Mayan glyphs. But the other side is the original Erinsi. And yes, it looks a lot like Sumerian."

Before I can say anything else, Ixchel types "ninhursag" into an empty text box in the middle of the weird website.

The music stops and a new page appears.

It only takes a few seconds for it to sink in that we're looking at the secret documents of the Sect of Huracan. Protected by a fifteen-letter sequence that is known only to people who have the formula of hip33. By a password that's written in ancient Sumerian.

"You need the Adaptor to open the Revival Chambers," I say, breathless. "And the Adaptor needs the Key. I guess it opens some kind of biochemical lock mechanism."

Lorena says, "Hip33 has the same formula as the Key. . .!"

"Yeah. . ." I laugh. "Hip33 is the Key! Just like Arcadio tried to tell me in his postcard message: What Key Holds Blood."

"I wonder. . ." muses Ixchel. "Why 'Ninhursag'? She was an ancient Sumerian deity. A goddess."

The password-protected information on the website is organized into surveillance documents, details of Erinsi technology and some other sections that require further security clearance. We click swiftly through until we've found a page of technical drawings of three Revival Chambers.

The Erinsi chambers in Mexico, Iraq and Australia.

"The NRO control the chamber in Iraq. We control the one in Mexico, but it's empty. And the Sect found the one in Australia."

Ixchel asks, "Do you think they'd leave any Erinsi survivors alive? Wouldn't the Sect just kill them?"

"If they could get inside, probably. But what if they can't?"

Lorena asks, "Why shouldn't they be able to get inside?"

I grin. "Because . . . I nicked their Adaptor!"

"He did too," smiles Ixchel. "Right from under their noses."

"And without the Adaptor," Lorena says, "there's no way to open the Revival Chamber."

"The chief's guys didn't find the entrance. I bet that's because the Sect buried any sign of it."

"But now, thanks to quite astonishing ingenuity, Ixchel, my dear Josh, we have their maps. . ." Lorena seems delighted. "You really are such an asset to Ek Naab." Quite without warning she throws her arms around Ixchel. "I'm so proud of you! It seems no time at all since you were a little girl, wandering around the library!"

I stand very still, hoping I'm not about to get the same treatment. After a moment Lorena releases Ixchel, who's turned a bright shade of pink.

Lorena folds the computer printout with the hip33 sequence into a neat square. She drops it into the top pocket of her lab coat, a huge grin on her face.

"My dear young friends, this settles it, don't you think?"

"Settles what?"

"We must tell Carlos and the chief right away. I see absolutely no reason now why we should kowtow to the NRO. Even if they revived Cleopatra herself in those sarcophagi!"

Ixchel gasps. "If we can activate the fifth Revival Chamber, we can find our own Erinsi survivors . . . we won't need help from the NRO!"

I gulp down a huge breath. Loren's and Ixchel's enthusiasm is infectious, but I can't forget the absolute ruthlessness of the Sect. Yes – I stole their Adaptor from Simon Madison. They won't be able to get into the Australian chamber. But I wouldn't put it past the Sect to find another way to destroy any chance of reviving the Erinsi.

"Could be a long shot. But you're right. We have to try."

"I'll need to send medical aid," Lorena says. "To take care of any survivors you revive."

"I'll bet," I say. "Seventy thousand years in suspended animation must give you a terrible pain in the head."

But Ixchel's expression has turned suddenly pale. She stares past me, at the computer screen.

"Lorena . . . what's that?"

A message has popped up on the computer screen. YOUR IP ADDRESS IS BEING TRACED.

Lorena leans over the screen. An uneasy look enters her eyes. "Our computers can tell if someone is trying to trace an IP address. It means that going on to this website has triggered some kind of alarm. And now whoever owns that site is trying to locate the origin of your browser query. They're trying to find Ek Naab."

"Is there any chance that they can actually find the city from this?"

"Hopefully not," Lorena says. "That's why we install the IP tracing detection software."

"We've tripped a wire. . ." Ixchel says.

Lorena pulls the network connection out of the computer. "That'll put a stop to it."

I say nothing, try to bury the gnawing sensation of fear that's growing within.

The Sect know we're on to them. There's no time to spare.

Chapter 40

It's one thing to get permission to go to the fifth Revival Chamber. But Benicio was right; after what happened with the Muwan Mark II, there's no way that Chief Sky Mountain will allow me to pilot the Muwan.

"Let me fly Josh there," insists Benicio.

The chief stares pointedly at the brace on Benicio's leg. "You'll be confined to the cockpit. It's not safe." He's not happy about having his authority questioned.

"What, this old thing? Chief, you worry too much. If I need to get out super-fast, I'll eject!"

"Ixchel needs to come too," I insist. "I'm useless with those ancient inscriptions. If there's an inscription that means 'self-destruct', I'd be the one who presses it."

"You need a co-pilot," the chief mutters.

"But with Benicio, Lorena's medic, Ixchel and me, the Muwan is full!"

"All taken care of. I've requested Diego Ka'an," says Benicio. "He trained for the Sky Guardians before he became a medic. And there's always Josh."

The chief puts both hands on his hips, surveying his domain: the Muwan hangar bay. "I see. You seem to have this operation all planned."

"That's right," Benicio agrees, cheerily. "Josh, Ixchel, Diego, me. The crack team that's going to bring us back the last of the Erinsi."

Diego arrives, Lorena's Head of Surgery, a guy in his late thirties who I often seen training in the gym. He's wearing a heavy-looking backpack. From the tips of his fingers, Diego hands me a transparent zip-top bag. Inside I see the outline of the Adaptor.

We're really doing this: I'm going to activate the fifth chamber.

Diego relaxes when I accept the bag containing the Adaptor. He's relieved to be rid of it – the Adaptor is Erinsi technology that has the highest level of protection: one of the deadly bio-toxins. A single touch will release a poisonous gas that will asphyxiate anyone in a three-metre radius.

Anyone without the proper genetic protection, that is. I always assumed it was the Bakab gene. But now that I look at the Adaptor again, for the first time in over a year, I wonder. Tyler's words return to me.

Can any blue-blood use the Bracelet?

There's more to the Erinsi genetics than I'd imagined. And the Sect of Huracan seem to have worked that out, quite a while ago. They're way ahead of Lorena and her team. The Sect are recreating Erinsi abilities in their members. They've realized that those abilities are the key to using ancient technology.

We climb aboard. The Muwan hangar bay doors open. Benicio swoops the craft up high – so high that for a moment I wonder if he's going to try the Stratosphere Dive. But it's clear he's going even higher. Watching the pressure levels drop, Diego opens a panel under the co-pilot seat and removes three helmets with oxygen supplies.

"It's OK," Benicio breathes. "We're only going to be up here for a minute or two. Plot me a course to that Australian chamber, OK, Diego? I've downloaded the maps into the on-board computer."

Ixchel stares in wonder through the glass. "You can see the curve of the Earth. . ."

I want to look too but all my attention is taken up peering at the holographic projection of the maps of the Revival Chamber's location. It's in Western Australia, close to the mouth of an estuary. I watch Diego programme some landing coordinates, then take a closer look at the map. An entrance is clearly marked. But there's another tunnel that leads from the underground chamber. Has the Sect constructed a new entrance?

Turning, I find Ixchel looking at me in silence. She intertwines her fingers with mine. We don't say anything. Benicio is mumbling to himself, anxious. The tension needs to be broken so I plug in my iPod and select American Idiot by Green Day. Within seconds we're feeling better, buoyed along by positive energy. We listen to the whole album twice, and then just for luck, the International Superhits! album. I only switch to something different when Diego finally starts to complain.

At this height the land below looks like a gigantic, curvy atlas. The blue of the Pacific Ocean extends as far as the eye can see. After a couple more hours scattered islands come into view, dotting the blue to the south. Another hour passes before the eastern coast of Australia stretches far below, gradually disappears behind us as the country opens below, desert, unending desert in every direction until it fills every corner of the view beneath us like some impossible vision. Over the next two hours, lakes appear now and again, glittering in the red dust, sometimes white, sometimes pink.

Ixchel and I are dozing against each other, half asleep, when the holographic viewer springs into life; the route lights up, leading the Muwan to the location of the Revival Chamber. There are no landmarks, nothing.

In the middle of nowhere.

Benicio lands the craft and opens the cockpit. A blast of heat smacks down on us, hotter than anything I've ever felt. The exterior temperature gauge on the control panel reads 49 degrees Celsius.

"You couldn't have found some shade?" I mutter. Benicio shrugs. He's right – no sign of shade whatsoever.

We grab some sunglasses, remove our jackets and climb out of the Muwan. The sky is vast, deep blue with wisps of cloud like shreds of cotton wool thrown at random. The land burns red, like fired mud or the planet Mars.

There's no sign of anything or anyone, not even a road. Benicio stretches out an arm, holds his phone for a signal, following the image of the map. I cross-reference with a satnav programme on my own phone. The four of us begin to walk, shoes crunching on crusts of soil that hasn't been walked over for tens of thousands of years – if at all.

We easily find the original entrance to the chamber – an opening, about two metres high, in a rocky mound, as if leading to a cave. There's a door, metallic, rusted. It swings open at one push.

"This door isn't thousands of years old. . ." Benicio says.

"It's the fake door."

"I suspect whoever built it has long gone," Ixchel says.

Now we orient ourselves with the new map data; looking for the second, secret entrance. Did the Sect build the fake entrance? Or did they discover it? The metal door doesn't look all that old, just a bit weathered. Did someone else get there before the Sect?

So much time has passed since the Erinsi built these chambers. Millennia. How could they hope to keep a plan going for so long? Were the survivors of each chamber meant to take care of the others, so that eventually one group would last long enough? How much damage did Bosch do when he revived all the survivors of the Mexico chamber?

The sun blazes with implacable heat. The skin of my face and arms sizzle; the itchy beginnings of sunburn. We're searching a red desert for the hidden entrance to something that's been lost for an unthinkable period of time.

We continue, tracking the map until we arrive at an opening in the ground, barely wide enough for a person to enter. Benicio takes a torch from his tool belt and shines it inside.

"We're going to need rope."

I say, "How deep?"

"No idea," Benicio says. Sweat rolls into his eyes. He wipes his forehead with the back of his hand. With the toe of his boot he scores a line in the dust, near the opening. "See all the scuffs, the markings? Rope. Someone's been here. Not too long ago, either."

Diego steps forward. He's clearly come properly equipped. Diego whacks climbing posts into the rock and runs thin rope through the narrow pins. He ties the rope around his waist and hitches a couple of tidy knots. He hands me his medical backpack and one end of the rope while I watch him, conscious yet again of my inexperience. Every time I think I know what I'm doing, a guy like Diego or Benicio comes along to show me how much I still have to learn. It's kind of irritating.

We stand around the hole, casting short shadows in the unrelenting sunlight. As Diego disappears into the darkness, I clutch the Adaptor inside its protective plastic. One way or another, I'm going to have to go inside. Do what only I can do and use the Erinsi technology to activate the ancient Revival Chamber. And finally meet one of these ancient survivors of the Erinsi civilization.

The People of Memory.

Chapter 41

We wait. The only sounds are the steady scrapes of the rope on the edge of the gap, the occasional caw of birds. Very high overhead, two aeroplanes cruise by and their vapour trails cross. My eyes meet Ixchel's. I have to go down there, I know. Not her, not Benicio, just me.

Then Diego's voice calls. "Now, Josh, Ixchel."

We enter the hole and I grip the thin rope, steadying my feet against the rock. The descent is short, no more than five metres. Then I'm on solid ground. Diego is there, with a torch. He flashes it down a tunnel that leads north. Ixchel follows, her hand gripping my jacket.

Diego says, "It's down here. Do you know what to do?"

"Did you bring the Crystal Key?"

Diego takes a plastic tube from his pocket. He unscrews the blue lid and removes a wad of polystyrene. Underneath is a small crystal, no bigger than a tiny necklace bead.

"You put this into the Adaptor, and the Adaptor into the Container in the chamber."

"Like it says in the Ix Codex," I murmur, remembering the few pages that I managed to decipher all by myself.

"Let me check first," Ixchel says. "Just give me a few moments to read the inscriptions."

Diego hands Ixchel the torch and she pushes ahead, down the tunnel, into the chamber. After a second her body blocks out the light of the torch.

"I've seen it done," Diego tells me, "but naturally, I can't touch the Adaptor myself."

"You've seen it done?"

"Sure. The Revival Chamber in Mexico. It's empty, as you know."

Staring I ask, "But who . . . who opened it?"

"We're not supposed to discuss that."

"Come on, Diego, I'm practically on the ruling Executive. I'm supposed to know! Who opened the chamber?"

With some reluctance Diego replies, "Blanco Vigores."

"Did you say Blanco Vigores?" I say. I can't believe my ears.

"Yes."

"How do you know?"

"He sent for me once. He became ill . . . I can't really share medical details, Josh. I'm a doctor."

"I'm sorry." In the darkness, I blink rapidly. "This might sound like a stupid question but . . . are you sure Blanco actually used the chamber?"

"My guess would be that he did."

"On himself?"

In the shadows, I see Diego's shoulders bob up and down. "I can only assume."

"Is that even possible?"

"Without seeing the chamber in functioning mode, I can't answer that."

"Does the ruling Executive knows about this?"

"They do."

"Blanco has been . . . hibernating?"

"So it seems."

I think for a moment. "No wonder the ruling Executive have stopped asking questions about Blanco Vigores. Do they also know where he went?"

"All I know is what I just told you: Blanco Vigores used the chamber, at least once. Not long before he disappeared. And the Ruling Executive recently became aware of this."

Benicio's voice interrupts us as it travels down the pitch black tunnel. "Come on, you guys. What's holding you up?"

Ixchel calls back, "Just another minute . . . I'm trying to understand the syntax here. It's a bit complicated and I don't want to make a mistake."

I whisper, "No pressure, Ixchel. But . . . the Sect know we hacked their website. It can't be long before they come looking for us."

She turns around and shines the torch beam in my face the whole way back.

"OK. Here's what you do. Crystal Key goes into the Adaptor, and the Adaptor into the Container in the chamber, just like Diego said. You wait."

"How long?"

"It didn't say. The inscriptions say something like: Modify the Adaptor, insert into Container. Wait. Stand by with Fire Air."

"Fire Air?"

"Oxygen," Diego says. "I have a supply in the medical pack."

"To help resuscitate?"

"Exactly."

"OK."

Ixchel pushes past me in the tunnel. "OK, Josh. Your turn."

Trailing fingers along the rock wall, I follow Diego along the narrow tunnel. Why a second entrance? Who made it? It's not the original entrance, according to the Ix Codex. The Sect must have dug it themselves and blocked off the original entrance, once they realised other people knew about the chambers. Luckily though, we hacked into the Sect's secret website . . .

What if it's a trap? Without the Adaptor, there is no way that the Sect could have opened the chamber.

But I know the Sect well enough to know that they wouldn't give up so easily. As far as they're concerned, the world after 2012 is theirs for the taking.

My pace slows; my pulse quickens. What have the Sect left down here for us?

Diego comes to a stop before an entrance. He raises the torch, throwing a white glare around the chamber. Holding my breath, I take two steps forward and enter, for the second time in my life, that deepest secret of humanity's existence on the planet. The Erinsi. Holders of an ancient secret; the cycle of cataclysm that will be visited upon civilization.

I can't stop thinking about the words of those skeletal spectres from Mexico's Day of the Dead:

Como me ves, te veras. As you see me, so you will see yourself.

Our torches circle the octagonal chamber, identical in every aspect to the one Ixchel and I discovered under the Depths near Becan. Seven walls, each containing three sarcophagi carved from the same smooth-alabaster-like material as the Adaptor. A central altar, waist high. And everywhere, inscriptions; inscriptions that flow into each another, networks in a precise pattern.

The altar, too, is octagonal, inlaid with twenty-one stone tablets, each covered with similar markings as the lids of the sarcophagi. In the middle of the altar is a small depression.

Diego points. "OK Josh, this is where Ixchel and I have to stop. It's not safe to get any closer without the protective gene – or a gas mask. That's the Container. You place the Adaptor in there."

He hands me his torch. "Ixchel and I are going to hang back now, Josh. Don't touch the altar, especially the Container, until you hear my voice. OK? We need to be at least five metres away to be out of range from the bio-toxin."

He disappears back into the tunnel until there's only a brilliant point of light in the thick black.

"Make sure Ixchel's safe too," I call after them.

Diego hisses, "Obviously! OK. Now, Josh."

I open up the plastic bag and remove the Adaptor. My hands tremble very slightly as I fit the tiny Crystal Key into the small depression at the end of the Adaptor. Carefully, I turn the Adaptor around, until the intricate pattern of markings is facing me. Then I insert it into the Container.

For a minute, nothing happens. The minute stretches. Like the inscription said: Wait.

The next moments are reduced to a jumble in my mind. It begins with a faint pinkish iridescence from the inscriptions. The writing becomes projected into the air. The torch in the tunnel goes off; there's nothing but the pale light of those glowing inscriptions.

A small sphere of terrifying brightness rises from the central altar. I can't look directly at it. It floats about one metre above the altar and then begins to rotate, picking up speed with every rotation, until minute pulses of energy seem to be torn from its surface, rippling out like tiny solar flares. As the sphere spins ever faster, these flares of energy grew longer, until they're in danger of reaching me.

Instinctively, I drop to my knees, watching as above me, eventually, the tongues of light reach the sarcophagi. The caskets fill with a hazy, gaseous substance, a suspension of particles. The doors begin to slide open. Flares of energy continue to flow from the central sphere, which contracts, slows and finally disappeared into a tiny point of light, just above the Adaptor.

The air immediately around me crackles with static and a smell like hot, thick sheets of cotton flapping, dry as old bones. I taste salt on my lips. Awestruck, I touch a finger to my cheek, feeling a tear. The ancient rite of revival from which a great civilisation is reborn!

I'm dizzy, unable to speak. Shadows penetrate deep into the open sarcophagi. I'm afraid to use the torch to confirm what I already suspect. With a trembling hand, I lift the torch and point it directly ahead.

All twenty-one sarcophagi are empty.

Someone must have already woken them up! Did the Sect revive them, then slaughter the survivors? A million hopes seem to be dying inside me. Millennia of planning, all that energy expended to save civilization. All vanished to nothing.

The impossible waste.

Even the NRO can't help us now. The 2012 plan needed three Erinsi survivors to activate the moon machine. The NRO only has one.

Diego and Ixchel are as dazed as I am. A crushing discovery. We feel the weight of it all the way back to the surface.

When we climb out, Benicio is nowhere to be seen.

I'm still trying to orient myself when in the distance I spot the gleaming metal of the Muwans. Two birds, silver against the red rock and indigo sky.

Two.

I shade my eyes to look more closely. People are clustered around the aircraft. One of the Muwans is a Mark II. The second is a Mark I.

My throat constricts as I realize what this means.

The NRO are here.

Chapter 42

At first I walk; then I break into a run. When I reach Benicio and the visitors I'm way ahead of Diego and Ixchel. Ixchel catches up next. Instinctively, I grip her hand. Whatever is going on now, I want Ixchel close.

The second craft has delivered a man in who looks about thirtyish, close-cropped black hair with a high, suntanned forehead, his eyes hidden behind mirrored aviator sunglasses. He wears a khaki green flight jumpsuit covered with US Air Force insignia, his rank marked by two silver bars on his shoulder. The top buttons are open and I can just see a flash of red and blue on his chest – a tattoo of the American flag. He stares at me impassively. He has a sidearm prominently tucked into a shoulder holster, another smaller pistol at his waist.

With the Air Force guy is a very elderly woman with long silver hair that's pulled away from her round face in a simple ponytail; dark, narrow brown eyes; and skin that's pale, paper-thin. She wears a flowing blue cotton blouse and loose red trousers, sandaled feet poking from underneath.

There seems to be a twinkle in her eye as she gazes at me. Or maybe it's a trick of the light.

I face them, sweltering in the unearthly heat. Diego lines up beside Benicio. Eyes gravitate anxiously towards the new arrival's guns. There's no time, no option for any of the Ek Naab team to produce a weapon. We're at this guy's mercy.

"And so. This is the boy," says the woman, peering at me. Her voice is surprisingly youthful. I'd half-expected a witch-like cackle from someone so old. She speaks with a very strong foreign accent, not quite like anything I've heard before.

The pilot folds his arms across his broad chest. "Yup. This is Josh Garcia."

Ixchel's fingers tighten around mine. I address the pilot. "Do I know you?"

He sticks out his right hand. "No, son, you don't. I'm Captain Connor Bennett."

The name sounds somehow familiar, but I can't place it at all. My gaze goes to his shoulder, the military insignia. "Are you part of the National Reconnaissance Office, too?"

"That's right, son."

"You're one of the blokes who captured my father?"

He hesitates. "No. By the time I was put on this programme, your father had gone."

He doesn't say "disappeared into thin air".

I stall, biding my time, wondering if this guy knows about the Bracelet of Itzamna, that my father used it to escape from an underground prison. I glance back at the aged woman. Everyone in the gathered group is staring at her, except the captain, who can't seem to tear his eyes away from me. We're staring at her as it dawns on us all just who she must be.

With a dry mouth I whisper, "Are you. . .?"

She begins to smile. "Am I. . .?"

"One of the Erinsi? Are you Ninbanda?"

Her smile broadens. She has white teeth, amazingly well preserved. "I am the last of the Erinsi."

Beside me, I sense Ixchel flinch. "Wow," I breathe, staring. "Just . . . wow."

"Why," I manage to say, "are you here?"

"We had to find a way to meet you. We knew you'd come here eventually. You'd have to, right? To see it for yourself – the empty chamber. 'Happy are those who believe without seeing'," chuckles the captain. "But that's OK. I'd want proof too."

Now I'm exasperated. "What are you talking about?"

"The Erinsi," the captain states, emphatically. "They're all gone. Gone. Ninbanda is the last. So listen to her."

"If the Erinsi are gone, then it's over, isn't it? Because we need three."

Ninbanda smiles gently. "We do. But I believe that you, child, may have what it takes."

"Me?"

"You activated the Revival Chamber, isn't this true?"

"I guess. . ."

"Then you can help. My role will be to instruct."

I blink. "But . . . three?"

"There is another. Captain Connor Bennett."

The officer smiles and nods.

"Him?"

"Our genes are widespread now, Josh. It was planned thus. Survivors, revived every few thousand years by their own descendants, were sent into the world to reproduce. One hundred and five individuals extending the continuity of our civilization over countless millennia. Casting wide our genes. Waiting for the return of the superwave."

Captain Connor Bennett grins broadly. "You and me, kid, we're descendants. We're gonna save the world."

"The Sect," I say, stumbling over my words. "Are they . . . descendants? Do they have the gene too?"

"The way I understand it," the captain says, "their entire existence is based on it."

"The ones you know as the Sect of Huracan are descendants of the Erinsi," says Ninbanda, pronouncing the words carefully. "But they don't wish to share our dream of life, the development of humanity, of continuity. They dream instead of cataclysm, of death. And the rebirth of an elite. Yet they saw to disrupt our plans. That is our tragedy, Josh; our own children sought our destruction."

A better tomorrow for the best.

I bite my lip, force myself to remain silent about what I've seen of the future, resist the impulse to touch a finger to the Bracelet of Itzamna under my sleeve. Ixchel feels the same tension, I know.

Neither the captain nor the Erinsi survivor has mentioned the time-travel device. Maybe they don't know?

"Will you help us, Josh?" says the old woman, with a kind, hopeful smile. "I've waited so long. But without your help, there can be no solution."

"So what do you say, buddy? Are you going to share the final secret? You Ek Naab guys have always had the most important piece of the solution."

"What important piece?"

The captain guffaws. "The location, of course. The location of the moon machine."

Ninbanda murmurs, "As was written in our Temple of Inscriptions."

Ixchel is silent, but I feel her entire body tense up. I stare back at the old woman. "If it was written on those walls in the Temple of Inscriptions, then it must be in one of the Books of Itzamna."

There's a faint but unmistakable panic beginning inside me. The NRO guy and this Erinsi woman are so sure that the location is somewhere in those inscriptions. But people in Ek Naab have been trying to find that information for years.

What if somehow, that part of the inscription wasn't copied?

What if the location of the moon machine is lost for ever?

Captain Connor Bennett is suddenly still, rigid and alert, disturbed by something. Then I hear it too. An aeroplane. But not high and distant, like the commercial aeroplanes that leave their trails across the blue.

This one is low, approaching fast.

The captain shoots a steely glance at Benicio, then me. His voice is harsh and abrupt. "Did you send someone else?"

"That is not a Muwan," Benicio says, quietly. We all follow his gaze. Now we see it, a small aeroplane, a propeller-driven jet. It descends even lower. Heading directly for us.

The captain throws a protective arm around the old woman. She's bewildered. For a second I sense how fragile she is. Frail, aged and vulnerable. And with her, all of civilization.

Captain Bennett asks sharply, "Is there any way that the Sect could know you're here?"

I stare, dumbstruck for a second. "We . . . we accessed their website when we were in Ek Naab."

Ixchel adds grimly, "They were trying to do an IP trace. But that couldn't lead them here . . . could it?"

The aeroplane is less than five hundred metres away, dropping by the second. The captain explodes with fury. "That website is a trap! The Sect use it to track people who know their secrets. If you were on that site then it's gonna be pretty obvious to the Sect that you'd come here next." He reaches for his sidearm and yells at Benicio, "Get your people in the birds. Get out, asap. Stay in radio contact. We're going to have to rendezvous somewhere else."

I grip Ixchel's hand even harder. We head for the parked Muwan.

The sky erupts with explosions.

Bullets rain down from above, spattering the cracked red earth, throwing up clouds of hot dust. Someone in the aeroplane has a machine gun trained on the ground – firing directly at us. Random death, ready to rip us apart at any second.

I don't let go of Ixchel's hand, but we sprint faster, heads down. The terror is unreal. I lose my sense of where any part of me is; all I know is the speed and the zing of the bullets. I hear Ixchel breathing hard beside me, no energy wasted on words. Fifty metres to cover under a cloudburst of deadly gunfire.

At the edge of my vision, the very edge, I catch glimpses of the others racing forward, Diego slightly ahead. Benicio is slower, limping, dragging his wounded leg. The captain and the Erinsi woman lag even further behind, I guess – I don't see them.

A riot of gunfire. From close behind me there's a dull crack, a moan, a cry of anguish. The aeroplane swoops over us with a high-pitched metallic drone. I'm suddenly rooted to the spot, hearing the sobbing from behind me. The old woman crying, "No . . . Connor. Please, no."

Benicio passes me with thunder in his eyes, pressing ahead to the Muwan. Ixchel and I glance at each other in despair. The aeroplane is turning around. Any second now it'll be back for another pass.

Captain Connor Bennett lies on the ground, one hand outstretched, clenched into a fist. His foot shakes for a second; his lower body trembles. But he doesn't make a sound.

In a hollow voice Ixchel says, "They'll kill us all."

Diego appears beside us. He grabs my arm just above the Bracelet of Itzamna, pushes me angrily. "Get into the Muwan. Take the woman. Get to Ek Naab, no matter what. That's an order, pilot!" Dazed, I stare at Diego for a second, then see Benicio climbing into the Muwan. Ixchel tugs at the old woman. "Please," she says. "Hurry."

Diego insists, "I'll look after the captain. Protect the Erinsi woman. Go, Josh!"

Tears are streaming down Ninbanda's face, her eyes creased with sorrow. In the sky, the aeroplane approaches. I hold her hand tightly.

"Not Connor," she mumbles. "No . . . I couldn't bear to lose him, too. . ."

"Ninbanda, we have to run!"

We stumble the final few metres to the Muwan. I climb in first, hauling Ninbanda in after me. Benicio lowers the cockpit cover as the aeroplane passes above, throwing down a screaming hail of bullets. Pockmarks pepper the windows, but the glass holds. Ixchel is trapped below, sheltering under the body of the craft. We hear the aeroplane turn again. As I scrabble for the co-pilot headgear, I spot Diego dragging the wounded captain out from under their Muwan.

Brave guys. Captain Bennett must still be alive.

Benicio opens the cockpit and I pull Ixchel into the Muwan just as bullets spatter against the body of the craft. Ixchel tenses abruptly, her face screwed up with pain. When she's inside I notice that Ixchel's blood is smeared all over the edge of the window.

"Ixchel!"

From the passenger seats she says shakily, "I think . . . think I'm OK."

"You're bleeding!"

Ixchel looks up, trembling.

Ninbanda takes a closer look at her ankle. "That's a very unpleasant graze. The bullet must have caught you on a ricochet. It stings, I'm certain of it."

"Good to know you're alive," Benicio tells me, curtly. It sounds as though he's a bit angry with me for getting him – and Ixchel – into another scrape. I watch his eyes when he looks at Ixchel. He's pretty shaken, as much as I am. "I'm going to get us out of here. Strap yourselves in."

The Muwan begins to lift. Ixchel's injury seems to have focused Ninbanda, who asks me for a first aid kit. Panting slightly, Ixchel shows her where there's one in the back. Benicio takes the Muwan up very suddenly, so swiftly that we're pressed tightly into our seats. Within seconds we're out of danger. But the other Muwan is still on the ground.

"We can't just leave them. . ." I begin.

Benicio cuts me off. "You know, maybe the Sky Guardians is not the career for you. You seem to have a problem with orders."

Red earth opens up beneath us, extending in every direction. The Muwan is a silver spot on the ground. Benicio changes course and we soar into the heavens. Straight for the deepest blue.

Chapter 43

Over the radio, Benicio exchanges some urgent words in Yucatec.

"The ruling Executive want you back right away, Josh. And the Erinsi woman."

I fumble for an earphone and plug it into my ear. "Let me talk to them. . ."

Benicio flips a switch and I hear the chief.

"Josh, is it true – do you have one of the Erinsi with you?"

"She's the last of them! The chamber was empty!"

An air of finality enters his voice. "We're finished."

"No – the Erinsi says that she can tell two others what to do. But they need to have the Erinsi gene."

"What?"

"The gene that the Sect call 'jelf'. It allows only Erinsi to interact with their technology. Protects them from the bio-defence, or allows them to activate things. Like me with the. . ." I stumble, stop just in time to avoid saying "the Bracelet of Itzamna". "Like me with the Adaptor. I can touch it, Simon Madison can touch it. Other people die."

"That's what it's all about? Using Erinsi technology?"

I can hardly get the words out fast enough. "The Sect of Huracan select people who have the Erinsi genes. That's why they think they should rule. That's why they want 'a better tomorrow for the best'!"

"How does this Erinsi gene make them 'best'?"

I think for a moment, putting the pieces of information together. "It must be because of hip33. The mind-control drug gives them powers over ordinary people – everyone else! That must be left-over Erinsi technology, too. And the Sect worked it all out. They found the drug, learned how to use it. The reverse-engineered the Erinsi technology. Just like Bosch did, with the time-jump device."

The chief goes silent for a moment. I guess he's conferring with the rest of the ruling Executive. Then Montoyo comes on to the line. "Josh – are you saying that you can substitute for one of the three Erinsi?"

"Yes."

"That still leaves us short of one."

"I've been thinking about that. . ." I breathe. "The NRO captain who brought the Erinsi, he has the Erinsi gene too. They wanted to use him, me and the Erinsi lady. But the NRO guy has been shot. I'm not sure he's going to make it. So. . ."

"Yes. . .?"

"I reckon we use Tyler," I say triumphantly.

"Tyler?"

"The Tyler I brought back with me," I say, dropping my voice to a conspiratorial whisper. I really can't let the Erinsi woman find out that I've been travelling in time. She'd probably try to take the Bracelet away from me – after all, it is Erinsi technology, and not something that the Erinsi had planned to release into the world. "You know . . . that Tyler? In his timeline Tyler was chosen by the Sect. Which means he must have the Erinsi gene too."

Ixchel and Benicio are staring at me now, mystified. I put a finger to my lips, praying that they'll get the hint not to mention the Bracelet of Itzamna.

"Tyler?" repeats the chief. "No. The boy is in no condition to withstand a trip to the moon."

"What? Even if he agrees?"

But the chief seems to ignore my question. "Has the Erinsi woman told you how you're getting there?"

257

My heart sinks. The location of the moon machine is the Erinsi's final riddle – and it looks like no one has the answer.

I look back at the Erinsi woman. She's helping Ixchel to bandage her wounded foot.

"Ninbanda?" She looks up. "Ninbanda . . . how are we going to get to the moon?"

For a few seconds the fragile old woman seems puzzled at my question. Finally realization seems to dawn on her.

"Ah . . . you mean to activate the moon machine?"

"Right," I say, nodding.

"My dear child," she says, and there's almost disappointment in her voice. "What made you think that the activator is on the moon?"

"It isn't?"

"The Erinsi did not achieve manned travel to the moon. The moon machine is activated by a laser – which is located on Earth."

"So you do know where it is?"

Now she sounds irritated. "Listen to my words, child. I know only that the activator simply cannot be on the moon."

The Erinsi woman remains tight-lipped on our journey back. Everything I say on the subject results in nothing more than an enigmatic silence. I can only hope that Ninbanda will be more talkative in front of the Ruling Executive.

Ixchel and I communicate through wordless gazes and the touch of our fingers between the seats. It's not easy to keep my mind from the gaping void of our possible failure.

Was it all for nothing? The whole elegant plan ruined by Bosch and his dumb meddling with technology he didn't understand?

When hours later we land in Ek Naab, a medical crew is already there, ready to receive the second Muwan carrying the injured captain. They've radioed that they finally managed to get into the Muwan without anyone else being injured, with one of the pilots giving cover by shooting at the Sect's aeroplane. Sounds as though the Sect didn't stick around too long once their target started fighting back. With a little help from Benicio and me, Ixchel staggers out and immediately sits down on the floor of the hangar, rubbing her bandaged ankle. Benicio heads off towards the medical crew, to brief them about the captain.

Chief Sky Mountain and other members of the ruling Executive – Lorena, Lizard Paw, Rodolfo Jaguar and Montoyo – arrive. Tyler is at the chief's side, his arm in a sling. Ninbanda takes my hand, steps out of the Muwan and climbs down a staircase that's brought up against the aircraft. I stand at the top of the staircase and watch the chief welcome her to the city.

"Our honoured guest. We've guarded your secrets for over a thousand years. All we need now is the location of the moon machine. And your guidance to activate it."

"My guidance, you'll have. But the location was given to you. As it is written in the ancient inscriptions, the location is the key. I know it not."

Realization takes hold over the next few seconds.

Montoyo speaks up. "Excuse me . . . you don't know the three-dimensional map location?"

"No. So much detail could be lost; memories can degrade during hibernation."

He looks flabbergasted. "So . . . even if we could get you there, you might not remember how to activate the moon machine?"

"There will be inscriptions to guide us. And a vocal instruction – a simple response that is imprinted into my memory."

Tyler begins to chuckle. "This is sick, man! The old lady has to say a magic spell."

259

The members of the ruling Executive seem to have been struck dumb.

I stare at them all and take a step backwards, leaning against the open cockpit. This cannot be happening. No. I refuse to believe that the Erinsi wouldn't have left us the location of the moon machine.

Urgently I say to Ninbanda, "What did you just say . . . the location is the key?"

She turns to me, smiling. "Exactly."

"And you've got no idea where the key is?"

"No. All I know is that the information was on our Temple of Inscriptions."

"Yeah, I know, the ruins near Izapa. Bosch-I-mean-Itzamna copied it all down into his books. So it has to have been in one of the Books of Itzamna."

"Yes. But don't expect a vital piece of information like that to be plainly stated."

It has to be in code.

My eyes lock with Ixchel's; I can tell she's thinking exactly the same thing as me.

"Surely not. . . The key location? Ixchel – the key!"

Ixchel frowns, gazing back at me. "Could it really be so simple?"

I climb back into the cockpit, grab the headset and bring up the menu for all basic flight programmes, just as I've done in every lesson I've ever had

The chief sounds puzzled. "What's the boy doing?"

Ixchel replies, "All our technology comes from instructions in the four Books of Itzamna, and the specifications for the Muwan Mark II are in the Kan Codex, yes?"

Now the chief looks dumbfounded. "Any pilot learns that on his first day."

I call out, "Well, that means that code in the Kan Codex can translate into a pre-programmed flight plan in the Muwan."

"What Josh is saying," Ixchel concludes, "is that the information we need could be in the on-board computer."

The chief looks stupefied. "How would such a thing be possible? If the location of the moon machine were in the program bank, we'd know!"

From inside the cockpit I call out, "But the actual location is in computer language! You'd only see that particular flight program come up. . ."

Ixchel completes my sentence, ". . . if you were to search for it. You'd have to know the exact sequence of letters. The exact fifteen letters!"

"And it never even occurred to us to look," the chief says. He sounds almost ashamed.

"Why would it?" I say. "Ever since Lorena's team found the fifteen letter sequence that's inscribed on the Adaptor – we thought it was only a chemical formula. But what if it was BOTH? A chemical formula AND the name of a flight program. The location is the key."

Montoyo's reponse sounds like laughter. "The key location has been in the on-board flight computer all along?"

Leaning out of the cockpit, I give him a grin. "Totally! There are lots of pre-programmed flight plans and manoeuvres. My personal favourite is Crazy Benicio – that's full-on. I bet you anything that the location we're looking for is one of them."

Montoyo's enthusiasm seems to have infected the other members of the ruling Executive. Lorena says, "Josh – that's astonishing. Go ahead – try it!"

I type an A. The list of manoeuvres appears. I type in the rest of the fifteen-letter sequence. And there it is. One of the hardwired basic flight programmes, taken directly from the Kan Codex: location AGYLIHRPPREIKGR.

Not exactly a sequence you'd type in by accident or coincidence. Hiding in plain sight. Unless you understood that the fifteen letter sequence of the Key peptide is also the key to the location of the moon machine.

On the holographic projector, I see the route being plotted out as data is pulled into the programme. The red line flows west, across the Pacific Ocean.

I call to Ninbanda and Tyler. "Get in! I've got it!"

Shaking with excitement, I try to steady myself as I strap into the pilot seat.

Once again . . . What Key Holds Blood. Arcadio's message to me on those postcards keeps getting more prophetic.

Two Muwan engineers perform flight maintenance checks as Ninbanda and Tyler climb inside. The chief calls across the hangar to Benicio, ordering him back into the Muwan. But Ninbanda won't hear of it. She becomes stern, even hostile. "This was always planned as a final journey for descendants of the Erinsi. There can be no witnesses."

With a nervous glance at his watch, the chief backs down. Tens of thousands of years after their civilization ended, one of the Erinsi still holds all the cards.

Before I get into the Muwan, I tug at Ixchel's elbow and take her to one side.

"Well, I guess this is it," she says, but her smile is an anxious one.

"I'm going to finish it this time. Then our worries are over."

That actually makes her laugh. She hugs me tight. "Yeah. Impossible to have any problems in life apart from the end of the world."

"Hey, don't knock it! I'm looking forward to only worrying about exam results and getting a job and all that other stuff. . ."

Ixchel kisses me and I don't hold back. Who cares if the rest of them are watching?

Then I'm in the sky again, at the helm, Tyler by my side. I take some time to show him the controls once more. He might as well practise if he's going to remain in Ek Naab. Ninbanda sits quietly in the rear passenger seat. Her mood has become, quite suddenly, rather sombre. We watch the route appear in holographic form.

"Where are we going?" asks Tyler.

I peer at a transparent network of lines in the air. "I'm guessing Indonesia. . ."

Ninbanda makes a tiny sound, somewhere between surprise and sadness. "Lake Toba. Well, well."

"Of course!" I say. "Lake Toba is in Indonesia. Bosch told us that the original Erinsi civilisation was destroyed by the supervolcano that created Lake Toba."

"Indeed. The ancient Erinsi is now known as 'Indonesia'."

Our Muwan drifts, a lone arrow fired against a fearful destiny. My thoughts drift along too, as I wonder what we'll find at the mysterious, secret location. It seems impossible to grasp that those years that Tyler lived, an apocalypse I merely glimpsed, could soon be nothing more than a nightmare.

The descent begins. Detailed images of the land below appear. Tightly knitted green, forest hues. A gigantic ring of deep blue water; a lake. At the water's edge the blue gives way to a low white mist rolling in from nearby forest-coated peaks. In the middle of the lake, a vast island. Even from hundreds of metres above, I can't see across to the other side.

Ninbanda leans forward. "Those who survived the supervolcano acquired a marvellous expertise in tunnelling, at living underground. Why live under a sky of ash that yields nothing but poisonous rain? We believed the winter would never end. And just when it did, when we began to recover, to return to our homeland . . . from the centre of the galaxy came the superwave. We didn't know what it was, what had happened, for decades. Finally we came to understand the nature of the superwave: a cosmic event that was destined to repeat every twenty-six thousand years – the same period as the precession of the equinoxes of our planet. We prepared. By then we were too few to survive as we'd been. And we knew that however great we became again, it mattered not. One day the superwave would return."

I murmur, "So you made the plan."

The Muwan slows even further, lowering us on to the middle of the island.

"Lake Toba," says the Erinsi, gazing down. "Oh my dear children, if you'd seen our city." She smiles at me once, very sadly. "What is left, the very little that is left, lies sunken hundreds of metres below, at the bottom of the crater. Destroyed by a volcanic eruption, the explosion of a caldera, a cataclysm of terrifying violence."

The Muwan landing protocols kick in. With a practiced hand, I guide the craft to a landing spot as close as possible to the flashing light on the route map. We fly in low, swooping over palm trees and the dark wood of steeply sloping roofs that peek out from the green. Lakeside settlements disappear behind us as the Muwan enters deeper towards the island's interior. To the last remnants of a lost world.

Chapter 44

We land at the edge of a forest, high on a ridge. In the distance I see a narrow road stretching out, not more than a few kilometres away. The landscape is parched, green in patches but drying fast. "Keep your visor on," Ninbanda tells me. "The aircraft computer can relay the location to your visual cortex."

"How do you know so much about flying a Muwan?"

I hear a faintly smug smile in her reply. "My dear, who do you think built these craft?"

"What – you?!"

"No, child, I'm of a more recent generation than those who devised the 2012 plan. But my mother lived in the last living city of the Erinsi. She designed the holographic interface of the craft you know as 'Muwan', which we called 'sparrow hawk'. Her specifications are incorporated into the instructions in the book you call the 'Kan Codex'. She told me many stories of the days when she flew in such a craft."

I lead us into the forest, blinded by the visor, stumbling over tall grass that I can't see, just following the map in my head.

"There's an entrance," I tell them. "In the ground. About a hundred metres in."

We move slowly, at Ninbanda's pace. I want to keep checking back with the Muwan but she tells me not to worry. "It's no longer your concern," she murmurs. Tyler and I give each other an ominous look. What does that mean?

Finally we reach the opening. A stone slab in the ground, no more than a metre across. Ninbanda removes a bottle of water from her pocket and kneels down. She cleans the surface, first with the water, then with some wet wipes from a packet. When it's clean I see that there are three faint depressions, inside which the stone gives way to the same strange alabaster-like surface of the Adaptor. She hands us the packet of wipes. "Clean your right hand," she says. "The bio-sensor needs to react with molecules produced by your skin. It is sensitive to contamination."

Then, following her lead and in a concerted action, we all place the heel of our right hand in the depressions. It takes several moments before anything happens. Then I'm aware of the vibrations of machinery, deep underneath the stone. Ninbanda sighs a little and stands. Hesitantly, Tyler and I also stand. The stone slab starts to rise. Inside is a cubicle, a tiny life-pod, just big enough for one person. Ninbanda indicates Tyler. "Let this one go first. When the capsule stops, get out and stand back. The capsule will return to the surface."

With one last, nervous look at me, Tyler steps inside, turns around and frowns as the capsule begins to descend. He disappears into the earth. I wait, filled with anxiety and excitement.

Turning to Ninbanda, I ask, "Why are you called Erinsi? People of Memory? What do you remember?"

"We remember the secrets of others. Just as you and your family remembered our secrets."

"But . . . whose secrets? Were there others before you?"

She smiles. "Yes. But not of this place, not even of this universe. We never knew them. They also died. Not just their world; their universe. As it collapsed, they sent a radio signal. Unthinkably old, it came to our universe, to us, through a black hole. Days, weeks, months of continuous data. Their world memory. In a universe where everything dies, they found a way to transcend death. The body must die, yes. But knowledge . . . knowledge is eternal. They bequeathed this truth to us. As we now bequeath it to you."

I'm still riveted by the ancient woman's gentle smile as the capsule arrives above the ground. Dazed, I step forward and feel my stomach lurch as the ground falls away. I grip the sides of the pod, trembling with fear of the unknown. The capsule burrows deeper, deeper into the earth. The rich smell of warm clay fills my senses. Then after what seems like an eternity, the pod lands. In the pitch black, I hear Tyler's voice.

"Josh . . . is that you?"

I take a torch from my flight jacket and turn it on Tyler. He looks frightened. The first time I've really seen that.

"You scared?" asks Tyler, hesitantly.

"I'm bloody terrified, mate."

Shivering, we stand in what seems to be some kind of antechamber, not very big at all, maybe two metres by three. We wait for the capsule to return. Three minutes later it does, and Ninbanda steps out. She looks calm, serene. The second that she steps into the centre of the chamber, part of the wall ahead begins to rise. A door opens.

Ninbanda leads us inside. We follow her through a tunnel that passes two more stone doors, both closed. Then we reach it. Another chamber, similar in feel to the Revival Chamber, but without the sarcophagi. There's a hexagonal centrepiece covered with inscriptions.

"Bit dark in here. . ." grumbles Tyler. It's sounds as though he's trying to lighten the moment, but I suspect he's as tense as I am. This is totally unknown territory for both of us. No one's been in here for tens of thousands of years.

Ninbanda takes out her water bottle and begins, once again, to wipe the surface of the altarpiece clean. She hands us each a fresh wipe. "Clean hands, please."

My hands feel numb, but I do as she asks. Then I watch as the woman takes up a position beside the centrepiece. She crouches, examining the inscriptions, lightly running her fingers over the carved stone.

Standing again, Ninbanda places both hands on the surface. From the edges of the chamber, a soft pink light begins to glow. As its intensity increases the inscriptions on the centrepiece become visible. Ninbanda instructs us to stand as she does, at the other points of the hexagon, each with a hand over the remaining sectors. She shifts the position of her hands, rests them beside a panel of inscriptions on the centrepiece. Some of the inscriptions are illuminated from behind, by a sequence of gently blinking lights.

"Learn the sequence," she says. "Take a moment to study it – it is quite simple, only five symbols. Then touch each symbol, in the correct sequence."

Tyler and I stare with furious concentration, trying desperately to memorize the incomprehensible symbols.

"Ixchel would have been much better than me at this," I mumble, trying to cover my nerves. "At least she'd know what the symbols mean. . ." But I'm sweating hard. Utterly terrified. What happens if we get it wrong?

"Take your time," the woman says, gently. "We've all come a long way. There's still enough time for this."

Eventually Tyler says in a steady voice, "OK. Got it."

The pressure is immense. I stare at the inscriptions, trying to think, to clear my mind of the million thoughts that are whirling around. Is this the end, is this my destiny, or does it always end the same way?

After another minute I let my breath go. "OK. Ready."

Ninbanda touches something and the entire panel of inscriptions lights up. I keep repeating the sequence in my head. Going first, she presses her five symbols. There's a low crackle, then a sound. A series of musical notes, in a strange rhythm, repeated. It sounds something like Morse code.

A transformation comes over Ninbanda and she starts to speak. A stream of strange-sounding syllables flow from somewhere in the back of her throat.

Then with round, staring eyes, Ninbanda turns to us. She seems to be looking right through Tyler and me. Despite the fact that she doesn't seem to see us, she nods.

At Ninbanda's signal, we touch the symbols on the panel of inscriptions, one after the other, in a steady sequence. From inside the centrepiece there's a deep, sonorous click. A second passes. I catch the look in Ninbanda's eye.

Now she's nervous.

Another second.

"What. . .?"

Ninbanda shushes me harshly, waiting, listening.

Another second. Then the sound of a final click.

The Erinsi woman breathes a sigh of absolute relief.

"That's it?"

She swallows, a little shaky.

"What . . . that click?"

"The laser beam just sent a signal to the moon. It takes about a second and a half to get there . . . then a second and a half for the reply. We just had the reply. The energy device is activated." She sighs again, but without any obvious satisfaction. "Thank the gods. It's over. I can finally die in peace."

There's something very final about the way she says that. Final and also immediate.

"What . . . what do you mean, die?"

She looks up at me, a curious, bland expression in her gaze. "None of us will leave this place."

"What are you talking about?"

"In about five minutes a gas will be released. It'll put us all to sleep very gently. We will never wake up."

Tyler and I stare in stunned silence.

Ninbanda's voice seems to come from outside of her, as though she's completely detached from the words. "Some secrets must be buried with the Erinsi."

Somewhere down the tunnel, we hear the sudden grinding of stone.

"Run!"

Tyler and I race through the tunnels, half-blind. My torch scatters light in a crazy pattern before us. The door to the antechamber is closing; a shrinking black rectangle. It's already too low to walk through. We sprint; I rapidly pull ahead as Tyler struggles with his injury. When we reach the door my heart almost stops. It could already be too late.

I dive feet first, slide beneath, let out a sharp yell as the stone slab almost pins me under its crushing weight. Squirming, I manage to free myself.

There's no way that Tyler can squeeze through the gap. From each side of the door we both grip the bottom edge of the stone slab, heaving, straining muscles against the ancient mechanism. We slow its progress, but can't budge the door any higher.

"We just need to jam something in, wedge it open," I shout, panting with effort. "Then I'll go up and get some tools from the Muwan. There's got to be a way."

"Have you got something?" Tyler says.

"Try the torch." I shove in the torch, propping it upright in the opening. The slab descends as we let go. In another second there's the sound of cracking glass. The torch begins to buckle.

There's desperation in Tyler's voice.

"Piece of junk! You got anything else . . .?"

My hand goes to the Bracelet of Itzamna under my sleeve. "I've got something that's solid metal . . . should be stronger. . ." My fingers tremble as I fumble, pushing up my sleeve, tugging at the Bracelet.

Then I understand. As I pass the Bracelet of Itzamna through the remaining gap under the stone door, the torch begins to give way.

"Tyler, listen. Use the Bracelet. It's your only way out, Ty! To time travel! It'll get you out of there, take you right back to Oxford. Your Oxford, Ty."

Tyler's voice sounds faint. I see his fingers reach for the Bracelet. "What . . . what do I do?"

The torch buckles; the door collapses, now less than five centimetres from the ground. And still it squeezes, slowly crushing the remains of the torch.

I drop down, lie flat as I speak through the gap. "Listen carefully. You ready? When you want to go, Tyler, when you're ready, you press down on the Crystal Key. Your fingers can't be touching any other part of the Bracelet. Press down hard. The Bracelet will go weird and bits of it will start to move. Don't be scared. There's a countdown. Then . . . you'll go. You'll go back to where we started – back in Oxford."

"Back to the EG Centre? Oh great, man. So they can shoot me all over again."

"No – the Bracelet will transport you to roughly twenty metres from where you left. And . . . this bit is important, Ty . . . you'll arrive ten minutes before we left."

"Ten minutes?"

"Yeah, it's a safety default. For exactly this kind of emergency. You'll go to approximately where we were, ten minutes before. Make sure you get out of there! Go back to the Muwan, in the uni parks. It's yours now, Ty. It's yours."

I wait for Tyler to answer, hear a tiny chuckle in his voice.

"So. I'm going back."

"I'm sorry."

"Don't be. I'm not. This was all good, mate. It was fine."

I swallow. "Tyler, you're . . . you're the best friend I ever had. I mean it. The best."

"Yeah, yeah, Mariposa, whatever," he says with a laugh. "What was that riddle again?"

"Riddle?"

"Yeah, the one on the postcards. The one from your old mate, Arcadio. I'm Arcadio, I must be. I've got the blue eyes; I can use the time-travel bracelet. Looks like I'm going back to my reality. And somehow, I'm going to leave that flyin' saucer for you to find in 2014."

I whisper, "Please . . . not like this!"

"My crew need me too, Josh. So - that riddle. You'd better tell me. Hurry up."

Mouth as dry as dust, I say, "It . . . it's written on a piece of paper. In my parents' house. I mean – other-Josh's."

"Heh, so it is. Perfect," says Tyler. "I'll drop in for a cup of tea and some of your mum's cookin'."

"Tyler . . . I'm sorry. I didn't mean to get you mixed up in all this."

"Hey. I was feeling a bit harsh about stepping out on my boys in Jericho, you know what I mean? Maybe I am livin' inside the trunk of a dead tree, like that Camus bloke wrote in The Outsider. But I got used to it. It's time to get back to my boys."

"Ty. . ." My voice breaks.

I hear Tyler catch his breath for a second. He exhales slowly, resigned. "Allow it, man. You can't stay anywhere for ever."

The torch holding the stone door open is squashed completely flat. Deep inside my chest I can feel something tearing wide open. Alone and trembling, I stand. I'm grateful, so grateful that in the end, someone shared this responsibility with me.

I hope Tyler understood that. I hope he knew.

BLOG ENTRY: WAKE ME UP WHEN SEPTEMBER ENDS

As I floated in the stratosphere all the way back, nothing but a silver streak in the sky, there was a mist in my eyes. In memory of my friend, I played the same track over and over.

The radio was chattering with people in Ek Naab wanting to talk to me, but I needed the solitude. I'd let them know that I was alive, the job was done and Tyler was gone. More than that, I didn't want to discuss. Instead, I dedicated those few hours to Tyler. A Tyler that I'll never meet again, in all probability. Because the boy I know in Oxford will grow up in a world where all the opportunities of modern life are open to him. He'll go to college and study, meet someone to be with for the rest of his life. He'll become whatever he wants to be.

Yet that other Tyler exists too. In another reality, where his life took another path. All the courage and determination, as well as the bleakness, the anger; everything that made him the man I saw is inside the boy I know in Oxford, right now.

And although it makes me uncomfortable to think about it, the potential that other-Josh had – to choose the stupidest time to walk away from his family – that potential exists in me too.

I'll never forget Tyler's words before that door closed, locking him inside the tomb. How accepting he was. Deep down, he knew where he belonged. As hard as that life was, he wanted to return. What mattered to Tyler in the end were his responsibilities, the people who relied on him.

For the longest time, I thought about all that. Travelling in time had been making me feel disconnected, as though I'd lost my anchor. Other possibilities, other realities, seemed so tempting. The fact that in one universe I could be making a different choice somehow made it all right to do whatever I wanted. Finally I'd experienced a reality that helped me feel more grounded in my own. Maybe I'd found some essential part of myself, an inescapable core. Like Tyler, I knew where I belonged.

Back in Ek Naab I received the hero's welcome I'd secretly always wanted. The entire population turned out, crowding the area around the black *cenote*. My fellow student pilots grabbed hold of me; they carried me on their shoulders through the streets.

The sky flickered red with handfuls of hibiscus petals tossed into the air. I spotted my mother's face at the periphery. She was next to Carlos Montoyo. He pulled his tight grin and gave me an ironic salute. My mother smiled and blew me a kiss. For the first time in a very long time, I saw no trace of sadness in her eyes.

The crowd released me when we reached the market. And then I was face to face with Ixchel. She didn't hug me right away, just looked me up and down a little. I could feel people's eyes on us. Every second that passed made me feel more awkward.

Eventually she broke the tension, grinned broadly and threw both arms around my neck.

"Anyone would think you'd just saved the world."

"It wasn't me. It's like you told me once: I was just the button-man."

Ixchel laughed. "You know something? You shouldn't listen to me too much."

"Could you write that down on a card? I might want to remind you sometime. . ."

The crowd, having seen the moment of our reunion, began to disperse. I heard calls for an impromptu pool party.

More than anything, I wished Tyler could have been there to see it.

BLOG ENTRY: SIXTEEN

My sixteenth birthday came at a pretty crucial time for Ek Naab. The medical team finally released Captain Connor Bennett, who spent weeks in their care. The National Reconnaissance Office agreed to swap the captain for our Muwan Mark II, which was still "in their custody", no more questions asked. Benicio had tried to make sure that Captain Bennett hadn't been able to watch the final approach to Ek Naab. Hopefully, the location was still secure. But I guess time will tell. We just have to trust them, for now.

I wondered about the plan to use hip33 against the NRO. The NRO had surprised us by turning up at the fifth chamber. We were completely unprepared.

It wouldn't have been a nice tactic to use against someone who, in the end, was trying to help. Would it even have worked, given what we now knew about Captain Bennett? If he had Erinsi DNA, if he was a descendant, like me, then he would be immune to the effects of hip33. Tyler told us that a blue-blood couldn't be influenced by someone using hip33.

But later, Lorena discovered something else that made us all wonder. Captain Bennett had an identical twin, a scientist called Dr Jackson Bennett. Jackson Bennett's name was on research papers that had found something similar to hip33 biology, but in the fruit fly. Maybe the NRO already knew a lot more about hip33 than we might have guessed.

Why hadn't Jackson Bennett been asked to be the third member of the team to activate the moon machine? I remembered something that Ninbanda had said through her tears, when Connor was shot – "Not Connor . . . I couldn't bear to lose him, too. . ." Had something happened to Jackson? Why did she seem so close to Connor and his brother? Could they have been the ones who actually revived her? I began to realize then that there'd been a lot more going on than I'd ever known; other people who I knew nothing about, risking their lives to bring about the ancient plan to protect the world from the superwave.

Everything returned to normal, with the NRO still jealous over Ek Naab's hoard of ancient technology. Yet somehow, finally, we'd reached a kind of truce.

What topped everything for excitement was the breaking news about a strange energy phenomenon near the moon. It was amazing and also kind of weird to suddenly see everything we'd speculated about for years being openly talked about on the television and in social media.

The superwave emerging from the galactic core couldn't be stopped – the scientists in Ek Naab had feared that much. But the moon machine could protect us. Now we were finding out how. Scientists started recording incredible data in cosmic ray detection, and all sorts of other stuff that I didn't understand. Something bizarre was happening on the moon; that much was clear. For weeks people tried to make out it was a natural phenomenon.

The conspiracy theorists, of course, they knew better. I went back to my old ways for a while, hanging out on the Internet discussion boards, enjoying all the crazy, wacky theories that were being posted.

Aliens got the rap most of the time.

I toyed with the idea of posting what had really happened. It wasn't close to as outlandish as some of the theories. And who would believe me, right?

With all that going on, we didn't get around to much of a party. Well, we had a bigger party in mind.

Dr Banerjee got her moment in the sun, too. She published her article in some top science journal. Once other scientists understood the implications, it spread across the planet like wildfire. Or like the energy bubble that seemed to be radiating from the moon. Around the time that people understood what was happening at the centre of the galaxy, the space agencies managed to get a shuttle out to the edge of the moon bubble. They did some experiments and realized – it was a gigantic force field. Growing in radius every day. And it would entirely shield the Earth – for three days.

After that, the power would run out and the field would collapse. By then the gigantic electromagnetic pulse would be on its way through the rest of the solar system. No problem for all those uninhabited planets, but it looked pretty bad for all those scientists who had probes on Mars and for the poor old Voyagers. There was some hope that the Voyagers would be shielded in part by the "heliosheath" – the outer layer of the heliosphere where the solar wind is slowed by the pressure of interstellar gas. But there was also a good chance that their systems would fry and we'd lose all contact with them.

All this would happen on December twenty-first to the twenty-third, 2012. No one missed the significance of that. But how? everyone asked. Who did it? And how did the Mayans know?

Hey. I'll never tell.

Chapter 45

Ixchel gives me a little shove. "Get up, lazy. You have to get that application for Harvard in today."

I roll over in the hammock and frown. "Did my mother send you?"

Ixchel takes a backwards step towards the window, a glass of water in one hand. She leans out, tips the water into flowers in the hanging basket overlooking the narrow alleyway below. "I sent myself. If you're coming with me to university, you'd better shape up."

"You're too good for university," I tell her. "You should be teaching there."

"Ha ha. Maybe one day."

I sit up, glance out of the window. The sound of a band rehearsing comes wafting in from the marketplace. Preparations for the biggest party Ek Naab has ever seen – on December twenty-third. The same party is being prepared all over the world.

The day the world didn't end. Funny to think that when these parties were planned, almost no-one outside Ek Naab and the NRO knew that the 'Mayan apocalypse' threat was actually real.

Well, didn't they have a surprise, when the force field began to form?

"I've been thinking. . ." I tell her.

"Yes?"

"I know we've both got offers for Oxford. But maybe I actually want to go to Harvard."

She purses her lips in thought. "Is this about Tyler?"

Despite myself, I feel my cheeks burn. "Tyler? No. He's going to study capoeira in Rio, in Brazil."

"It's understandable if you feel weird about seeing him. I can imagine it won't ever be the same for you, after meeting the other Tyler."

Sometimes this girl knows just the right thing to make my eyes misty. With my eyes, I plead with her silently. "Can we not talk about all that?"

Ixchel looks at me as if she's thinking about going further, but stops.

"Look, I grew up in Oxford. I want to go somewhere new."

"Well. . . " Ixchel grins. "We don't always get what we want."

I stand up. "Ixchel . . . I mean it. I want a new beginning."

"Seriously, Harvard?"

"I just feel like I should be moving forward. Not back."

"Do you have any idea how cold it gets in Massachusetts? I couldn't handle it."

"OK, then somewhere else."

Ixchel nods, thoughtful. "I think we should both apply to various schools. Keep our options open. See where we feel happiest."

"You're going to love Oxford, though," I groan. "All that history, all those ancient colleges. You won't be able to resist."

Outside, people are carrying trays of food, stereo speakers, paper decorations to hang from the lampposts, huge baskets of flowers. Ixchel and I give the baker a hand with an enormous blue-frosted sponge cake. The party's being held around the black *cenote*. When we arrive, I see Montoyo in earnest discussion with the chief. When I turned sixteen in August, Montoyo stood down as my proxy on the ruling Executive, let me finally succeed. But already there's talk of him joining again, this time as an official proxy for Blanco Vigores. Who, so far as anyone can tell, has simply vanished. Like mist.

A bigger question is this – what is the point of Ek Naab now?

We'll worry about that after tonight.

Tonight, the galactic superwave hits the solar system. By midnight, it'll crash through Earth's atmosphere. On the other hand, maybe that mysterious force field around the moon will protect us. That's what the space scientists tell us is going to happen.

And if you can't trust space scientists, who can you trust?

When Montoyo notices me, he breaks off his conversation with the chief and strolls over.

"Your mother received a call today. From Susannah St John. She wants to invite us to celebrate in Tlacotalpan."

Ixchel and I exchange a glance "You mean," I say, "instead of here?"

"That's right."

"Why doesn't Susannah come to Ek Naab?"

"She says they're having a really wonderful party. A proper Veracruz fiesta. Great food, live salsa music, *danzon*, all those marvellous things."

"Sounds all right," I say. "But we've got our friends here. I'm going to play some songs on my guitar. Don't you think we owe it to everyone here, after all their years of work?"

"Josh – let me assure you – your duty to Ek Naab is done! And after all, you can party with your friends any time."

"Not like tonight."

Montoyo is really trying hard. "Josh, your mother wants to go. She's hungry for some 'real Mexico'."

"I'd like to go," Ixchel says, tugging at my hand. "I love Tlacotalpan. And the people in Veracruz have incredible parties."

"What about Benicio? We should hang with him tonight, don't you think?"

Ixchel grins her cute, lopsided grin. "You know perfectly well he has a new girlfriend. He'll be with Roxana. I guess maybe you want me to see them together . . . you want me to see that he's really and truly over me?"

How little she knows – if there's even a chance that Ixchel might be jealous of Benicio's new girlfriend, I definitely don't want to see it.

"It's got nothing to do with that! Just that, you know, he's been a big part of all this. Massive. Honestly, I'd be dead several times over without Benicio."

"He knows that; we all do."

"And he's family."

"If it's about family, then maybe you should do what your mom wants?" she says.

"Hmm," I mutter, hunting for another tactic. "Anyway, I thought you couldn't stand Susannah St John. . ."

"I guess I was wrong about her. Since Tyler is Arcadio. Come on," Ixchel says. She smiles. "*Para bailar a la bamba, se necesitó un poco de gracia. . .*"

"To dance the bamba, I need a bit of grace? OK. See – there's the whole problemo. Grace. On the dance floor. I've got none."

"Not true," she insists. "What about capoeira? That's a dance."

282

"Not the way I do it. . ." I grumble. "Look, OK. We'll go. But let's at least say goodbye to Benicio. And don't expect me to dance."

We leave Montoyo to get back to my mother and head for the marketplace. Benicio is there, setting up the party with some students from the Tec. His new girlfriend Roxana is one of Lorena's medical students. A really pretty girl, who I think has been after him for a while. Ixchel's right; Benicio seems more interested in Roxana than in where Ixchel and I plan to be at midnight. We help with the set-up for another couple of hours. When we say goodbye it's casual, as if it were just another day. Maybe it's too big to acknowledge, the fate we've been spared by the presence of the giant force field that emanates from the moon. It would be good to think that two guys who once fought over a girl could eventually become really good friends. That's what I want now, for Benicio and me.

When the goodbyes are over, we head for a Muwan that waits in the hangar, Montoyo and my mother in the passenger seats, Ixchel up front with me. We fly to Tlacotalpan. This time, the NRO don't bother us – if they even notice we're in the air. We find a hidden place to leave the Muwan, about two kilometres from town. The rest, we walk, mostly in the dark, watching out for swamp frogs hopping across the road, their eyes glowing green when they catch the passing beam of a car's headlamps.

All the taxis are full, lines of cars arriving from nearby towns and hotels in Veracruz for the party of the century. There are some pretty big-name bands on the bill tonight. Every type of music from salsa to dubstep.

Susannah told us to meet here in the main *zocalo*. We arrive to find the fiesta has already begun. There's a band in the central gazebo playing old-fashioned Latin dance hall music, trumpets blaring. A dazzling light show of powerful multi-coloured beams that meet in the air above the central square. All the surrounding buildings are decked out in *papel picado* – traditional Mexican paper decorations in red, white and green, the colours of the Mexican flag. There's a Mayan theme too – people walking around in traditional Mayan costume, which actually freaks Ixchel and me out. I guess we're the only people here to feel that way, but I don't mind admitting that the sight of one guy dressed like a fierce Mayan warrior, face painted in red and black like that thug Rain Son, gives me a nasty scare.

The ancient Maya were right – that's what some of the New Age types are saying. There was something significant about the date of the end of the Mayan Long Count Calendar. The date that the human race realized that We Are Not Alone. That Someone or Something out there in the Universe is watching out for us. A global shift of consciousness. Gratitude to replace all our selfishness. Etcetera, etcetera. In the end I can't bear to listen.

I can't forget that for our reality to be saved, Tyler's reality had to suffer the consequences of the galactic superwave. Without visiting that future, I would never have made the connection about the key location. There wouldn't have been three people to activate the moon machine. Maybe this is the only reality where we're spared from the superwave.

Hard to forget that when you have people you care about in the other place.

Staring into the *zocalo* I watch the graceful gliding of couples dancing *danzon*, men dressed all in white with loose *guayabera* shirts, red neckerchiefs, white shoes and panama hats, women in bright-coloured dresses that sway with their hips. Ixchel points and murmurs "Look. It's Susannah."

She's right. Susannah has her hair tied back with a red carnation and she's dancing very smoothly with an elegant mover, a guy about the same age as her, dressed in crisp white cotton. When she sees us she smiles, waves a red fan at us and finishes the dance with a flourish. Her dance partner turns, takes her hand. She leads him over to us, fanning herself delicately.

When they're up close my jaw drops. Susannah smiles, first at me, then at Montoyo. He leans in and kisses her warmly on the cheek. So does my mother. But I can't budge, can't stop staring at her partner.

"Is he here?" asks the elderly gent, with a grin. His glazed eyes stare at a point just over my shoulder.

"Yes, my dear," replies Susannah. "Josh Garcia is standing right in front of you."

I stammer, "Blanco Vigores. . ."

Chapter 46

My eyes are riveted to the old man. Then to Montoyo I say, "Did you know he was here?"

"Susannah told me earlier today."

"Blanco. . ." I repeat. "You're here. How? Why?"

"Because," Susannah says, with tenderness, "he came back to me. After all those years, finally, he did."

The significance of her words takes several seconds to land.

"You?" I gasp. "Blanco? You're Arcadio. . .? But what about Tyler? I mean, how?"

Blanco removes his hat and I get another shock. He's not bald. A neatly cropped scrub of short silver hair covers his scalp. Blanco steps forward. "Young Josh. I'd like to talk to you, alone. Would that be acceptable? Perhaps you'd be kind enough to take me somewhere quiet? Maybe by the river."

As the old man fumbles for my arm I take his hand, place it on my shoulder and say to Montoyo, "You once told me you'd met Arcadio. Did you know that he was Blanco Vigores?"

"No. It was a long time ago, Josh. Blanco convinced all of us, with his appearance of age. In the past few months, since Blanco went missing, I admit that I began to wonder. But Arcadio made me promise never to speak of our meeting. On pain of certain death!"

"I have some experience of time travel," Blanco admits, a touch ominously. "And some idea of how things may turn out."

"So you're not really old?"

Blanco laughs, a short, sharp bark of a laugh. "As you can see, young Josh, I am quite advanced in years!"

"But you've always looked the same age," Montoyo says. "An aging, bald, blind man."

"You used the Revival Chamber," I say. "Didn't you? Diego Ka'an told me, the Head of Surgery. That's where you used to disappear to, all those times you went missing."

"Yes, every week or so I'd put myself into hibernation for at least a month. Decades passed in Ek Naab, while I aged by a mere handful of years."

"That's how you stayed the same age for so long."

"A bald head doesn't show the hair turning white," Blanco tells us all. "I was doing a good job of slowing the aging process, it's true. Until the Sect of Huracan discovered the Revival Chamber." He turns to me with a melancholy gaze. "Young Josh, will you let me explain? Listen to the confession of an old man?"

We leave the group as the band starts up again. Blanco's hand lies firm on my shoulder. I'm thinking furiously, my mind racing as I lead him through the crowd and towards the palm-lined Malecon, the pier beside the wide, dark water of the River Papaloapan. A fireworks display is being prepared on a barge on the opposite bank. We find an empty bench and sit.

"If you're Arcadio, then what about Tyler?"

Blanco's hand goes to the red cloth around his neck. He fingers it almost nervously. He peers at me. It's eerily as though he can see me looking back. "Haven't you guessed, Josh?"

And then it hits me. I shrink back.

"You're . . . you're him. You're other-Josh. From Tyler's reality."

With a nod, he replies, "Yes, I am."

I gaze out across the water, to the opposite bank where reeds and sugar cane sway in a gentle breeze.

"Wow. That's not what I expected, after what I heard about how you walked out on your family."

"Don't judge me too harshly. I was very young. I was in love."

"With Emmy?"

There's a sudden, joyous smile. "Yes! Emily. Dear girl. Did you know her too?"

"Yes." I shrug. "Never occurred to me that she might like me."

"Most of all, I was in denial. Many of us were. The most surprising thing about the end of the world is just how few people recognize that the moment has already passed."

"But . . . you're the one. You fixed things. If you hadn't written me those postcards. . . You did all this."

"No. We did it. You and I, together. With a great deal of help from our friends."

"Hang on, didn't you tell me you found the Bracelet of Itzamna in Izapa?"

"Yes. In this reality. I travelled back here with the Bracelet you gave to Tyler. Right back to those woods near San Cristobal."

"You told me that you almost died when you first used the Bracelet."

"Yes. Foolishly, I first tried without instructions. In my own reality, it took me years to find the Ix Codex, the instructions. Many more years to translate the book. Are you trying to catch me in a lie, young Josh? I've always been careful with what I've told you. But I've never lied."

"Your accent is weird."

"I've lived all over the world, in so many times. I once went fifteen years without speaking English! I don't know where I'm from any more."

"I'm glad you're not really bald. But am I going to go blind?"

He laughs. "That's what you've been worried about? No – the blindness was from a chemical accident in the laboratory."

"Jeez – thank goodness for that! I didn't like to ask."

The old man chuckles. "Ah, youth! Well, thanks to Tyler, I was able to escape my own bad choice. Tyler returned to his own reality and found me in the Emergency Government Centre."

"Ah – that explains why Andres couldn't find you. Tyler had already gotten you out!"

"Heh. Precisely. He took me away, back to his friends in Jericho, then back to my parents. He gave me your message. We did what you made possible. We moved Tyler's group away, found somewhere to start again. Tyler was an inspirational leader. Eventually, when I was in my late twenties, I gathered up enough courage to use the Bracelet of Itzamna. I knew that it was still anchored to this reality, you see. I merely had to find a way to change the default setting to return me to the woods near San Cristobal, rather than the underground bunker in Lake Toba." He gives a short laugh. "It only took me five years."

"And you came back, just because of what Tyler told you, about becoming Arcadio, sending me those postcards and saving this world?"

Very simply he says, "Some destinies are unavoidable."

"Oh," I say, relieved. "Good. I mean, not for you, obviously . . . but. . ."

"So all this time – there's been two of me."

"I'm no more you than if we were twins. We share the DNA we were born with and some commonality of upbringing. You must have seen enough to know that we were different."

"It's kind of nice to have a twin."

"And we share a destiny, too, young Josh. Don't forget that."

289

For a few moments, we're silent. "Your mother mustn't know," Blanco warns, his tone suddenly dejected. "I'm relieved I can't see her. There are things I don't wish to remember."

"Is that why you didn't come to the funeral when my dad died? You didn't want to see Mum?"

He nods, very sombre.

"What happens," I say, with a rush of anxiety, "to Sofia? To Eleanor and Andres?"

"Tyler takes them away too. Menorca, Josh, in the Mediterranean Sea – one of the few places not to become affected by the plague. Their strict no-fly policy during the sickness allows them to hold out against the Emergency Government. The population there are able to readjust to a life without technology. They catch fish; they grow olives, tomatoes and oranges and swim in the blue, blue sea. It's still a hard life, but much better than existing in that desolate village by the lake."

"So you read those books," I say. "The ones I left in your bedroom?"

"Ah yes. I read them many, many times. Borges and Calvino. Most influential," he chuckles. "Indeed. As you can probably tell from my name."

"Your name?"

"Borges," he says with a smile. "And Calvino. Think about it."

I stare at his smiling, unseeing face and am glad that he can't see me blush. "Right. Of course! Your name - an anagram. Staring me in the face."

"The truth often does."

"So did Tyler tell you all about that strange old Erinsi woman?"

"He did. What a marvel. The last of her kind. I've always envied you a little, for meeting such an extraordinary individual."

I can't suppress an ironic laugh. "Tyler can't have told you everything. That Ninbanda was, like, totally suicidal. I mean, I can just about understand that she might have been trained for a suicide mission, but to drag me and Tyler into it, to die in that bunker, all to protect the Erinsi secrets. . . It's just . . . madness!"

"As Tyler might say," Blanco murmurs, a touch of longing in his voice.

"If you knew about Ninbanda, why didn't you tell us that the NRO could be trusted?"

He looks puzzled. "What makes you say that?"

"Ninbanda knew, didn't she, about the 2012 plan? She must have told the NRO. And that's why they were obsessed with finding Ek Naab and the Ix Codex. At least, that's what we figured out, Ixchel and me. The NRO wanted to save the world from the superwave, too."

Blanco shakes his head firmly. "We can never be certain of that. Ninbanda's motives may have been pure – yes, this is possible. The Erinsi took extraordinary pains to ensure that no single person could ever execute the 2012 plan alone. Cooperation and secrecy were built into the solution. Those of the final generation, who would eventually execute the plan, were willing to die in the act of protecting the planet from the superwave. To sacrifice themselves for the continuation of civilization. The NRO, however, were always suspect. Their leadership is subject to the changing winds of democracy. Who could say what a given administration might order them to do?"

"Well, yes, I guess the Erinsi didn't trust anyone who wasn't willing to die when they went into that bunker. But I think Captain Bennett would have been up for it."

"I suspect that Captain Bennett may indeed be an unusually brave man."

"Yep. Braver than me."

"You can't know that. You didn't know that the final journey might be one-way."

"At least Bennett didn't have to give his life, and Tyler and I had a way out."

Blanco gives a rueful sigh, perhaps at being reminded about time travel.

"So now you're back with Susannah. Why did you leave her?"

"Eventually the inevitable happened: the Crystal Key burned out and the Bracelet of Itzamna stranded me. For many, many years I lost my memory. Memories returned rather slowly. I wasn't able to get back to Susannah. It took years of working with the top scientists in the world, trying to find a way to make that blasted Key peptide." He sighs again, this time deeply. "The truth is, I grew old."

"Josh. . ." I say our name tentatively. He responds with a curious half-smile. "You time travelled loads of times, didn't you? What were you doing?"

"Ah! Things which are best left in the past."

"You're not going to tell?"

Gently, he shakes his head. "Time is fragile, young Josh. By now even you should understand."

"What does that mean – 'even' me? You're me. We're the same."

"We were the same. And then our lives took different paths."

"What about me? Will I time travel again?" I think silently of Bosch's comment in his letter to me: All I know, *tjommie*, is that you and I will meet again. Can't tell you when and where, but we do.

Was Bosch referring to meeting Arcadio? Had he seen the resemblance between us? I couldn't tell what answer I wanted to hear. Did I want Blanco to reassure me that I'd be staying in my own time? Or was some part of me hoping that Bosch's prediction would come true?

Blanco's smile widens. "I have no memory of meeting you in any other time but this. My dear twin, I'd deduce that from this point, your future is a blank slate."

292

BLOG ENTRY – THE WORLD-DIDN'T-END PARTY

Midnight came and went and the world didn't end.

I received an email from Dr Banerjee a few minutes after midnight.

Hey Josh Garcia,

I've been thinking about you, what with it being the end of the world and whatnot.

I don't know how you did it, kiddo, but you did it. I'm guessing you time-traveller types are secretive about your methods. If you ever feel the need to share a little, like how that thing on the moon actually works, where it came from, how you do the time-travel thing, I hope you won't forget your friend down in Telescope Country. Anything, really, would be a bonus. And I'd be up for keeping your secret too. Seriously, I'm just curious.

Cheers,

R.M. Banerjee

P.S. Still reading your blog, btw. Intriguing. I sense you've missed out (or password-protected?) the best stuff, though. Too bad for me! But I guess you've got better things to do with your time than entertaining a scientist while she looks at the night sky. By the way, did you hear the news about the Futurology Institute? It's just had the official opening! Wonder what new plans your "Sect" has now...?

I check on the Internet and see that she's right. The building has been completed in record time. Bit of a disappointment for the Sect of Huracan, the way things turned out. But no one should underestimate them. People with power, money and influence don't let go of their ambitions easily. And the Sect has set their aims pretty high.

Blanco Vigores and I returned to the others. I left them celebrating, walked through the deserted backstreets of Tlacotalpan. Music was everywhere, and the hum of excited voices, the clink of glasses from each old house.

I strolled back to the riverbank and stood at the edge, staring into water as dark as that in the black *cenote* of Ek Naab. All the time I've spent gazing into that black mirror – it would add up to days by now. It's as though the answers to everything could be found in the pool's reflection. Yet I never could discover anything new.

A stray firework was released somewhere in the square. A green and blue chrysanthemum of sparks burst overhead, every detail reflected in the river.

I heard a voice next to me and turned around. It was Ixchel, watching me watching the water. She was smiling as if she wasn't sure of herself for once, as though she might be intruding. She wasn't, though; of course not. I took her arm and guided her to stand next to me at the water's edge.

"I've finally figured it out," I whispered. "The water tells the future."

"It does?"

"Yes," I said and I pointed into the river. "The only part of the future I know, the only thing I'm sure about."

"And what is it?" she asked, still gazing at me. Until I made her look. Until we were both staring at our reflection, side by side in the water.

When she got it, her voice did a little jump and she went, "Josh!"

I turned and held Ixchel close until I could feel her heart beating against mine.

"Mission accomplished," I whispered. "We're both still here . . . we're still together. That's how it's going to stay."

Ixchel hugged me back and started to say something, but then she stopped and squeezed me even tighter.

The moment could easily have been ruined: someone else could have come by, a party might have got out of hand and spilled on to the streets, one of us could have got sad, thinking about the people we'd lost, but it didn't and we didn't and the moment was perfect and we stayed like that for ages, holding each other, and every word I said to her came from a place of ultimate truth inside me.

I opened my eyes and over Ixchel's shoulder I saw sparks from the fireworks, a shower of them landing in the river. Light falling into water; the darkness swallowing all that brilliance. No one was there to see it but me.

As for this blog, it's time to close The Joshua Files, because a place where I can get rid of all these things going on in my head is ultimately an escape. And I'm done with escaping. I only want to be here, now.

Acknowledgements

Many thanks to my editors at Scholastic Children's Books UK, Clare Argar and Jessica White for their enthusiasm and vigilance in helping me to complete Josh's adventures in this final instalment. Grateful thanks to Alex Richardson and Alyx Price of SCB for taking such good care of me on publicity trips. To a collected gang of marvellous, inspired authors without whose constant support I would have no-one to hang out with in coffee shops or inflict with my latest ideas: especially Susie Day, Sally Nicholls, Bill Heine, Steve Cole, Lucy Coats and Mark Robson. Big hurrahs for my former editor Polly Nolan and lovely agent Peter Cox, both wonderfully supportive and talented and - luckily for me - still interested in my writing. Thanks also to all the readers and book bloggers who've supported the Joshua Files series, especially Jens Hildebrand for feedback on the manuscript and Darren Hartwell (The BookZones) and Vincent Ripley (Mr/ Ripley's Enchanted Books).

Immense gratitude to Dr. Reba Bandyopadhyay of the Department of Astronomy, University of Florida, for advice on the astrophysics-y bits of *Apocalypse Moon*, without which I might as well have been writing about magic!

Eternal thanks must for to my daughters Lilia and Josie for being lovelier than strawberry cream cake, and my adorable husband David for his tireless work and energy. It can't be easy to be married to an author- we don't exactly let our minds inhabit the real world. Never mind the practical work of book-keeping, doing the taxes, computer technical support, marketing advice and keeping the household going when your wife disappears into a manuscript.

M.G. HARRIS

M.G. (Maria Guadalupe) Harris was born in Mexico City but moved to England as a young child. Before becoming a writer, M.G. worked as a scientist and ran an Internet business.

On regular visits back to Mexico, M.G. became fascinated by Mayan archaeology and made several trips to Mayan ruins in Yucatan and Chiapas. One such trip planted the seed of the idea for *The Joshua Files*. While recovering from a skiing accident that resulted in a broken leg, M.G. began writing *Invisible City*, the first book in the Joshua Files series, on a laptop next to the bed.

M.G. is also the author of GERRY ANDERSON'S GEMINI FORCE ONE. She writes for young adults as M.G. Reyes.

When not wandering around the exotic settings for her novels, like Mexico, Brazil and the Swiss mountains, M.G. and family live on a quiet street in Oxford.

INVISIBLE CITY

M.G.HARRIS

The Mystery: What really happened to Josh Garcia's father?
Ancient Artefacts: The Ix Codex, a book of Mayan inscriptions lost for over a thousand years.
Key Locations: Jericho (Oxford, UK); the Mayan ruins of Becan (Campeche, Mexico); and Catemaco, a lakeside town of witches in Veracruz, Mexico
Mysteriously Stolen: A copy of *Incidents of Travel in Chiapas, Central America and Yucatan* by John Lloyd Stephens
Mysticism: Dream-talking, the witches of Catemaco
Action: Car chase; escape into the Caribbean sea; hunted in the misty crater-lake of Catemaco

ICE SHOCK

M.G. HARRIS

The Mystery: Who is behind the strange coded postcards from Mexico and what do they mean?

Ancient Artefacts: The Adaptor, the Bracelet of Itzamna

Key Locations: The ruins of Godstow nunnery (Oxford, UK); the underground rivers and caves of Yucatan, Mexico; a mysterious riverside town of Old Mexico; the snow-capped volcano Mount Orizaba (Veracruz, Mexico)

Cheekily Stolen: The Adaptor

Mysticism: The spirit-dream of two long-dead young lovers

Action: Midnight chase and fight around Port Meadow, Oxford; lost in the caves; deadly crisis on glacier of a volcano

ZERO MOMENT

M.G. HARRIS

The Mystery: Who is Arcadio?
Ancient Artefacts: The Bracelet of Itzamna, the Crystal Key
Key Locations: The giant sand dunes of Natal, Brazil; the tropical jungle of Brazil; the lakes and mountains of Switzerland
Bravely Stolen: The Crystal Key
Mysticism: A message from beyond the grave, a disturbing spirit world
Action: Dune buggy chase; capoeira fighting; time travel; car chase across a mountain pass

DARK
PARALLEL

M.G. HARRIS

The Mystery: What's happened to Josh's memory? Why is the Ix Codex suddenly "mostly blank"?

Ancient Artefacts: The Bracelet of Iztamna, the Books of Itzamna

Key Locations: Ancient Calakmul; the Mayan Riviera; the National Museum of Anthropology in Mexico City

Mysteriously Stolen: The Ix Codex

Mysticism: Time travel, alternate realities

Action Highlights: Motorbike race; knife vs capoeira fights; shootouts and chases with Mayan warriors

APOCALYPSE MOON

M.G. HARRIS

The Mystery: What is the actual location of the moon machine? Who is Arcadio?

Ancient Artefacts: The Bracelet of Iztamna, the Adaptor, the Key

Key Locations: Lake Bacalar and San Cristobal de las Casas in Mexico, post-apocalyptic Oxford and Lake District in England, Lake Toba in Indonesia

Cheekily Stolen and lost: By Josh, a Muwan Mark II.

Mysticism: Time-travel, post-apocalyptic possibilities

Action Highlights: Muwan chases, motorbike chases, midnight shootouts in a forest, a lightning raid on the enemy's stronghold.

The Joshua Files on the Internet

Video trailers, articles and more at

themgharris.com

MG's YouTube Channel

youtube.com/user/mgharrisauthor

Joshua Files on Facebook

fb.com/joshuafiles

MG's blog

mgharris.net

The Descendant - An Alternate Reality Game

The mystery continues online.

Fourteen-year old Josh Garcia (of *The Joshua Files*) is troubled enough by his own adventures. But when his godfather PJ Beltran is murdered in Mexico City, Josh helps PJ's 13-year old daughter to solve the mystery of his murder.

If you've enjoyed *The Joshua Files* or *The Descendant* then the Alternate Reality Game (ARG) will give you a whole new insight on the story, the chance to eavesdrop on the characters online.

Your first clue?

Google *where is Gabi Beltran*

For more information, videos and clues, see

fb.com/thedescendant

18217307R00189

Made in the USA
Middletown, DE
26 February 2015